JAMES PYNE

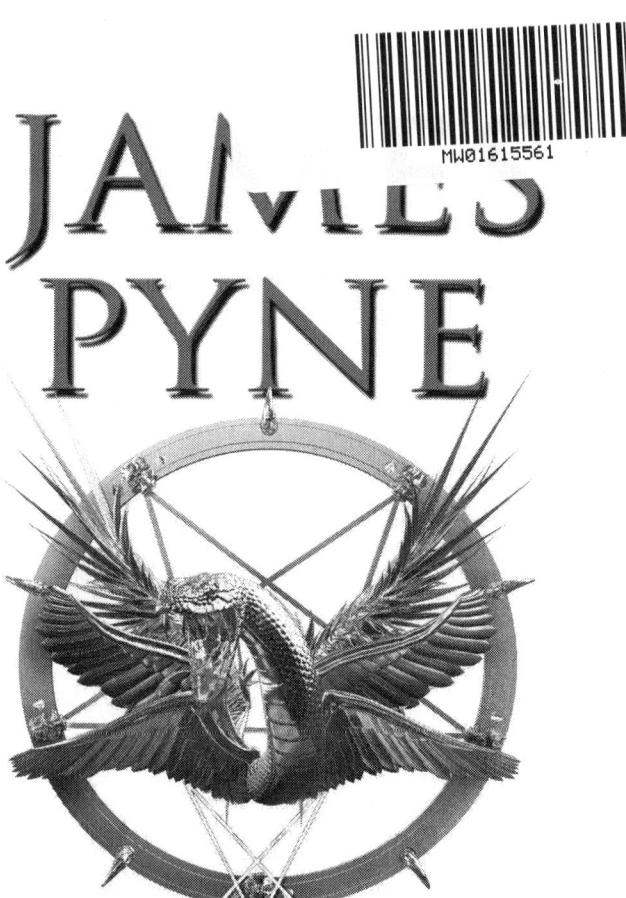

BIG CRANKY
FALL INTO DARKNESS

PUBLISHING

Dedicated to
Momzy, Father, Sister, Brother,
and my forever muse, Elle.

"The road up and the road down are the same thing."

—*Hippolytus*

"All the gods, all the heavens, all the hells, are within you."

—*Joseph Campbell*

EL VERSUS THE PIG

JAMES PYNE

The End

El

El whipped another rock at the frightened pig. He stood on the middle rung of the pigpen mocking its screeching and oinking.

"Oink. Oink." With one hand on the rail, El pushed his nose up, making his nostrils flare wide, the gums of his top teeth showing in all their pinkness. "Oink. Oink."

"Real tough, kid."

El stepped down from the fence. He turned to see his mother in a magenta sari, the secrets of the universe embroidered on its material in an ideographic language El had yet to decipher, but would, and when he did, look out cosmos. A dark ponytail cascaded down one side of his mother's neck, her bottle-green eyes refracted into amber when she glanced down at the penned pig, then back to sparkling green when looking back at him.

The expression of her lips was impossible to read. She could be mad or indifferent. Or was it just her resting bitch face? El snickered at that thought. Regardless, he didn't want to remain in her presence because it meant more lessons when he just wanted to play. He was still a boy in terms of maturity, even though mortals thought he was no more than ten years old. As an immortal, he was ten thousand years old with another six thousand years of fun he should be looking forward to, not being forced to grow up before his years. What bullshit.

"Where are you going?" His mother grabbed him by the shoulder of his tunic. Her face was set against a sapphire-blue sky. "You have that pig to make things right with."

"It doesn't feel." He tried shaking loose. It felt like she was going to lift him to her face. Instead, she released him with a minor shake. "I was just having a little fun."

"The pig has feelings. It feels the pain you inflict upon it."

The swine wallowed in the mud of its sty, always at its happiest when El's mother was present. They were in the middle of nowhere. There was no farmhouse nearby, just hills of rolling green pastures in every direction. An empty blue sky with a slow approaching sunrise lit up a wooden chair and table that hadn't been there a minute ago. A crow's feather was stuck in a bottle of ink and a sketchpad lay next to it on the table. A shifty breeze messed El's shoulder-length hair in complete disorder.

"Instead of understanding your creation, you torment the holy hell out of it. I shudder at the kind of king you will become, a childishly cruel one. Now go sit down and make things right. We have little time."

"Drawing's not my thing, you know that. Can't you just snap things into creation after I describe them to you like you did with the pig?"

"No. It's time for you to be hands on and take full responsibility."

"But I don't draw well."

"I have the solution for that, kiddo." His mother smelled of rose oil one minute. The next it was cinnamon, and the next scent after that was something else El found pleasant, but he didn't know what it was, so he called it Mommy smell. But when she smelled like turnips, shit was about to fly, and if he was smart, he would flee for safety for her words stung like a thousand hornets.

"The quill and ink are extensions of your imagination," she continued. "What you envision something to look like in that stubborn head of yours, will appear on paper no matter how talentless your hands. Imagine a certain scent to go with your creations and it will come into existence. Paint this planet in with life with your best thoughts. Show me this dimension will be left in good hands."

"This planet's too small for my big ideas." It really was, taking no more than ten minutes to fly its circumference, something he couldn't do right now thanks to his mom making his wings lame. Translation, he was grounded until he got things right. "I want a bigger canvas to work with."

"Baby steps, my son."

"I'm not a baby." He pouted and stomped.

"Prove it." She turned from him and faded from view.

"This is your fault, pig. You tempted me."

The pig snorted at him.

His fists clenched. "Are you mocking me?"

The pig shied away, trembling. It was the first time El had seen such an expression coming from it and it bugged him. He really was just having fun.

"I guess I can let you out." He opened the fence gate with a long creak.

The pig eyed El's every move.

"I give you freedom."

It fell back on its side, splashing mud up on El.

"I should—"

Mother would be watching and grading his every move. Best do what she asked so his wings would come back to life and fly him off this dump. El plunked himself into the chair. He would get the pig back another way. But first, a little harmless test run.

El dipped the feather into the ink, slid away an excess glob on the rim of the bottle, and drew stick people on the sketchpad, grinning like a hyena.

Stick people sprouted from the rolling hillsides, unraveling, and rising to full height. They were all around him, in bold-typeset black, standing there like a silent army waiting for orders.

"Just keeping it real, Mom. I'm no artist."

The ground shook. The stick people collapsed into twigs that took root, flourishing into patches of lush green forests. Not his doing. That was his mother passively reminding him to smarten up.

He looked over at the pig. It stood at the open gate, sniffing its freedom. It looked back at the mud, stared out at the rolling hills, then back at the pool of mud.

El waved away the pig. "Stay in there for all I care."

The sky needed clouds. The very tiny planet looked like it was getting dry. The tallgrass was already turning yellow and sunburnt in places, and now with trees sucking up the groundwater, everything was drying up faster. He dipped the feather-point into the ink jar and decided on the number of rainclouds needed. Too many would flood the planet.

He hated this game. Becoming king in the image of his mother was boring, too much order with no chaos. How would anything evolve into anything worthwhile without some anarchy here and there? The universe needed things that didn't make sense, to confound all living creatures, spur them into seeking answers for things that had no answers, leading to them discovering profound things along the way.

The pig wobbled by, stepping to El's left

"Mother says I need to make things right with you. Setting you free is one thing, but giving you choices, instead of rules is the greatest gift of all, yes?"

The pig just stared at the rolling hills of green grass, the blue sky and the scattered forests, no doubt unsure what to do.

El imagined a bridge, then drew one. It slowly materialized in front of the pig, stone-grey, arching all the way up to the sun, looking like nothing he would draw, but true to his mind's eye.

"Come on, go up it. Or what about this?" He imagined a giant lake of mud and drew it. It materialized to their right. The pig oinked with excitement, curly tail wagging. It started towards the sludge, then stopped to glare up at El with distrust.

If the ungrateful swine was going to be like that, then he would give it a reason not to trust him. He just couldn't resist the devil on his shoulder. He grinned.

"Exactly! Maybe there's a pig-eating monster in that lake, not even I know for sure. But from way up there on that bridge, the muddy lake will be transparent at that height, allowing you to see if there's a terrible monster in it."

The pig looked up at the bridge, then back at the Lake of Mud.

"Fine, then."

El dipped the quill into the ink jar, imagined what the pig's favourite food might be and drew it. In front of the pig appeared three tubers for it to taste. More popped into existence all the way up the bridge.

The pig munched on one and its eyes lit up, no doubt finding it was the best tuber ever. It tried another, then another, nosing its way up the stone bridge, tail wagging at every step. The farther it waddled up that bridge, the bigger the grin on El's face.

"That's it. Fill your gluttony to heart's content."

The pig had the lack of knowing when it was full. El had created it like that. Not knowing when to stop eating might have it blow up any second, curly tail still wagging while it ate every tuber it came to.

El laughed aloud at the thought of it blowing up.

"I hope you don't!" he shouted up at the pig, looking at the sun. "A much better fate awaits you."

Something he had whispered into its creation was the capacity to feel pain; it was extremely sensitive to that. The anticipation of the pig becoming smoked pork had him in a fit of giggles. He would claim it was an accident of course.

Suddenly, everything went dark, like the sun's flames had been blown out. A moon flashed above, then starlight, as if time had sped up.

"What the hell, Mom?"

He flicked the feather into the darkness and threw his hands up in exaggerated defeat, and just as the quill touched the wooden table it split into a million splinters. The chair exploded, too, sending El hard onto his bum.

"Mom, you always ruin everything."

He folded his arms, refusing to stand.

"Pig-headed like your father was," his mother said, not yet appearing in sight. "Look, kiddo, like your father I will be moving on to the next phase of our existence. I feel the eternal energy pulling me into the next reality." She materialized into view. "And you are not ready to be the keeper in this one. But you are all that's left of our bloodline."

"Things are going to change then." It did sadden him that she would be leaving. It was the main reason for his rebellious nature, hoping she would remain here until he grew into adulthood. It didn't seem right for her to abandon him at such an early age. "You'd better not leave because things will be different."

"Why do you want to inflict so much misfortune?"

"Pain will be another form of scars, to remind them of what can hurt them. They'll grow stronger because of it."

"They already feel horrible pain when losing a part of their body. They die, they suffer from the loss of loved ones, and many find that grief is the worst kind of agony. Why do you want to give them cruelty? What point is there in that?"

El sprung to his feet. He marched proudly around his mother, as if sizing her up, which of course he wasn't, but if anyone saw them from a distance, they would think that's exactly what he was doing.

"For them to be truly enlightened beings, to maybe even surpass us someday, they need to know fear and unimaginable pain. They need to know true evil. Throw those things in with the pleasures of life, and they'll be better for it. Your way of guiding them along with commandments stops once I take over, Momzy. They're going to be figuring out things on their own. If they blow up the universe while doing so, that's no concern of mine. Do you really want to leave me behind, knowing this?"

His mother sighed. "What will I do with you, El? You truly are terrible. Threatening the wellbeing of the universe if I leave? We will meet again in the next reality when you are ready. Don't be afraid. I will always be with you. Your father will be too."

"If it's for the greater good that you go, leaving me to suffer from such a loss, then it's for the greater good that they suffer. They'll be better for it, according to your way of looking at things. You'll see. My vision of how things should be will—"

El tripped over the pig, sending him face-first into chunky swine excrement.

"You have such big plans for the universe, yet one of your creations"—his mother leaned back from laughter, pointing—"a simple pig has tripped you up."

*

Long before the most seductive of angels, Aphrodite gave El the not-so-affectionate nickname Big Cranky, and long before he created humans in his image, the universe was void of life for the umpteenth time. Everyone had blown themselves up and El couldn't understand where he had gone wrong. Every planet ended the same. Some of the inhabitants reached the stars and met up with other races, and not long after that they obliterated each other over insignificant sections of space. He didn't interfere, not even when the last planet with life upon it was close to expiring, for he had held onto the hope that they would figure things out in time and finally vindicate his efforts.

So, here he was starting over. Again.

This time he would pair everything up. Everything would have its own balance in beauty and chaos. Male and female. Night and day. Moths and butterflies. On and on the list of opposites went. He would get things right this time. He would find the missing puzzle fragments. He would get his answers to what had gone wrong that day everything changed.

El would backtrack. Relive it all and not just through his own memories. Through everybody's. He would do whatever it took to make things right next time.

The Throne Planet

The Order

No angel knew for sure if Heaven existed in the same dimension as the faraway planets they babysat or harvested. Not even Hephaestus, the chief blacksmith and runemaster of angels had that answer, or he wasn't telling, for he was also the only portal maker besides the Almighty. Sure, the celestial lungs of angels could breathe the light helium and hydrogen of outer space, but their wings couldn't carry them far in the vastness of the universe. There was just no way of knowing. It was one of those questions forever haunting angels.

The throne planet known as Elysium, its ancient name too long to write or pronounce, was filled with many wonderments, like clouds that morphed into ghostly creatures flapping about, enjoying whatever time remained of their sentient life before bursting into vapor again. Other places of tranquility were the Hanging Gardens, the Lake of Souls, the Musical Meadows, and the Serene Sea. And like all planets, it had its volatile regions like the Forbidden Zone with its ancient ruins the younger generations knew little about.

One of the most popular places on the throne planet was Rainbow Ridge, a collection of crystal mountains, each with its own vibrant colour pulsating as if there were a beating heart inside. Angels meditated there. Others enjoyed the scenery while on leave from one of their assignments. But what it was best known for was the birthlings conceived there. Whatever the reason, everybody left there feeling better about themselves.

The cobblestone courtyard of the Almighty's throne area rose into thirty-three steps, stopping at a black crystal throne where he sat. It pulsated a red glow whenever he sat upon it, mimicking his heartbeats. The living quarters for the Order of Angels surrounded the throne like an ancient stadium reaching for the sky with everything that was part of it affectionately known as the Nest.

Each living quarters had a doorway at north and south. Along the bottom lived the Elders and Counsel of Twelve members like Cronus, Zeus, Odin, and Calliope, the latter being the Almighty's only daughter. Others dwelling along the bottom tiers were the greatest musicians, and poets such as

Apollo. Residing in the middle section were the peacemakers like Shiva and Shangdi. Along the top two floors were the Seraphim under the command of Lucifer and his protégé, Michael, along with other warrior clans like the Death Dealers commanded by Gabriel, whose apprentice was the firecracker Muerte.

The whole purpose of the Order in those days was to guide mortals to enlightenment, with the occasional Harvest taking place, as per the Almighty's discretion.

Everything was about to change.

Order from Chaos

Lucifer

Angels weren't sexless like most mortals believed. Though immortal, they did procreate. The catch — and there always was one when it came to immortal life — was that a female angel would mature in appearance by seven years every time she gave birth.

Males could father ten birthlings before showing any signs of ageing, and even then, it was hardly noticeable. No female these days dared to go past two cherub births. Then there were warriors like Zeus fathering hundreds to his stable in preparation for the day when it came to ruling his own House.

That wasn't the case with Lucifer, only son of the Almighty, brother to Calliope, husband to the beautiful and ambitious Lilith. She and Lucifer parented no birthlings with no plans of having any soon. It had nothing to do with keeping up appearances. They simply weren't in a rush and having adopted Athena, Zeus's shunned daughter . . . Well, she gave them a good dosage of parenthood. Lucifer loved Athena as his own, but she provided more than enough headaches.

Lucifer, golden hair down to his hips, had a deceptively smug expression, for he was one of the most approachable of angels. Lilith strutted with a hint of arrogance Lucifer couldn't soften, her dark hair tight in a ponytail tipped with a metallic claw that when whipped, tore through mostly anything, or at least left a memorable mark.

They followed Lucifer's father along a trail through the Hanging Gardens, a range of mountains carpeted by every species of flower ever imagined into existence.

It was an odd feeling walking with a father who didn't look much older than himself—average muscular frame, nothing bulky like one would expect of the Supreme One of Everything. He sported a white tunic which most angels wore in leisure, or when in emissary mode to an assigned planet. It was traditional attire from the days of his mother, he would say when one of the younger generations tried wearing something different. He walked with careful consideration of every step, frustrating both Lucifer and Lilith into a slow pace.

Lucifer was armoured in black dragon bone from the first firebreather he had ever slain. Usually only worn for battle, it was impregnable to any force except his father's will.

"All living things on six planets are dead right under our noses," Lucifer said of the recent catastrophic events on nearby planets. "And you act like nothing's wrong."

"The universe is compensating," his father said. "Balancing itself out. This must happen, as unfortunate as it is. Surely it's an interstellar plague."

"Nonsense talk." Lucifer was sure his father knew what was really going on. He just wasn't saying for whatever reason. It was always about secrets when it came to good old Father. He didn't even want the others to address him by his name. There were days when Lucifer would annoy him by calling him El, sometimes in front of an audience. Everybody was to address him as their Lord or by some other ego-stroking name. It was amusing when Aphrodite called him "Big Cranky" in front of everyone, because then the younglings would do it, much to his annoyance.

"Tell us what's really going on, Father. Stop with the secrets."

"Impulsive as always. Order from chaos then?" his father said, looking over his shoulder with slight irritation. "Does that work for you, son?"

"I see no order," Lilith said, her white-marbled armour streaked in black swirls complementing her swagger. "I see only chaos."

His father didn't look back, only walked on, the vibrant flower bushes of fall colours thickening, branches swishing against Lucifer's armour.

Lilith continued, "The mortals on every planet are beginning to fight amongst themselves, some with neighbouring planets, like a sudden sickness has come over the entire universe. An ancient presence looms, has returned, is the feeling I'm getting."

"She's sensitive to such things, Father, but you're much more connected. Why won't you tell us what's really going on? Or has my wife suddenly become more powerful than my almighty father?"

Lucifer and Lilith had just returned from one of the planets nearest theirs. It had been silenced of mortal noise, the only remaining sounds those of rushing tides and trees rattling in the howling winds.

"Ebb and flow," his father said, ignoring Lucifer's attempt at goading. "Everything must balance out. Something like this was inevitable."

"Everything sentient was dead, right down to the smallest insect," Lilith said, looking at Lucifer with a look of disbelief. "How's that natural? All their energy drained, not so much a spark in them. Murdered, plain and simple. Plagues don't pile up bodies to be found. You're hiding the truth, and you know it."

El clasped his hands behind his back, as he continued leading them though the Hanging Gardens, his knuckles whitening.

"I sense nothing out of the ordinary." He sniffed orange flowers, the scent of citrus fanning Lucifer's way. "Everything is as it should be."

"We're not stupid!" Lilith shouted. "Stop treating us like younglings."

"Mind your tone." Lucifer's father stopped longer than usual to inhale the mustard yellow flowers growing out from a boulder. "Being my son's wife puts you under closer scrutiny, not less."

Lucifer placed a hand on the bosom of Lilith's breastplate, easing her back before she did something impulsive. It was all over her face, she was ready for an argument. They continued along the winding trail, the bushes closing in the further they went.

"Before you say it, it's not an advanced race of mortals making their mark," Lucifer said to his father. "There's something different. I felt it on every one of the dead planets. Something from long ago. Like Lilith says, you're treating us like we're dimwitted."

His father turned, his expression grim. "Are you challenging me?"

"I know what I felt—"

"You know nothing." Black rose vines crept all around them. "Leave me with my thoughts."

"This is what it's come to?" Lucifer said. "Suddenly, not even you are usual."

His father glared at him.

"Are you going to strike me?" Lucifer didn't budge, clasping his hands behind his back, chin up. "Or put me over your knee and spank me?"

Would he? It certainly looked that way.

A tiny smirk came over his father's face as he turned away, walking onwards. "Your spunk is familiar, a mirror image of my early years. Yes, the signs do point to a calculative intelligence trying to get our attention by leaving a trail of unfathomable carnage." He looked over his shoulder at Lucifer. "Pair off our best, including Gabriel and Muerte. Send them to the planets neighbouring the ones affected by this familiar destruction. I will share more of that later." He stopped, his head slightly tilted to one side, not completely looking back. "Perhaps they will find out where our missing brethren are."

"Missing brethren?"

"Yes, you are the only ones to return from the first expedition."

"What? And you can't sense where they are?"

"Let me work on that." He waved them away.

Lucifer clenched his fists. This time it was Lilith who gently touched his chest plate, shaking her head no.

"You would strike when I'm not looking?"

"No, Father, but you're frustratingly stubborn, keeping secrets, refusing to see logic."

"You see through the eyes of a babe." He didn't look back, one hand beneath a barbed red rose. "You both will not be going on this expedition."

21

"Stop protecting me."

"You are relieved of duty for now. Take a break, everything will be fine. I will call upon you if needed."

"You insult us in this way. They'll notice and see favouritism—and over something you say is of no great importance. What will they think of our House?"

"My final word on the matter."

As they turned together, their wings spreading, their king said, "Thank you both for being forthright with me, but I strongly urge a different approach next time." He glared over his shoulder. "Be glad you didn't do this in front of others."

El sniffed again the barbed roses hanging from the vines as if they were rapture to him, once remarking that their smell reminded him of his mother when she was at her happiest.

Not looking back, he finished, "Otherwise, the result would have been unfortunate."

The Stubborn Protégé

Gabriel

Gabriel was playing the part of babysitter, assigned to Muerte by their Lord. When Gabriel asked why him, why not Lucifer or Michael, the Big Guy replied, "She's an impossible brat just like you were at that age. Who better to season her?"

This was Gabriel's punishment for giving the Big Guy grey hairs back in the day.

"What's your rush?" Gabriel shouted to Muerte.

They were flying towards nowhere in particular while looking for anything unusual.

"Can't keep up, old relic?"

He still looked about her age, having not fathered any younglings. He was married to his duties and wouldn't have it any other way. She was a refreshing spark, though, shaking away the cobwebs of tradition.

"You need to stop throwing caution to the wind."

"You sound like one of the Twelve."

"Low blow."

She was referring to the Council of Twelve and their reputation for taking eternity coming to a consensus on anything from being top heavy with bleeding hearts. It was a position he had turned down centuries ago. Diplomacy wasn't his thing. Not his kind of war. No glory in that.

"I can strike lower if you like," she said, following her words with a playful smirk, then a wink.

Like Gabriel's, her wings were black, the only difference being that hers were crimson-edged. A scythe was holstered along her back, the blade gleaming in the rays of two suns. It was all over her that she was itching for a fight to gauge the durability of her pearl-black armour. Four long blades were fitted on each leg like a second layer of armour. When activated, the multipurpose blades pushed out of her leg armour, to be used as swords. They also rose into a horizontal position while she spun, slicing her enemies in poetic flow. They had been gifted to her by Hephaestus when he had a crush on her before marrying his half-sister, Aphrodite.

"Don't you remember the anticipation of your first battle?" Muerte looked over at him, wisps of clouds briefly hiding parts of her. Icy-white hair, black lips on a pale face, eyes that weakened a male to her words if they weren't vigilant. "Or are you so old you've forgotten?"

"I remember." His hooded black cloak drawn over his white armour, flapped in the wind, and his straw-blond curls blew all over the place. Considered an equal to Lucifer in looks, Gabriel refused such compliments, many times stating, "Let Lucifer's vanity be quenched while I have the glory in battle."

Gabriel continued, "To rush into combat is inviting defeat."

"They're just mortals with advanced technology," Muerte said of the inhabitants of the butchered planets. "We'll cut through them in seconds, leaving them to their natural evolution. They'll forget we were even here generations from now. We'll become nothing but figures in their myths."

"The vanishings of our comrades aren't the work of mortals."

No mortal in the universe could overtake an immortal, with the average angel being five times the strength, wounds healing in seconds. Most mortal blades and weapons had little effect, yet almost an entire battalion worth of angels had disappeared like they never existed or were finger-snapped into nonexistence. Those who had gone missing were of the older generation of angels, all of whom had strong rumblings against their king. Rebellion was faint in the air, with the House of Cronus and his ambitious son, Zeus, rumoured to be pulling the strings.

Then there were the whisperings involving their Lord's commanding of Lucifer and Lilith to dispose of the discontents. Nonsense, of course. Lucifer lived by the Twelve Commandments, especially the first: Thou shalt not kill another angel.

"You worry too much," Muerte said. "We're Death Dealers, our touch alone evaporates mortals instantly, and weakens immortals to their knees" — she twirled the scythe blade lying across her shoulder — "then off with their heads." The scythe blade stopped a mere inch from Gabriel's neck.

She grinned and flew off.

"She will be the death of me," Gabriel muttered to the heavens.

A Lover's Influence

Lucifer

"He cannot see where our sisters and brothers are," Lilith said to Lucifer, as they strolled through the Garden of Eden in casual, knee-length togas. Here in this orchard of colourful delights nothing killed, nothing starved, everything got along. The only catch was they could never leave or they would burn into ash. Every planet out there had such a garden, but none lasted long in mortal hands.

It was early morning, and the stars were still out, the two moons—one blood red, the other electric blue—sinking below the horizon opposite Rainbow Ridge. Fluorescent flowers marked the winding path. Lilith held her hand out to a snake coiled around a branch. It curled around her arm, then stretched along her shoulders, its head resting within her cleavage. They walked on.

"I wonder if your father is omnipotent as he proclaims."

Lucifer wondered too. All his life he had believed his father was the epitome of infinite power, infinite knowledge, and infinite presence, but lately, he was seeing a father unsure of himself, frustrated, plunging into brief temper tantrums. The recent cleansing of all life on those planets was getting to his father, almost driving him mad in his inability to see the culprit. Or a haunting past had returned and the thought of that had him losing his mind. The latter Lucifer strongly considered was the logical answer for his father's sudden uncontrolled rages. If the House of Cronus saw such vulnerability, they would make a run at the throne, which was their right, as it was any House's right.

"Mark my words, Lucifer, the monster doing this wants our attention. Who could blind your father to their presence? Commit such swift genocide in our backyard for so long without detection?"

"He once spoke of an ancient enemy that our kind long ago vanquished, but he trailed off into silence, thinking twice about telling Calliope and me anything more. It was like he wanted to share this burdensome secret so badly but telling us would somehow change our feelings towards him. Soon I will pay a visit to my old mentor, Baiame, and get some long overdue answers."

"There are hints all over this planet of a great war, Lucifer, yet he tells us nothing of these ancient ruins, even the Forbidden Ruins your beloved Baiame guards with all his heart like a past he doesn't want to let go. The victors tell the stories and what have we noticed about the mortals when it comes to the winners? It's usually the bad ones who win but rewrite themselves as the good guys. What if your father was the bad one?"

"He has his faults. We all do."

"I'm just saying what must be said." She patted the head of the serpent still within her cleavage. "Don't you think it's odd, those speaking the loudest against your father have disappeared? All Elders, at that. And his excuse is that he can't sense them? When has your father ever admitted to being wrong, or clueless about something? Quite out of character, don't you think?"

"Are you suggesting my father has something to do with this?"

"Quite conveniently, his biggest distractors are now seemingly out of the picture."

"It makes no sense. Why would he wipe out all life on those planets?"

"A ruse from him, or sheer lunacy. Who knows how his mind works?"

"You seem to know."

"Husband, I've always been forthright with you." Lilith placed a hand on the side of his face and gave him a peck on the lips. It was her way of calming him before things got heated. "I could be totally wrong, but I'm not the only one thinking it, am I?"

No, she wasn't. The thoughts she spoke had been plaguing him all day.

"He has removed us from the picture," she said. "What is our fate?"

They entered the narrow mountain pass leading to the Lake of Souls where along the horizon, Rainbow Ridge lit up the evening sky in flickering multicolour hues.

MUERTE VERSUS THE TENTACLES

JAMES PYNE

The Arrogance of Youth

Gabriel

Gabriel was searching for Muerte. She had suddenly nosedived into the thick layer of fog covering the planet, mountain peaks and treetops the only things visible above it. She had withdrawn her scythe, shouting that a giant black tentacle had just lashed out of the haze. She had then disappeared before he could stop her.

Odd. Something so careful to hide its presence now revealing itself could only mean a trap. Blinded by a blanket of white deepening into a thick grey, he kept an ear out for her, the coolness of the mist entering his nostrils refreshing him. One of Gabriel's gifts was sensing life and how much of it, but he hadn't sensed one living thing here. No birds. No insects. No animals.

"Only a matter of time before you fall!" he heard Muerte shout just below him. She sounded frustrated by her opponent's refusal to do just that.

Gabriel landed in a crouch, observing the fog at ground level was thinner. There was Muerte, wings closed over her body like a second armour, in an intense battle with creatures he had never seen before. Their muscular shapes defied logic, freakish things leaning heavily to one side, barbed and spiked, yet swift and unrelenting, their tentacles shrinking from sight, then whipping out from other areas of their bodies.

Gabriel stood up and drew his sword. He hurried toward her, giving a war cry to split the creatures' attention. They looked his way. Two lumbered towards him.

Muerte whipped her leg blades at the tentacle monsters, collapsing them, willing her swords back to the side of her legs or hands, throwing them again. She could will inanimate things according to her imagination, even bend them. The monstrosities pounced out of the thicker areas of fog, wolf-like things that stood up on their hind legs, hunched over from bulky backs.

"Come at me then." She motioned them forwards with both free hands.

"She's mad with war." Gabriel cut down the incoming Tentacles. Both exploded into acidic liquid stinging any exposed skin. That's what they were. Tentacles. They couldn't be anything else. Over the years, Gabriel had overheard Elders speaking of such beasts, with them quickly going silent at his approach. His hearing was sharper than they realized.

With her scythe still along her shoulders, Muerte spun a good twenty feet in the air, cutting down the taller deformities that dropped slowly and clumsily. She landed in a crouch at the heart of the circling wolf-like beasts, leg blades sticking out at different levels, one arm out, the other still holding her scythe along her back.

She willed the leg blades to spear through every deformed thing that came at her, then they returned and speared through them again. The last collapsed without half of its head. The blades reconnected with her armoured legs.

Muerte's face peeled from her icy-white hair as she slowly looked up and said, "Hope those two I left you weren't too much trouble."

"Your arrogance will expose you," Gabriel hollered. "Not everything's this easy to slay. Something was evaluating you, playing with you. This isn't done."

"I touched some of them." She stood up. "They're empty. They've no minds of their own. Like these." She motioned down at her leg blades. "They're controlled by something else. I couldn't even drain them of their energy."

"Well now," Gabriel said as hulking shadows silently appeared in the fog all around them. "A fine mess we're in."

They were as tall as any beast of legend. The ones Muerte had just cut down slid back together or combined with fallen comrades into unimaginable horrors.

"Looks like you get to have some fun after all." Muerte turned away from him.

"She's a lively one," an unfamiliar voice said from within a patch of denser fog. A shadowed figure appeared, not much taller than Gabriel. Humanoid, muscular, tentacles hanging from the outer side of its beefy arms and shoulders. It walked slowly, its posture cocky, like a seasoned warrior. Shaded, bat-like wings rose and folded closer to their full length.

"Show yourself," Muerte said. "I'd like the pleasure of seeing your life leave your eyes."

The creature laughed. The fog kept rolling around it, as if it controlled the elements.

"The arrogance of youth," it said.

"How's this for arrogance?" Muerte jumped up into a spin, her leg blades rising and one by one detaching from her. They joined together into a giant sword, spearheading the murky thing in the fog, sending it flailing backwards and away from sight.

She landed on all fours, cat-like, looking up at Gabriel as mist swirled about her.

"How can you not be impressed?"

Mood Swings

Lucifer

They continued walking through the Garden of Eden, talking about all manner of things, while the snake remained hanging from Lilith's shoulders, head resting within her cleavage, yellow eyes intent on Lucifer. It hissed at him, like it was whispering his name. They would enter the mountain pass soon. In another hour, the two suns would be up.

"There will be a time the throne will be yours," Lilith remarked.

"If it comes, it comes."

"A fresh outlook is needed for the universe."

"Such ambition leads to a path of blood."

Lucifer dreaded such weight on his shoulders. Impossible to please everyone with everybody complaining about the tiniest of things. He didn't see himself having the patience his father had. And this was his father's creation; he had nothing to do with it. Why would he want to inherit such a mess?

"Do you enjoy doing his bidding?" asked Lilith.

"You're in a mood."

"I'm hormonal, yes. Many thoughts and feelings are mixing together."

She leaned into a fig tree in full fruit. The serpent slithered up into the leafy branches, its head sliding into view, slanted eyes intent on Lucifer.

He thought about willing it into flames.

Lilith's serious look softened into one of playfulness. "Enough of politics. How about something more appetizing to go with the mood of our present surroundings?" She sashayed towards him, white and crimson roses glowing in the background. "Do you think some maturity on this face would look good on the wife of the future ruler of the universe?" She winked, just before jumping into his arms.

"A child is the last thing I'm thinking about." He lowered her gently to the ground.

"And when?"

"So eager to have your own heir to the throne not yet mine?"

She smirked at that, turning away, leaving him unsure about her sudden mood changes. Everybody close to his heart seemed to be losing their minds except his sister, Calliope.

Fearless

Gabriel

"How can you not be impressed?" Muerte said again, after sending her leg blades spearing into the angelic-shaped Tentacle.

Secretly, Gabriel admired her enthusiasm and impulsiveness. A carbon copy of him at her age, the Big Guy was right about that. And from what he knew of himself back then, nagging him only made his arrogance worsen. It was best letting him learn the hard way. It looked like she was going down the same path of discovery and setbacks, assuming they made it out of this current predicament in one piece.

"Have you forgotten about them?" Gabriel pointed with his sword, then shook Tentacle guts from it.

The Tentacles appeared in the valley fog, monsters of all shapes, sizes, and deformities. The scent coming from them was one of rot. One towered so high its upper body disappeared into the thicker veil of fog. They trudged into view, eyes where a mouth should exist, the rest of their misshapen faces just as illogical. They were assorted colours of a dull grey, lizard green, pearl black, or a mix of those colours, all marching to the same drummer, that much was apparent.

Gabriel sensed no life in them, not even from the one that spoke.

Muerte unsheathed her main sword while holding the scythe along the back of her shoulders.

"They're not moving," she said. "Obviously, they have second thoughts thanks to me."

"Obviously," Gabriel said in a sarcastic tone. "I wasn't sure before, but yes, you're positively insane. Hephaestus!" he shouted.

"What are you doing? We're not cowards."

Any time someone uttered the name of Hephaestus, no matter the location, he was able to zero in on the speaker and open a portal.

"They don't attack because I don't will it," the angelic Tentacle said from a dense patch of fog. "And your portal maker friend did not hear you."

"But I killed you." Muerte raised her sword, breathing heavily, adrenaline pumping through her.

"You amuse me," the angelic Tentacle said. "This entire army is an extension of me." Its shadowed arms rosed with its side and back tentacles, as if in striking mode. "I'll tell you the secret to defeating all of them." It folded its meaty arms. "If you defeat me, they all collapse into slumber. But while I'm awake, they'll multiply. They'll regenerate no matter how many times you cut them down." It paused. "You have one of two choices. Defeat me or join—"

"First option," Muerte said, charging at the angelic Tentacle.

A huge tentacle coiled around Gabriel's chest, pulling him upwards. His wings spread out before another feeler spiraled around them.

"Muerte!"

She slipped into the fog, becoming a dark figure amongst the shadowed Tentacles making room for their king's coming skirmish. Muerte's shaded body twirled, the Tentacle King leaned back, the point of the scythe blade just missing its throat. Its tentacles reared up, recoiling above its head, and like stingers they lashed down at her. Muerte scythed any feelers coming at her. They sprouted back to their original lengths at unreal speed.

Gabriel pounded at the huge tentacle lifting him quickly to a misshapen face with uneven eyes, nose, and mouth. His blade-tipped raven-black wings hacked away at the massive tentacle, right to left, left to right, leaving only minor damage.

Gabriel looked down to see the Tentacle King gripping Muerte by the throat, its arms folded over its chest. It slammed her to the ground. Stomped her chest. The wind carried the copper scent of her blood, flaring Gabriel's nostrils, filling him with anger—and dread—that those bladed tentacles were going to cut her to pieces.

"Muerte!" Gabriel shouted down as the Tentacle King slowly lifted her to its face by one tentacle, her body limp. Suddenly, she sparked to life, head-butting its nose.

"Insolent brat." It tossed her to the ground. Stomped her face.

"I will kill you!" Gabriel shouted down at it. As he struggled to get loose, the grip of the feeler tightened. "Your army will fall before me as I stand on your lifeless body."

He had gone to that place he had never gone before, where the Almighty had told him he would someday go and that day he would taste his full potential and the heavy burden that would carry. The rush of panic. Of uncertainty. The sight of a vulnerable Muerte mockingly toyed with sent him into an uncontrollable rage, draining his captor of energy. The tentacle slid from him as he landed in a crouch. The giant Tentacle slammed into the ground, exploding in a cloud of dust within the light fog.

"That was unexpected," said the Tentacle King, lifting a lifeless Muerte high above it. "But it changes nothing."

The Burning of Souls

Lucifer

They cuddled against a fat-trunked oak, its huge, gnarled roots stretching out into the Lake of Souls. One arm hung over Lucifer's bent knee, the other leg yawning out. The blueish-grey spirits wordlessly drifted amongst each other, sometimes in the shape of their earlier incarnations, snaking around trees growing along the bank. Sometimes the wraiths passed through them, sending chills through Lucifer, humbling him into deeper thought about his immortality.

Questions flooded his thoughts. What if an angel perished, did they end up here? The belief was that once an immortal was dead, it was a done deal, no coming back. Adding to the pessimism was the fact his father wouldn't give him a straight answer when asked if angels had recyclable souls. Instead, a somber expression clouded his face, as if he were remembering something devastating from his past that he preferred buried forever.

"We call them mortals," Lucifer said of the spirits swirling around each other in playful abandonment. "Yet if we're slain, apparently we don't come back while they're reborn into another life form somewhere in the universe. I don't feel very immortal knowing that."

"No angel has killed another angel in our time," Lilith said, her head beneath his chin, her breath warm against his neck. "It's bound to happen sooner rather than later. It will start like it does with the mortals. One angel kills another. The fallen is avenged leading to another casualty. Two in a snap of a finger gone from existence. The death seed then planted, sprouts two more leaves, their names Hate and Revenge. More angels perish. There will be no coming back from it. But you have nothing to worry about. You're of his blood and can't be killed unless by your father or maybe your sister."

"But you can die."

"Stating the obvious."

"Which means a part of me can be killed too."

Lilith squeezed him tighter. She was his perfect match. Like him, she took no guff from anyone, especially the male persuasion, always making it clear that she was equal or better and proving it through sharp words or in combat. And if anybody crossed him behind his back, she made quick work of them for all to see. She never let him get lazy in the mind. She was always at his side and always wanting good for the Order, like a true queen.

"I sense the day is coming soon when one of our kind is slain," Lucifer said. "It feels like I'm screaming from the future inside my own head, or someone is, warning me of something unspeakable happening. I just don't know who. Or when."

"What has brought on this mood, Lucifer? The planet's suddenly devoid of life? Come now, your father did it. You know this in your heart. No one else could've done it."

"If you're right, then that's cause for concern."

"They're just mortals. They come back here, then they go back out there somewhere."

"First they experience a cleansing." Something Lucifer never told anyone was a vision his father had shared with him when he was still a youngling. He had never been sure if it was something invented by his father, but it had looked and felt real. "Their flesh and bone burning from them. A nightmarish place between this reality and another. A portal opened by my father is the only way there. The virtuous get a quick exit to the Lake, with their flesh burned away by intense fire, painful, but mercifully quicker compared to others. They fuel a hellish train as if they were coal. It has a skull face as its locomotive, flames exhale from its nostrils with every soul forced into it, over and over, until their sins burn away. The most wretched are chained to walls and slowly dismembered, aware to the very end, their head always thrown last into the furnace. It's not something anyone would be in a hurry to experience and so many just have."

"I didn't know." Lilith stared out into the Lake of Souls.

"It makes you pause with deep thought, yes?"

A soul passed through her. The expression on her face, like she just experienced mortality for the first time.

"It makes me think how sick your father can be."

"He says it's for their own good, makes them stronger for the next life."

"What point is there in burning their past lives away? How will they evolve, learn from their past mistakes? Why not just make them immortal like us?"

"There are many things I've not shared with anyone, but that stops tonight. No more secrets between us. We'll need to be at our strongest and most connected for what I sense is coming. If my father has truly gone mad, then what will stop him from killing angels next?"

"It feels like he has already started."

She snuggled into him.

The morning star rose over the Rainbow Ridge, brightening the colourful glow of the blinking mountains, a signal of the illumination that was coming. She held him tight as the morning star grew to its brightest. Next to come were the two rising suns, the whole effect created by Lucifer's mother to mark his and Calliope's births. It was one of the few things he knew of his mother.

"Someday you'll learn the truth about her, Lucifer."

The Tentacle King

Gabriel

Gabriel held his sword firm and true, surrounded by these hellish beasts. Not one made a move towards him. They emitted no feelings, no life. They were empty vessels remote controlled. Was this Tentacle King afraid to lose more of its army? Unlikely—it didn't seem perturbed by anything. Regardless of the outcome, Gabriel was ready to fight his way through the blockade to rescue Muerte from the fiend's clutches.

"You could try," the Tentacle King said from within the thick of the fog, Muerte limp in one of its tendrils. "But I'd drain the last of her life before you reached me." It pulled Muerte closer to its face. "She has a curious mind. I can't quite penetrate its chaos without permanently damaging her."

48

Tentacles shuffled from each other, creating a path to their king, as if daring Gabriel to try rescuing Muerte.

"You're from the same spark, close friends or devoted lovers in this life. At the beginning, thirty-three sparks from the swing of El's sword on the rock face of the tallest mountain of your planet created the original Order. The same spark is always attracted to its other pieces. That's your lesson for today on the universe, suckling."

The Tentacle King paused, drawing Muerte closer.

"Yes, that's what you both are. Death Dealers. I could burrow deeper, but neither of you have anything I haven't seen before." Its shadowed side remained to Gabriel, not once looking his way. "What do I do with you two then?"

Gabriel couldn't charge into the fog. Even if he got by the Tentacle King's army via air or ground, it would kill Muerte without pause. He was sure of that much.

"What are you?" Gabriel was stalling, working out his next move.

"Here." It tossed Muerte to Gabriel between the line of Tentacles. She rolled to his feet, ghost white. "And here." Her sword arrowed by the two lines of Tentacles, impaling the soil next to her head. "And these." The shadowy thing tossed Muerte's leg blades, twisted around her scythe. "A peace offering, if you wish. Or the reality of it, you are no threat to me."

Gabriel focused on the enemy at either side of him, ready to drain them into dust. But there were so many of them, and an incapacitated Muerte wasn't helping matters.

"You have my word . . . Gabriel." It knew his name. "My army will let you leave intact."

He couldn't get them both out of here without the Tentacles swarming them, or the taller ones swatting them like flies. Reluctantly, he sheathed his sword. Gabriel crouched, lifting a limp Muerte into his arms, his wings still in full bloom. He looked for the lowest point of the surrounding army, where he might escape in flight with her.

"Why do you follow El?" the shadowed Tentacle King asked, turning to Gabriel. "I was once his friend, until he betrayed me. Wars followed until he and his minions eradicated my brethren. He thought he'd ended me. Ridiculous. I am a true immortal. I've existed in the shadows for eons. Your kind and I have almost crossed paths before. Even you, Gabriel, walked mere seconds from me. I've watched his lunacy play out the same way, rebooting the universe, starting over, always the same result. He can't fathom why nothing changes, when it's so obvious."

"Tell me," Gabriel said. "How is destroying all life on planets any better?" His straw-blond curls brushed Muerte's face. He still barely detected any life in her. "It appears you've killed many of my kind, yet you expect to have my ear?"

"El has the Order annihilate entire planets when he concludes they are a mistake. I'm simply speeding things up and erasing all his blunders." The Tentacle King's tentacles relaxed at its sides. "I'm still undecided about your kind. Don't worry, I haven't killed any of your compatriots."

It nodded up at the hazed sky. The fog gave way to the rugged shoulders of the taller Tentacles where the missing angels were perched. They, like Gabriel and Muerte, had been sent to investigate the genocide of the planets in the surrounding area.

"Aether?" Gabriel said of one of the former members of the Council of Twelve, relieved of his duties for being too loud with his opinions. "Caelus? Uranus? Hyperion, even you?"

All Elders. They silently stared down.

"They've been around a long time and see things my way," the Tentacle King said. "Like you do, Gabriel. I know your doubt. I've been there. I don't need to read your thoughts. It's in your eyes, in the tone of your voice."

Muerte moved a little in Gabriel's arms.

"My words fall on empty ears while you're concerned for her," the Tentacle King said. "You love her."

Gabriel looked up to see the Tentacle King make its way out of the fog.

"Oh, you do. But someday that love will be your undoing. That kind of amity always is. It never gets old with me. Always amuses me how foolish and soft love makes your kind."

It stepped out to reveal itself.

Dark hair down its chiseled, angelic face, branching down its massive chest. It was a mix of dark green and deep blue and swirls of midnight black. Tentacles protruded from the sides of its muscular arms, shoulders, and back, eyes amongst the suction cups, all weaponized with bladed ends. His talons looked like they could tear away mountain rock like flesh. His ancient bat-like wings stretched as far out as the Almighty's.

"Tell El that Cthulhu is coming for a visit. Now go before I change my mind and make you the first immortals to die in a long, long time."

A Foreboding Ringing

Lucifer

The Gjallarhorn blew so loudly it caused heavy winds throughout the planet Elysium. When the horn blared, angels in the universe could hear it no matter which assigned planet they were on, starting out as a ringing in their ears.

They stood up. Held hands. The morning star faded from view during the completion of the double sunrise. Rainbow Ridge lit up into streaks of every colour imaginable.

"It appears, my dear, that the genocides and vanishings of our sisters and brothers now have an origin."

"To new beginnings, husband."

"What do you mean?" It seemed an odd thing for her to say. "Another vision?"

"Yes."

"Are you going to tell me?" Glimpses of the future were one of her gifts, more than his or anyone else's.

53

"First, we witness this mystery unravel, then we talk about my visions, King Lucifer."

An Ancient Game of Chess

Gabriel

"We must strike now!" Muerte shouted up at the Almighty's throne, with Gabriel at her side, making sure she didn't do something stupid. Both were still in their war armour. "He's getting stronger."

On the outside, Muerte had fully healed. Inside, Gabriel feared she may never recover. He could see it in her eyes, a madness setting in.

The homes of every angel in the universe surrounded them like they were in a towering coliseum, reaching twenty-two floors and split unevenly into three groups, the warrior cast on the top levels, with everyone able to hear with equal clarity.

Gabriel was embarrassed. The entire hierarchy of angels knew the only reason why Muerte and he were standing here was because they had been soundly defeated and sent back as messengers. They were Death Dealers, proud, never retreating, always fighting until victory. He'd had that chance to fight the Tentacle King but instead let his heart overrule his honour.

"I would do it again," he shouted. "Though it is our tradition to never retreat, I could not risk her life."

"No one is judging you, Gabriel," Lucifer said, standing next to his father's throne. Lilith leaned into her husband's side. Lucifer's sister, Calliope, stood alone on the other side, quiet. "You made the right decision. Otherwise we would still be in the dark."

The Almighty remained neutral, no doubt reading their minds. Though he had given his word never to violate anyone's privacy, no one believed it.

"Heed my words"—Muerte looked up at the angels standing or crouching at the doorways of their living quarters—"we still outnumber his army, one that we can defeat by his downfall. The time to fight is now. He's been watching, studying us for a long time. He knows of our weakness for stalling, for discussing things until we're covered in dust. He won't see us coming. His arrogance will be his ruin."

"Muerte's right.," Gabriel stepped forwards. "Waiting allows his forces to grow. He's nothing we've seen before, a monster born from our bedtime stories and myths."

"They multiply at an alarming rate by his feeding off souls," Muerte continued. "He has burnt these images into my mind. He's determined to devour every soul, including dimming the Lake of Souls of its life. He has a keen interest in that, but not before slaying you, my Lord. You're his greatest prize."

The Almighty maintained a stoic expression on his smooth, bronze face, sitting there in his usual drab white tunic. Every angel was looking at him from all levels of the Nest. He didn't fit the profile of the oldest living thing. He seemed youthful, not much older than his offspring, yet he was older than any Elder.

"Nonsense!" Odin shouted. In ice-blue armour, he stood along the wall of the bottom floor next to his best friend Zeus. Both looked ready for war. "Our Lord would have sensed so many misplaced souls."

"I saw it in my mind, everything."

Muerte didn't acknowledge Odin with a look, much to Gabriel's amusement. There was an unfriendly history between the two. She had bettered him in swordplay once as his pupil and he made her pay for it in the next round.

"Images of Tentacles reaching throughout the entire universe, every planet, moon, and sun. And you" Muerte looked up at their Lord — "his tentacles rolled your body down to his feet. Your face dried up like a statue and blew away into dust."

The Almighty's eyes widened, and the crimson pulse within the back crystal of his throne sped up, then returned to its usual steady rhythm. Gabriel could clearly hear angels whispering to each other, remarking on their king being in such shock. However short the moment was, it left its negative impressions.

"Hyperion would never betray us," a white bearded Zeus said. He wore the crimson armour that the rest of his bloodline wore to show solidarity. "Or the others. She said it herself." He nodded at Muerte. "This creature tried reading her mind, left things in there. She's a unique breed of our Order, one not easily influenced or infiltrated. Such a power that can even scar her mind is foreboding." Zeus looked up at the Almighty who looked in deep thought. "It may have Hyperion and the others under some form of mind control."

"He," Muerte said. "Not it."

"Zeus is partially right." The Almighty finally spoke. "The younger are more easily swayed. But Hyperion and the rest are first generation, seasoned and impregnable to such manipulations. Cthulhu attracts his own kind of lunacy. They've joined him willingly."

"He says you're mad" — Muerte stepped forward — "and that you murdered his kind."

"Enough, Muerte." Gabriel held her arm, keeping her from going any further. She shrugged loose and continued towards the throne steps. They had already discussed this, agreeing that it wasn't wise to air out such grievances in public. They were to request a personal audience with their king to discuss the Tentacle King's claims.

"Is this an act of revenge?" Muerte stopped at the steps.

Lucifer, in his dragon bone armour, placed one hand on the hilt of his sword. Calliope, in a knee-length tunic, bent over and whispered something in her father's ear.

"All those planets drained of life because of some old hate he has for you?"

"Mind your mouth." Lucifer descended halfway to the top step, hand still clasping his sheathed blade, his three sets of wings raised. "Last warning."

"We must strike now." Muerte didn't back off. What spunk. "You of all angels, Lucifer, must agree."

"It makes no sense!" Odin hollered in his booming voice.

"I agree with Odin," Zeus said.

Missing from Zeus's side was his father, Cronus. Odd, considering the circumstances. It wouldn't go unnoticed by their king. Another slap in their Lord's face? It was no secret they disliked each other.

Odin continued, "It could enter through one of the portals our Lord has left open throughout the universe and ambush us. Yet this Cthulhu doesn't. He even gives up the element of surprise by revealing his identity and location, tells us we can defeat his army by defeating him? He shows heights of arrogance not even Zeus can reach." Laughter came from others while Zeus glowered at his friend. "No, something's not right with this story."

"It's not a *story*, Old Beard." Muerte glared at Odin.

"The age-old problem of youth," Odin said, "always thinking emotionally. Stupid youngling."

Gabriel squeezed the handle of his sword.

Odin did the same, grinning. Daring him to try.

"Stand down, you two!" Michael shouted from the parapet walk of the Nest, standing in place of Lucifer with the silver-armoured Seraphim. Other warrior casts like the black-armoured Death Dealers stood below the Seraphim along the ledges of the upper levels. "Emotion is getting the better of you all. It's what this new enemy wants. Divide us. Scare us into doing something stupid."

Michael was Lucifer's protégé and second in command of the Seraphim. The Almighty's most loyal.

"Many more races will become distant whispers if we continue stalling." Muerte put one foot on the bottom throne step, no further, no doubt her way of sending a message to Lucifer that she wasn't backing down.

Gabriel readied himself to stop her doing something irrational. He didn't think she would, but he needed to make appearances that he was ready. He would fight by her side against anybody but the Almighty if it came down to it.

"Are you going to sit there and give excuses?" she continued. "Or are we going to strike now?"

"Rest now, both of you, while I discuss this with the Twelve," the Almighty said. The Twelve consisted of the likes of Zeus, Odin, Lucifer, and Cronus, if he showed up. "You exhibited bravery today, Muerte, when most would flee against such insurmountable odds." He leaned forwards. "Sometimes bravery makes us shortsighted. You're lucky to be alive." He stood up. The tips of his vast, heavenly white wings curved to either side of Muerte, flapping a gentle breeze of calla lily scent.

"You old fossils take forever to decide things, slowing the rest of the Twelve down," Muerte said. "Stop biding time, my Lord. Are you scared of him?"

Lucifer clenched the hilt of his sword, taking another step down, and said, "You'll be represented well, Muerte, I promise. Now remember your place."

Gabriel stopped next to Muerte. "She speaks the truth. We must act now. The Twelve are notorious for taking an eternity to make decisions. They're too divided these days. Cronus can't even be bothered to show up, even after the great horn is blown."

"What are you implying, Gabriel?" Zeus looked ready to withdraw his sword. "Consider your next words carefully. My father has his reasons for not being here."

"That your father is self-serving, with eyes for the throne," Muerte said before Gabriel could speak. "He can't be trusted."

Zeus started drawing his sword from his scabbard.

"As stated, Muerte, your viewpoints will be heard." Lucifer smirked down at Zeus; no doubt amused as Gabriel was at his annoyance. Lucifer turned to walk back up the steps. Before he reached the top, his wings lowered and he looked back over his shoulder, down at Muerte. "Are you sure the growth of his army depends on souls?"

"It's more like he feeds on them, allowing him to make more of these Tentacles."

Lucifer nodded at her, then made his way back to his father's side.

"He wants us to chase after him," the Almighty said. "This is a game to him. He's been strategically planning this for a long time. He didn't just snap into existence. He's been around longer than any of you."

"This isn't a game of chess." Muerte pushed off from the bottom step, backing up towards Gabriel. "We mortals and angels aren't pawns to be sacrificed for an ancient feud. Do those who don't have hearts for war a favour and meet this Cthulhu on a faraway planet to settle your differences."

Muerte turned away,, her black, crimson-tipped wings spread out. She flew upwards, leaving the Nest, and out of sight.

"My Lord, she's still hot from battle. I'll counsel her."

The Almighty nodded with approval, no clear anger in his expression. The heartbeat of his throne had slowed down, not sped up like Gabriel expected. It was a good sign no punishment was coming Muerte's way for speaking out.

"That's right," Odin shouted at Gabriel. "Chase after her like a lovesick fool."

"One of these days, Old Beard." Gabriel's dark wings spread wide as he turned away from the throne to fly after Muerte. "You will fall before my feet."

Prophesied King

Lucifer

"Zeus loathes you and thinks you a weakling," Lilith said from the dais of the throne, "but the coward won't say it in earshot."

Lucifer's father was way up there atop Mount Titan, waiting for the remaining Twelve to show up. A gnarled butte, Mount Titan overshadowed the Nest and during midday gave a beautiful view of the sparkling blue of the Serene Sea backgrounding Rainbow Ridge.

"There will be a day you and Zeus fight for the throne."

Lilith not only saw visions, but she picked up thoughts, the type that were loud with ill intent.

"You forget I feel strong emotions, too, and I'm quite aware that the mere sight of me greatly perturbs him. Share with me this vision you had about a war amongst our kind."

"Perhaps I should wait until after the meeting. Giving you such images to think about may cloud your decision-making."

"Enough teasing."

She put her arms around his neck like she was ready to kiss him. "A great war comes, one between our kind."

"With these Tentacles?"

"They're not in this vision. Neither is your father."

"When is this war?"

"I don't know."

What did that mean? The fact that the Tentacles weren't in this vision, meant there was a good chance they had been defeated at some point, but angels fighting amongst themselves in a great war, in the modern age, was unthinkable. What of his father? Outside the view of her vision? Had he fallen? Could the universe even survive such a shock? The greatest thinker of the angels, and closest confidant to Lucifer's father was Baiame, who had once told Lucifer that if his father's blood died, everything would collapse upon itself, shrinking into nonexistence.

"And what else, Lilith?"

"And at the end of this vision, you're standing at your father's destroyed throne in battered and bloodied armour, as king."

In Sync

Gabriel

He found Muerte sitting cross-legged on the tallest peak of the Rainbow Ridge overlooking the Lake of Souls to the west and the Hanging Gardens to the south and the Serene Sea behind it. Each mountain pulsated its distinct own colour along with their own heartbeats.

Gabriel landed behind her. She didn't look back.

"Mind the company?"

"Depends," she said, still not looking back, "if you're going to nag me or not?"

He sat next to her. Her snow-white hair grazed his face from a sudden breeze, strains of it tickling his nose and filling his nostrils with the scent of daffodils.

"I agree with what you said back there," he said.

"You're just saying that to set my ears up for some loud chiding."

"They've become stale." Gabriel had once been just like her, always looking for confrontation. "I saw doubt in the Lord's eyes. It's like he didn't expect this. His throne at one point even warned of rage."

"He isn't all knowing," Muerte remarked. "He's as vulnerable as we are."

"Don't underestimate him." Gabriel sat with one leg bent up, his feathers accidentally touching hers. He willed his wing away from hers. "When it's all said and done, I always put my faith in the Big Guy."

"Then you're as *stale* as the rest of them."

Muerte went back to staring at the sunset. The pulsating mix of colours on Rainbow Ridge flashed on her face the darker it got.

"I do agree we must attack soon," Gabriel said. "I also agree we must do it on our terms. We're all on the same page, but we're all too stubborn to see that."

"More like they're all too stupid to see what's coming." Finally, she looked at him. It wasn't quite fear he saw in her expression, more like she was searching for answers in his expression. "You were there. We shouldn't be alive. Cthulhu has the power to take immortal life with ease. It's a game to him, just as it is to our *wise* leader. And both have their own armies they'll lead into battle, eventually leading to the two of them fighting it out so why don't they just do it now and save the rest of us the horrors the images burnt into my mind promise."

"You, looking for a reason not to fight? How you've grown so quickly before my eyes."

"I'm looking out for those who've never seen battle of any kind, the thinkers, the artistic. To outnumber the enemy we'll need everyone, and that's a lot of unwilling hearts."

For a while they silently sat there. She moved Gabriel like no other, lighting a fire inside him and another under his ass. She made him feel alive, made him care about things again. He thought about something he had been hesitant to do, an urge growing stronger every second.

Her wing slid along the edge of his.

"You know what? Sometimes we should just follow our hearts," he said. "Screw it."

Both hands gently clasped her face as he kissed her deeply, eyes closed. His face pulled back from hers. Soft, watery eyes stared back at him, then they embraced while Rainbow Ridge pulsed in sync with their heartbeats.

Hairline Crack

Calliope

The Twelve had just voted seven to five in favour of not attacking now. Calliope had gotten a look of disapproval from her brother, Lucifer. He had told her long ago that there would be a day she would have to vote in favour of war despite her desire for everlasting tranquility throughout the universe. And today was that day to the shock of everyone. It was no surprise to anyone that Odin, Zeus, Cronus, and Lucifer voted in favour of an immediate response. War was the only thing the four of them ever agreed on. But this was something different. This wasn't a planet of mortals they were dealing with.

Muerte and Gabriel were fearless, and it was unprecedented to see them unnerved like that. How tempting it was for Calliope to read their minds, break her covenant with the Order, but she didn't have to. Her yes vote was decided before she even attended the meeting.

"Cronus, your absence earlier was noted," her father said, still in his tunic like the majority of the Council. Those voting yes for action were the only ones armoured, including Calliope, much to the displeasure of her father who was overprotective of her.

"I needed time to think," Cronus replied, his lips hidden within his bushy red beard.

"About?"

"The future of my House. Every father must hand over their legacy at some point." Cronus, in the crimson armour all his House wore, didn't shy from her father's glare. "Even you. To that." He nodded over at Lucifer.

With a loving presence, Calliope tempered her brother by putting her hand on the armoured chest, causing him pause, enough time for him to come to his senses and not confront Cronus for disrespecting him. Calliope was the strongest empath of them, outside their father, and the surge of anger emanating from her brother was the kind that led to physical confrontations. Lucifer sat back from the Round Table, which was made of all stone, including the seats and their backrests.

71

The giant tablet looming behind them had the Twelve Commandments written in eternal flame. At dark, its blazing laws were clear from Rainbow Ridge.

"I thought you were made of hardier stuff, Ra," Lucifer said, looking over at one of the Order's most decorated warriors, who was in his humanoid form as all Shapeshifters were. A strict rule by their father, all must be in their angelic form. This was much to Ra's displeasure, along with the angel sitting next to him, Shiva, who preferred his four-armed and blue-skinned form. "You've grown lazy, like the rest of the Elders at this table."

"Brother, honourable Ra is just being cautious. He's been around a long time."

That was her brother, finding another way to burn off his present anger spurned by Cronus and that smirking Zeus. That was one smug face she would like to roundhouse kick. She didn't share such feelings aloud. No one imagined she had such dark thoughts, but she didn't like the House of Cronus. Not one bit.

"The Death Dealers are right. We must strike now." Lucifer slammed his fists down on the table, causing a hairline crack to form on its surface. Impressive, considering the stone was impregnable with only their father able to obliterate it. That was the belief, anyway. Their father smirked widely at Lucifer like he was the proudest father ever, as odd as that seemed, for lately Lucifer could do nothing right. No, it was a forced smile. A different feeling was coming off her father, as if he'd had enough surprises for the day. And was that fear? Surely not.

"While we waste our time sniffing around like dogs for faded footprints," Lucifer continued, "this new enemy is waiting on one of the nearby planets. Where else would they be? It's not even a day since the Death Dealers returned. It shouldn't be hard to find these Tentacles. As much as I disapprove of Gabriel's hasty and barbaric tactics, under the leadership of myself and Michael, the Seraphim and Death Dealers will soundly defeat this enemy."

"Make sure you're doing the talking," Zeus said. "You speak more like your wife with each passing day."

Lucifer bit into his bottom lip, then said to their father, "Enough innocents have died, unless that's what you want?"

"What are you implying?" their father demanded, leaning against the backrest of his throne.

"You don't seem overly concerned about the genocides on these six planets," Lucifer said. "The inhabitants were the most peaceful and enlightened in the universe who exceeded your expectations. As their reward, their planets were portalled closer to Elysium and your heart. Yet it's like they never existed to you."

Calliope wanted to tell Lucifer to back off, but he was right. She didn't detect any sadness from her father, only annoyance.

"Emotion can cloud sound judgment," their father said. "Their deaths will be avenged. They will be recycled into the universe, you know this."

"I'm also aware of the process mortals go through after death. Don't worry, Father, I won't speak of it. But I will say this, the Lake hasn't swelled with souls these past months, so where did they all go? The other side of the chessboard, that's where. Isn't that right, Father? An age-old game being played between you and this Cthulhu."

Calliope sensed the expected glee coming from Cronus and Zeus. Odin seemed annoyed, along with Ra. The others were of mixed feelings. Yet no ill feeling towards their father emanated from Lucifer, who was more frustrated than anything.

"I have fought Cthulhu," their father said. "His kind are not something to be taken lightly."

"But you eliminated all but one," Calliope said. "What is one of him? He surely doesn't exceed the strength of his entire race. He has a puppet army. Take him down and they all fall, freeing those souls from him, yes? You could do that, Father, and end all this right away."

A spike of emotion came from him. Fear, or at least doubt in his own ability to deal with this ancient enemy. Then, the harsh feeling softened into something like betrayal, as if he felt Calliope was betraying him.

"You forget, sister, he can't sense Cthulhu." Their father glanced at Lucifer as he spoke, fists balling up. "So, the Council is firm with its vote, then?"

"The Council has spoken." Their father scanned the table, making eye contact with every member as he said, "Search and report back. No contact with the enemy. Understand, Lucifer? Use reason, not emotion, to influence final decisions."

"Does this mean I'm back in service already?"

"You were never out of it. Zeus is right, you listen to Lilith too much."

Lucifer stood up, and looked down at the hairline crack in the stone, pointing at it while looking over at their father, saying nothing as he turned away and spread his three sets of wings. He dove up into the clouds in a bright sparkle, then dropped like a shooting star, and out of sight.

Calliope watched her father reach out to put his forefinger at the end of the hairline crack to seal it up, but instead, he backed off and left it there.

POSEIDON IN CTHULHU'S GRIP

JAMES PYNE

Shattered

Poseidon

These days Poseidon was very much in love with one angel, and one angel only. Her name was Posedia and she had done what most believed impossible—she had tamed the playboy in him. The last week or so, she hadn't been saying much and had been spending time with his father, Cronus, more than she had with him. Rumours were flying about that, but he didn't take much stock in gossipmongers. They were jealous of his relationship, just like they were envious of his newfound friendship with the Almighty.

And now Posedia suddenly was one of those angels questioning his chumminess with their king.

"He has only befriended you to cause division in your father's House," she said.

"You sound like my brothers," Poseidon replied.

"He looks at the House of Cronus as the biggest threat to his rule."

"He doesn't talk ill of my father."

"You're so gullible."

"He's been more of a patriarch to me these last few years than my own."

"And there's the division I speak of."

They glided over a snow-capped mountain range. Posedia and he were exploring one of five planets this ancient enemy might be invading while making its way to the throne planet. They were checking up the planet next to the one recently devoid of life, though Poseidon suspected the enemy was hiding within the Nibiru asteroid belt, plotting its next move.

Poseidon's thick, pointed beard stuck out of his horse-hair ornamented helmet. His crimson armour complemented his bulging muscles. His sword was sheathed, his trident clenched in one hand, the only weapon he really needed. The other paired off angels investigating the other planets in the coming hours would be Zeus and his unhinged wife, Hera. And Michael and his one-time apprentice Aphrodite. Hades would be with his niece Persephone, and Lucifer and his beloved Lilith. Poseidon and Posedia had left early in hopes of being the ones to find the approaching evil. First bragging rights and all that, but he hadn't expected Posedia to nag him along the way. Time to return the favour.

"You could have dressed the part."

He was referring to Posedia wearing just a blue cloth wrapped around her breasts and a scanty loincloth. He would have pestered her to wear armour, but she would only have gone naked. A quick healer like him made them an impossible duo to beat.

"What are a few scratches?" she retorted.

"Your combat skills are legendary, Posedia, but neither of us are Death Dealers. Two of their best were pacified quickly enough."

"When did you become such a nag?"

"Just giving you a taste of your own medicine." He winked.

"You're not fooling anyone. You worry too much about me." Posedia's blue-feathered wings flapped the scent of lily. "After all, I am the only of my gender who went the distance with Athena."

"You still lost."

She said nothing to that.

The shadows from their vast wings moved over a sudden thick fog covering the land, billowing up the mountains and the gargantuan trees where the inhabitants of this planet lived. They knew nothing of war and were close to their Lord's heart.

"The scent of fresh death hangs in the air," Poseidon said. "Muerte spoke of a swift fog, yes?"

"He's down there," Posedia said, nosediving into the mist.

He plunged in after her. They were supposed to report back to Hephaestus with anything unusual, then he would pass it on to the Almighty. If a portal opened, they were to return without incident.

The heavy fog gave way to a mountain of carcasses within a lake of blood. All life on this planet was here.

"Posedia," he shouted, landing on rocky ground.

"She's with me," an ancient voice replied.

Poseidon turned to see a shadowed figure mosey into view, its blade-tipped tentacles reaching for the hazy sky. His angelic face and body hinted of an unknown era of the Order. Poseidon bumped the hilt of his trident on the rocky surface. The ground rumbled. It was his warning. He wanted to vibrate the Tentacle King's flesh into pieces, but the unknown fate of Posedia crippled his resolve.

"She's back there with my army." The Tentacle King's bladed feelers made swishing sounds from cutting the air, like he was warning Poseidon back. "She's fitting right in."

"Release my wife."

That uncontrollable rage Poseidon was known for was surfacing. The butt of his Poseidon's trident hit the ground ten times harder. The rock it had impacted cracked.

A sudden wind cleared the fog around them.

"I'm not your enemy." Cthulhu's tentacles lowered. "I know what it's like to be used by El. He is not your friend. He will dispose of the Order when he bores of it, like he does with everything else. Now join me" — his tentacles reached towards Poseidon in a non-aggressive manner — "and together, with my army, we'll cleanse the universe of his diseased mind and create a golden age for immortals."

"Release Posedia now."

The impact of Poseidon's trident opened the crack in the ground deeper.

"Haven't figured it out yet?" the Tentacle King said. "She has joined me."

"What did you do to her?"

"It was of her own free will."

"You're lying."

"I am the harsh truth. Your precious El sits on a throne of lies. Then you choose him?"

"Always."

"A pity."

The scent of lily drifted Poseidon's way.

"Posedia?"

Before he could turn around, a great force slammed into the back of Poseidon's armour, sending him straight into Cthulhu's tentacles.

"Sorry, Hon," Posedia said from behind. "Make it quick, like you promised."

Tentacles tightened around Poseidon's body, pinning his arms. One tentacle swatted his helmet from his head. Another curled around his neck, pulling his face closer to the Tentacle King.

Poseidon, feeling his life slip away, looked back and whispered, "Posedia? Why?"

Her hair dripped red from the lake of blood she appeared to have been hiding in, licking it from the corner of her lips as a look of ecstasy came over her.

"I'm done with fools," she said. "And if you want to follow that old relic, then I'm done with you."

"Betray your own kind?" A tentacle pulled Poseidon's trident from his grip with little resistance. "Betray me?"

The tentacles tightened. Poseidon head-butted Cthulhu, who remained emotionless. Was this death? No pain. It was peaceful, making it hard to resist the comfortable blackness offered, the welcoming silence from the noisy universe, from the stunning betrayal by the only angel he had ever genuinely loved.

"You promised!" Posedia yelled.

The Tentacle King slowly released Poseidon to the ground, barely alive, left there with something worse than death. A shattered heart.

A Balance

Calliope

Cronus was the last to speak with Calliope's father before his long, flaming wings filled the air with the scent of burning coal. He soared through the night sky, dipping to the Nest, leaving only Calliope and her father standing at the edge of Mount Titan. His arms folded while they watched the sky wraiths circling each other before dispersing into clouds.

"They enjoy life more than any living thing," the Almighty said. "Imagine that. Ten minutes at best and they enjoy every second of it. No complaining. No ingratitude."

"Cronus is just trying to stir the pot."

Cronus had just given him fatherly advice when it came to Lucifer. The temptation was there for

Calliope to put Cronus in his place, tell him to take his own advice and apply it to Zeus. She kept her cool for the sake of her father, whom she sensed carried enough burden. The only vibe she got from Cronus was the usual greed for power. Even if she dared break the rules and explore Cronus's mind, she would only get surface thoughts as Elders were difficult to read.

"I was once impulsive like Lucifer. You'd think I would be more tolerant because of that, wouldn't you?" Her father smiled down at her. "There are days when I just want to spank him over my knee in front of everyone."

"You exaggerate. He has always been a good son to you. He questions his purpose in the universe. He's gotten bored with everything and then along comes your haunting past, promising glory to anyone who faces it. In his eyes, you're holding him back."

"Well, my dear, let's hope he has the guts to go with the glory. These are not mortals in the coming battleground. Dark magic is what we will be facing. Unimaginable horrors. The longer the battle, the stronger they will become. The source of their life will need to be quenched quickly."

With a gentle hand on her father's chest, Calliope stopped him from leaving for his throne.

"Father, what does Lucifer mean, that mortal souls go through another process before ending up in the Lake? His tone made it sound horrible."

"Another time, Calliope." The Almighty looked up at one of the green planets in the evening sky, as if he sensed something or was trying to pinpoint a location.

"Why do you tell Lucifer such things and not me?"

"You are persistent, daughter."

"Like my mother?"

"You represent the beauty of everything I've created." He always avoided talking about her mother, someone she and Lucifer had never known. "You are pure, always the soothing voice in this Council, where the rest of us have war and personal gain in our hearts. Yet today you voted yes for war."

"I would prefer you facing this old friend of yours, but that wasn't an option on the table. We can't stand and wait for an attack."

"I understand. It would not have been an easy decision for you. Do not lose focus on who you are. Remain that purity needed not just in the Council, but as an example for every angel. But these things you persist on . . ." He kissed her on the forehead. "You do not need to know. They will only darken you." He looked up at the night sky, and a look of sadness came over him. "Everything must play out naturally." He forced a smile.

"Then why sour Lucifer with these things?"

"A balance. It was you or him. He craves the power, the throne, then if he is worthy, he will carry the burdens I do or he will" — her father looked down at that hairline crack Lucifer had made on the table, then looked back up at night sky — "break under the pressure."

A Mutual Betrayal

Poseidon

Poseidon lay in a weakened state, heartbroken, wishing death would find him, the reality of the ultimate betrayal having ripped his soul to pieces.

It was the Almighty who found him.

"I sensed your brush with death," the Almighty said. He knelt on one knee, in golden armour ornate with etchings of mythical creatures. "He left you here for me to find. Where is Posedia? Suddenly, I cannot sense her."

"She betrayed me." It was embarrassing to say that. "Betrayed all of us."

"Cthulhu influenced her mind, Poseidon. She is of the newer generation, weaker to his words."

The Almighty helped him to a sitting position.

"I know her eyes. She went willingly like the others. I saw it. He burnt each of their betrayals into my mind, the last image always Posedia grinning down at me before walking off with *him*."

"I can't sense his presence."

"He teased me with images of future angels betraying us."

"Who?"

"He erased their faces from my memory."

"Think harder."

"You could dig yourself. You have my permission."

The Almighty never entered anyone's mind unless given permission, just like his daughter, or any mind reader. Poseidon had nothing to hide. El didn't look Poseidon's way, but he was inside there, his intrusion undetectable.

"Black spots," the Almighty said. "Much is missing from today. I don't even see his face—inked out before your view turns to him. All I see is Posedia's betrayal."

"All I see is her betrayal. Poseidon stared past him into the empty sky. "A dagger plunged through my heart."

"I won't lie." He helped Poseidon up. "You will not be the same. A bumpy road lies ahead. In the end you will do the right thing when it truly matters. You will be okay, my friend."

"How can you tell me you know it'll be okay? You don't know sorrow. You don't fear an end because you're truly immortal. Never have you experienced a lover's betrayal. You don't—"

"I have known the deepest of love." The Almighty clasped Poseidon's armoured shoulders. "And she crushed me as Posedia trampled you."

A Dreadful Realization

Calliope

Her father suddenly willed his armour to grow from him as he portalled from Mount Titan. He mentioned something about Poseidon, that his pain was unbearable due the familiarity of it and that only he could help him now.

These days, he treated Poseidon more like a son than he did Lucifer, but she now understood why. Their talk this evening had made things clearer. He wasn't harder on Lucifer than everyone else out of hate, but for the good of the Order. Lucifer was being groomed to take the throne, it felt like her father was making sure the throne would be inherited by someone worthy, someone hardened by ill fate.

What did that mean for Lucifer? What unfortunate things awaited him?

It seemed impossible that there would be an heir to their father's throne because he was indestructible, but she was beginning to question that line of thinking. When his eyes had widened at Muerte's mention of Cthulhu's name, a spike of what appeared to be dread had emanated from him. However briefly, it had been there. What did that mean? Could this ancient thing kill the Almighty? The thought of it horrified her. Was Lucifer even ready if such a day came?

Destructive Rage

Poseidon

The Almighty let Poseidon wreck the place and he was grateful for the gesture. It was a lifeless planet now anyway.

"She was everything to me." Poseidon slammed the butt of his trident hard on the slabs of rock, causing the mountain of flesh and lake of blood to drop from sight, leaving a large sinkhole. Such power was within him, but the trident created by the portal maker, Hephaestus, amplified his abilities tenfold.

"I'll kill him." He spoke of the Tentacle King as he took flight, gliding over the lifeless world. "I'll strangle him with those tentacles of his and drain his life by his own touch. I'll make her watch. She'll grovel. She'll beg for me to take her back. I swear it."

A calmness came over him as he added, "Then, at the peak of her begging, I'll enjoy the horror in her eyes as I drain her to within a whisper of becoming a corpse."

He waved the trident across his vision. The vegetation before him quickly dried out and disappeared in dust clouds.

"I'll bury her barely alive in the Forbidden Zone." He was referring to the ruins of Heaven's throne planet. The heart of the area debilitated even the strongest. Being entombed alive there would keep her weak until someone pulled her out—and it wouldn't be him. "She will know the feeling of fanged worms and mutant beetles gnawing at her regenerating skin. Insects crossing over her sight. Eggs hatching beneath her skin. She'll go mad at the sound of them inside her head. Not even insanity will save her from the reality of it."

He landed in a meadow and stamped the ground with the trident. A vast crack opened in the ground, swallowing trees. Hillsides collapsed into the huge, jagged fissure in the ground.

Under normal circumstances, he would laugh at his asinine threats, at such mad imaginings, but right now he meant them more than anything he had ever intended no matter how ridiculous he sounded.

"The agony of it." Poseidon pressed both fists against his forehead, and his wings of different shades of blue lifted him a mile above the wrecked topography of the planet.

He willed oceans to rise into huge tsunamis that washed away one third of the land's vegetation.

"Feel better?" The Almighty lowered himself beside Poseidon over the rush of water pushing over trees.

Poseidon looked back. "Yeah, thanks, I kind of do."

A Father's Guardian Angel

Calliope

"You are not coming," her father said of her participating in the coming battle. They were atop Mount Titan. The two suns were setting at the horizon along the Serene Sea backgrounding Rainbow Ridge. "I will portal you with the younglings to a safe location until this is over."

They were all that remained of the Twelve as they watched Lucifer fly off to prepare his Seraphim army for battle. Calliope and her father were always last to leave. She was always the one he confided in after any meetings.

The Death Dealers had found the Tentacles on a planet next to Elysium, prompting the Twelve to jump into action. It was obvious that an invasion of the throne planet was in the works. Now closed were all portals leading back to here. It was beyond her why they needed this to happen for them to take arms. It was like the Elders still had the last unspoken war heavy in their hearts and were in no mood to ever be in another one.

Or did they fear this Tentacle King? Did that last war the Elders and her father refused to address involve Cthulhu?

"I have as much right to be at your side as Lucifer."

"I will not have you tainted by war."

"You trained me in the art of fighting. I'm better than Aphrodite and you're letting her attend the theatre of battle."

He turned to her, his eyes squinting as they tended to do when he was serious. "I did not train you for warfare."

"Stop protecting me."

"You are not ready. You were trained to defend yourself, nothing more."

"You can't stop me. I've always stood up for mortals. Now it's time for me to fight on their behalf, and on the behalf of all living things."

"You are just like your mother."

He seldom said that. It warmed her every time he did.

"I am of the House of El." She got in his face. "I am no coward."

He smiled. "Spoken like a true queen. Stay close to me on the battlefield and watch your brother's back. His impulsiveness might complicate things."

She readied to fly off to tell Lucifer, who was sure their father would portal her somewhere without her consent, keeping her from this coming battle.

"Calliope, why the sudden interest in war? What is the real reason?"

If she told him, he might do exactly what Lucifer said he would do.

"Calliope?"

Frig it. She turned back to her father.

"I won't let him kill you. I won't."

The House of Cronus

Poseidon

A t one side of the two amassing armies was a tar-black ocean with corpses moving up and down in the waves, the tide littering the rocky beach with eviscerated mortals. At the other side of them, less than a mile away, stood a city in ruin. Above them, the Tentacles loomed along a rocky cliff, moving from side to side, their bladed feelers swishing the air as if in victory.

Poseidon stood with his siblings, Zeus, Hades, the twins Hestia and Demeter, and their father, Cronus, in his looming fiery presence, along with the rest of the bloodline under his House. There was a beauty to the sway of the corpses in the ocean, like they were getting one last dance in before washing ashore to begin their rot.

"Zeus, look!" Demeter shouted, pointing at their father, her hair a multitude of colours like her sister's. "Father, what are you doing?"

Poseidon watched his father, Cronus, point his sword at the Almighty then pretend to slice his throat with it, an outright threat towards their Lord. It was an action unheard of until this day. Cronus turned his back to them all, another great insult, and slowly crunched through the rocky beach towards Cthulhu's army. At the sight of Cthulhu with folded arms, his body shook from laughter.

Where was Posedia? He expected to see her at Cthulhu's side like the harlot she was. But now this, the House of Cronus falling before so many eyes.

"This day stinks of cowardly traitors," Poseidon said to Zeus and Hades, one at either side of him. "Our patriarch turns his back on family. Shames us. Look at the faces of our comrades, demoralized at the sight of this. Look how they stare at us with contempt."

"No, Poseidon, they look at us to take action," said Zeus, in his spiked, crimson armour, "to make things right."

"We will right this treasonous act!" Hades shouted. The ends of his braided hair were bladed, hanging down armour similar to what his siblings wore.

"Too much disappointment." Poseidon withdrew his trident from its holder attached to the back of his armour. "Too much treachery." He charged at his father with a war cry. "Face me, Father!"

"Poseidon, stand down!" Lucifer shouted from behind.

Cronus, that huge, ancient grey-haired warrior, dressed in craggy armour fissured by lava that dulled the impact of any blade, swung around, and powered down his sword.

Poseidon blocked the strike with his trident, sending him falling backwards from the impact. For him to go down so quickly with such good intentions at heart filled him with more rage. Doesn't good always prevail? Isn't that what they had been taught?

"Follow me!" Cronus hollered to his offspring, offering his hand to Poseidon. "Forget the Old Fool. His ways have long passed. Cthulhu is another victim of El's who has come for his pound of flesh. All of you, stand down, turn your backs on that tyrant and you will be spared. Otherwise, a harsh reality comes your way."

Poseidon swiped his father's hand away with the trident. At that moment, Zeus's thunderbolts slammed into Cronus, sending him flailing back with a boom. Poseidon pounced up at Cronus, only to be batted away with minimal effort, landing not far from the feet of his siblings.

"Pitiful display. I'm ashamed my blood flows through you. I shall erase that mistake now." The flapping of Cronus's wings created a surge of flaming wind that Hades threw himself in front of to protect his brethren, his skin being impregnable to fire.

"I offer you godhood," Cronus bellowed, standing a good two feet over the tallest of his children, Zeus. "And you spit in my face with such impudence. I am your father, not that fraud over there. You will see today what he's really made of."

Cronus pointed his sword at the Almighty, who placed a hand on each of his offspring, easing them back from defending the honour of their father.

Posedia squeezed her way between the other traitors standing at either side of Cthulhu and nestled into him. The sight of her cruel, flirtatious ways, that damn smirk of hers, steered Poseidon towards her, abandoning his siblings. He would win the battlefield by defeating Cthulhu and avenging his broken heart in one quick —

"Poseidon," Zeus shouted. "We must take Father down together. Personal vendettas must be put aside for this battle to be won."

Poseidon looked back to see Zeus struggling to his feet, slammed back down from a fireball, his armour melted into his skin, silent agony in his expression. The unconquerable Zeus was almost beaten when the main battle hadn't even begun. It was all planned. Whether they joined their father or not, it didn't matter. The Tentacle King simply wanted the threat from the House of Cronus eliminated.

Cthulhu's tentacles branched in all directions with both of his arms rising above his head, then he whipped all appendages forwards like he was throwing an invisible boulder. The Tentacles rushed ahead, rolling, staggering, taking long strides, ramping off the cliff and landing hard on the shoreline. The taller ones grabbed pieces of rock and whipped them at Heaven's army. The battlefield came alive all around Poseidon — the booming noise of flesh colliding, the vicious clang of metal upon metal. The war cry of the Order overcame the approaching storm of disfigured flesh.

That traitorous bitch. Where was she? It was hard to focus on anything else.

The Tentacles rolled and pounced with their bladed tentacles, slamming down onto Lucifer and his army of Seraphim, cutting away at them.

Posedia sauntered along with Cthulhu towards the Almighty's position. She shed herself of her tunic and entered the battlefield nude, bearing only a sword. She disarmed every angel charging at her, all screaming revenge for Poseidon and as much as it moved him to see such sisterhood and brotherhood, he wanted to be the one to thrash her. No angel had yet been slain, the strictest of commandments still followed by both sides. How much longer would that last? Poseidon would end it now before it got to that point.

A scream for help by one of his sisters stopped him. He looked back to see Cronus slamming

Demeter onto a boulder, cracking it, and her armoured body went limp. She was not dead but exposed and no longer relevant in this battle. Cronus drove her down one more time.

"Your own daughter." Poseidon stamped the rocky surface with the butt of his trident. Sand and rock flew up at Cronos, distracting him from doing any more damage to Demeter.

"You are such a disappointment." Cronus casually walked towards Poseidon. "Beaten by a broken heart. Pathetic. I would have thought you were made of sturdier stuff."

A lightning bolt slammed into Cronus's spiked helmet, knocking it off. Poseidon speared his trident into his father's armoured stomach, penetrating skin. Zeus hurled more thunderbolts. Hades and Hestia sent wave after wave of fireballs into the approaching Tentacles, incinerating them.

Cronus prepared to flap yet another wave of fiery wind. "You will burn for days," he shouted.

Poseidon whipped his sword like an axe into Cronus's chest, inches from his heart.

Cronus slowly dropped to his knees, his intake of breath close to a death rattle.

"You do have what it takes." He grinned up at Poseidon, then fell clumsily back.

"The House of Cronus falls." Poseidon stood over his father, pulling out his sword and trident. His father would recover soon enough. If he had any honour left, once recovered, he would leave the battlefield and await his sentencing. "And the House of Zeus rises."

"Poseidon!" Zeus hollered. "Look—"

The blade of a sword entered cold in his back, licking his heart with a frigid tongue. Its red-stained gleam protruded from his armoured chest as blood splashed out.

"I just can't help myself from breaking your heart." Posedia licked the side of Poseidon's face, as she slowly pulled her sword from him slowly. He collapsed where his where his father had fallen.

CTHULHU VERSUS CALLIOPE

JAMES PYNE

Light in Darkness

Calliope

Cthulhu and the traitors centered the Tentacles, the ones who had broken her father's heart the most, to see them with such legitimate hatred in their eyes, grinning big with eagerness. Calliope felt her father's pain. He would make them regret this, especially Cronus.

The battlefield was full of so much fear, such uncertainty, anger, betrayal. The animosity was strong with most of it emanating from Cthulhu towards her father. It was personal, more than just hatred for being the last of his kind. How was she seeing his thoughts? Nothing was ever this clear unless she focused. It was like he was sending them. All of this because of a bruised ego? No, not that.

Defeat was a minor setback, making him stronger. The confidence the Tentacle King was emitting made it seem like he could take the whole battlefield on his own.

His tentacle army rolled into view, slithering around each other, morphing into different tentacle deformities, it was as if he couldn't keep them into solid, logical shapes for long, as if he wasn't as strong as the Almighty when it came to creating life. No, winning the war was what mattered to him. To become the Supreme One. That was his aim.

"The Swallower of Souls," he whispered inside her head.

That's what she was feeling from this ancient evil. He was determined to humble her father in the worst kind of way. Calliope wouldn't allow it.

"I allow insight into my mind. Not even your father has access. We are connected now until one of us dies. You are much stronger for it, a gift planted deep inside your mind, for a later time."

She couldn't beat him in physical combat, but she could reach the good in him if she dared to explore his mind. Was it a trap?

"The good in me is long gone. He took everything from me."

"I'll drag Cronus along this battlefield myself," Lucifer hollered, snapping Calliope out of her trance. There was Cronus, smugly looking their way, pointing his sword and though she wasn't sure what had happened, she stepped forwards with Lucifer. "I'll show everyone what happens to defectors."

"Let them sort it out." Their father placed a hand on the breastplate of Lucifer's armour and hers but didn't take his eyes off Cthulhu, nor did Cthulhu's glare stray from him. "It's a family matter. The honour of their lineage is at stake along with the heart of the battlefield. Let tradition take its course."

"Cronus is more powerful than all his offspring," Lucifer said. "They will be soundly defeated."

"Father's right, Lucifer. Focus on the source of all this darkness."

Calliope needed Lucifer on his game. They all did. The fact that their father needed them all here spoke volumes of their exaggerated faith in his ability to vanish anything or anybody with the snap of his fingers. He needed them so he could do what he hadn't been able to do eons ago—rid the universe of this evil for good. She needed Lucifer focused because she wasn't sure their father could defeat Cthulhu on his own. Something different was emanating from their father, but before she could categorize it, he blocked her out.

"Stay close to me, daughter, but not that close. And suddenly you have more push. Why is that?" He looked back at Cthulhu. "Stay out of his head, Calliope. If he comes knocking again, leave the battlefield. His gifts come with a heavy price."

Cthulhu and Posedia strutted towards them as the Tentacles rolled and slammed into Michael's radiant armour, plowing through the Seraphim. The traitors spread their wings and took to the air, swords drawn, quickly met by members of their own lineages looking to keep the honour of their bloodlines intact. An anxiousness came over Calliope, and it was not just from her first taste of combat. The combined uneasiness of the battlefield wasn't helping. The only ones she felt were not showing doubt of some kind were Cthulhu, and, to her shock, Lucifer. No dread. No doubt why he was there. He was focused on being the protector of all angels, as he told her after she gave him the news she would be partaking in the battle. Suddenly believing his destiny to be the next king of kings, ambition now pushed him. Sense of honour motivated him. And his true love for their race fueled him.

"Look at how Poseidon abandons his sisters and brothers for his own personal revenge," said the mammoth angel Quetzalcoatl, pointing with his sword. Clasped in his other hand was a war axe he used to behead middle-sized dragons that tried taking the Nest as their own. "And Demeter falls because of it. I'll bash some sense into him."

Lucifer batted Quetzalcoatl's sword down with his own. "His heart is stronger than you think." He slew one of the tentacle things as Poseidon speared his trident into Cronus.

Calliope felt the admiration emanate from Lucifer for Cronus's offspring, especially Poseidon. It moved him as it did all angels. To set aside his personal demons for love of family was a beautiful thing to Lucifer, one she felt Lucifer wasn't sure he would have done himself if Lilith had betrayed him. But Lilith was there, protecting her husband's flank. And there were the Death Dealers led by Gabriel and Muerte, slamming into one third of the Tentacles like a black wave of destruction.

Overcast skies darkened, then rumbled and opened up into heavy rain. The Tentacles pounced at her father and Lucifer and the rest of the higher-ranked. Before Calliope could raise her sword, her father pushed her back from the coming swarm of Tentacles that smudged him from her view. The other angels were in conflict, leaving Cthulhu and Calliope facing each other.

She readied her sword.

"Go back to painting lovely things into creation," Cthulhu said, referring to her ability to draw characters into life, "so, I might destroy them." He smirked. "You're outclassed, my dear. Take my gift and be gone with you. You will be able to read your father's mind now." He waved her away. "I've been in your head. You don't belong here."

"I'll wipe that arrogance from your face. You will not hurt my father."

"I'll hurt him where it hurts most, then. Through you."

His egotism infuriated her, pulling from her a rage she didn't know existed. The fear of losing her father had her charge at him. She cut one of the tentacles away before he ensnared her. Cthulhu showed no signs of pain as a new tentacle grew back, lashing the air in no time.

His tentacles came down at her. Her aim wasn't to beat him in battle, but to subdue him, pacify his hate. Her touch changed the negative disposition of any living thing into an agreeable one, or vice versa, but that was not something she ever considered. It wasn't a gift she used often. She believed every creature had a right to evolve by its own free will. But this beast needed taming. She would make sure no angel died today, especially her father, who was needed now more than ever. What other monsters were out there in the universe plotting revenge?

Cthulhu's tentacles grew back as quickly as she cut them. One bladed tentacle came at her throat, gliding by it, letting her know he could decapitate her if he wished. She stopped avoiding the tentacles, allowing them to wrap around her. His cold embrace and deep whisperings inside her mind, soothed her as he pulled her to his face. Calliope looked for a glimmer of light, but if there, it was out of her reach, buried deep in absolute hate for her father. No time to find it as he drained her energy.

"His daughter in my death grip." Cthulhu's tentacle carried her closer to his face. "An eye for an eye."

"Release her and face someone hardened by battle!" Lucifer shouted. "Or are you a coward hiding behind your soldiers?"

Cthulhu said aloud, "Just like your father in his greener years."

"*We'll meet again,*" the Tentacle King whispered in her thoughts, chucking her aside.

She landed hard and in her severely weakened state, the impact of the ground broke her arm and winded her. Her head rolled to one side, facing Lucifer who was cutting down some of the Tentacles, and there, her father had quelled the onslaught and now charged at Cthulhu, eyes widened at the sight of her lying on the ground in such a helpless state beneath the clang of so many swords and bladed tentacles. Calliope felt his blind hatred and fear. She barely felt any light in him at all; he had become what she feared he would. And she had made it happen by facing Cthulhu.

An air burst filled the battlefield as the two behemoths collided. She didn't see much of the battle, only the end of it when strength returned. One of the benefits of being of the royal bloodline was that one healed quicker than others, but in this case the truth was she had almost died. She felt it. The Tentacle King's last words to her, "*We'll meet again.*" He could have killed her, the result of angering her father to a blind rage would have been the same, yet he hadn't. "*We'll meet again,*" he had said. Like he knew for sure. And never had she felt such love from her father give way to such darkness in the speed of a rising flame.

In the sky they battled, with Cthulhu's bladed tentacles tearing away into her father's armor, pulling pieces of it from him. A purplish-blue portal swirled into view with her father powering Cthulhu into it. It shrank from view. Minutes later, the Tentacles fell lifeless. It was what her father portalled back as that disheartened her and shocked the entire battlefield.

THE AGED ALMIGHTY

JAMES PYNE

A Mutual Suffering

Poseidon

It would take Poseidon days to fully recover from Posedia thrusting her sword through his back, missing his heart but shredding whatever decency was beating in it. Her latest treachery left him helpless on his back, unable to wipe the mud from his face. The Tentacles were as relentless as hyenas, yet there was nothing Poseidon could do but watch.

One of the Tentacles coiled its feeler around Poseidon's leg, its bladed end dug into his flesh, dragging him along the battlefield for all to see. Cthulhu smirked down at him, then turned his attention to Calliope. Done with him, the Tentacle catapulted Poseidon back into the chaos of war, but before sinking away into the mass of moving flesh he saw the Tentacle struck down by Michael.

Angel and Tentacle trampled Poseidon until Michael pulled him out. In flight, Michael carried Poseidon to an oak tree on top of a hill that was a fair distance from the ocean and the battle.

"You've done your part." Michael lay Poseidon gently against the oak tree. "I'll return when the battle has been won."

He returned to the battlefield, shrinking into a sparkling star in the daylight sky.

"Love is mortal," Poseidon said to himself. Should he be surprised? Immortality was a long time, more than enough time for the truest of love to fade. "Broken. Because of her. Never again will I allow another to have ownership of my heart. Look at this state I'm in, wallowing in my pity while my brethren fight. The once feared Poseidon, now a broken myth."

He couldn't even influence a puddle to rise into the tiniest of tsunamis to come crashing down on a nearby anthill. Pathetic. A shadow passed over him, then came back.

It wasn't Michael who had returned.

"It can't be."

The Almighty slowly descended to Poseidon. His wings remained partially spread, with pieces moth-eaten along the edges. Curly, grey hair tangled with his beard and draped his ageing but still muscular chest. His armour had been replaced by a cloak, with hood flipped back. He clasped Poseidon's trident in one arthritic-looking hand and landed with one knee briefly giving out. It was the Almighty, wasn't it?

"You're having a rough go at it," the Almighty said, planting the trident next to Poseidon. "Your part in Cronus's fall spurred new confidence. And the second betrayal by Posedia angered all who saw it and they cried, 'Avenge Poseidon,' and we never looked back. Thank you, my friend, for not abandoning me."

"You speak kindly, but why hasn't Michael returned for me? I'm a sorry sight, I know, best hidden so not to damper the celebrations. And you have aged. How's this possible?"

"He is defeated, that is all that matters."

It was difficult to see the one who treated him more like a son than his own father did in this sorry state. It was disheartening.

"Your wings are the only things healing."

"I feel most of it is permanent. The outer shell, at least."

"Not even ambrosia and nectar can help you?" Soon enough, they would be drinking the rosy-red nectar from the Holy Grail and eating mustard-yellow ambrosia from the Divine Bowl to speed up healing and rejuvenate war-torn bodies.

"It is beyond that, Poseidon."

It was then Poseidon realized that their immortal leader was about as eternal as they were. It appeared he could die too.

"Don't pity me, Poseidon." He smiled, something he didn't often do. "It was time for a fresh look. Besides, having offspring looking the same age as oneself is unnatural, yes?"

Poseidon tried laughing, but the thought of Posedia came to the forefront, dampening any cheerfulness in him.

"And my wife?" he asked. "Why haven't you brought her to me in an even sadder state than I'm in? Surely one of my sisters or brothers would have avenged my falling?"

"Zeus did."

"And why hasn't Zeus laid her before me?"

The Almighty turned away, looking towards the main part of the battlefield.

"I've interred Cthulhu in the depths of an uninhabited planet." He stood with less difficulty, though he kept one hand on a low branch of the oak. "His location on that planet will change daily."

"He's dead then?" Poseidon tried sitting up. "Again, what of Posedia?"

"He cannot die." He leaned to one side, like it pained to weight both knees equally. "He's endless. The more I tried to destroy him, the more I aged, as if feeding him—or was I killing myself while killing him?" He thought about it. "His army remains asleep as long as he's in his present weakened state."

"You avoid telling me about my wife."

"She's been soundly defeated."

"How did she fall?" He imagined his brothers, Zeus and Hades, belting Posedia with thunderbolts and fireballs, shriveling her into a lump of coal, barely living.

"She's gone with the rest of the traitors, that's what matters."

"Where to?"

"Not important."

"It is to me."

The Almighty scratched his beard, looking in the direction of a huge bluish-white portal whirling open. "Michael and the rest are transporting Cthulhu's army into the icy region of an unfinished dimension. His dark magic is strong and destroying them would only have their essence trapped in the surface of this planet, festering, feeding, growing, waiting for the return of their king. To a cold, desolate place they go."

"Answer me, where is she?"

"Far from you."

"You deprive me of my right to avenge myself? What right do you have?"

The Almighty said nothing.

"She's mine to do with as I please."

Poseidon wanted to crack this world in half. "Why won't you allow me vengeance?"

"I am protecting you."

"From what?"

The night sky was clear as it would ever be on that planet that evening.

"Answer me."

"I have told you before, I once suffered from the same thing as you."

"What does that have to—"

"I am protecting you from having to make the decision"—he turned back to Poseidon with a look of a great tragedy haunting him—"that I had to make."

The Rising Son

Lucifer

Lucifer left the battlefield through a portal opened by Hephaestus. The lower ranked had returned to the Nest but not him. He stood at the Council of Twelve table, behind his father's throne, hands clasped behind his back. Planets of varied sizes shone in the starry night. The nearest moon haloed the crown of the Nest. The sound of lively flutes and song filled the air as everyone cheered and clapped below, all waiting for the heavenly nectar and ambrosia.

Lucifer had no interest in celebrating victory. He had things to sort out.

Lilith's vision of him sitting on his father's throne plagued his thoughts. The battle just won was not the one she had envisioned, though he considered it. It was possible the warring she had seen were traitors versus the faithful, with the Tentacles out of range of her vision. But today none died. Angels perished in her revelation. Besides, the battle today didn't even feel like combat, not one he understood anyway. Cthulhu should have stayed back letting his army do all the damage, then enter the theatre of war after all his opponents had spent their energy, including Lucifer's father.

Still, it felt like it had all played out exactly the way the Tentacle King wanted. Cthulhu had come for something. The fact that he didn't kill Calliope was a mystery. He wasn't a follower of the commandments. And now Lucifer's father was in ruin, further proof that if Cthulhu had just let his army do the work, then strike, he might have been the victor instead of the vanquished. Wishful thinking on Lucifer's part? To inherit the throne that way was unthinkable, unacceptable, and that was assuming he could have defeated his father's conqueror. A challenge he would have accepted without hesitation, under the flag of avenging his fallen father.

A misty-blue portal opened, sending a brief chill through the air. Lucifer backed into the shadows of the Great Tablet with the flaming commandments casting a faint orange hue on the bellies of sky wraiths passing over. His father lumbered out of the portal, helping Poseidon to one of the Twelve's stone chairs. Zeus's, to be exact.

"Rest there, my friend." Lucifer's father plunked himself down in his own chair across from Poseidon. "The air is cleaner up here, reinvigorating like the spray from the Serene Sea." He leaned over the table, coughing and wheezing at every breath.

"You don't sound good." Poseidon looked ready to stand up. "In worse shape than me."

"Relax. I am fine."

"They'll worry about you." Poseidon leaned on one bent arm on the table. "They need to see you're okay."

Blood had wormed out of the sword hole pushing out of Poseidon's breastplate, now dried, a reminder, along with the Almighty's present condition, of everybody's mortality. Lucifer continued listening, feeling cowardly to be hiding like this, as if he were once again that youngling sneaking up here and eavesdropping on the original Council of Twelve.

"When you join the festivities, tell them I am fine."

"Of course." Poseidon said.

Lucifer's father let out a raspy sigh and bowed his head as if finding it difficult to stay awake, or deal with the pain, something he might be experiencing for the first time.

"I am promoting you as a member of the Twelve during my absence. You will sit in Lucifer's chair, and he, in mine."

Was this what Lilith had seen? Him playing the part of seat warmer? He had done it before with strict rules attached, the most boring gig ever given.

"Where are you going?" Poseidon asked.

"I need to sleep for a while."

"Lucifer is a fine replacement."

Lucifer didn't trust Poseidon. Never had. The fact of the matter was that Poseidon's actions on the battlefield were honourable, the first time he had ever impressed Lucifer with anything, and perhaps that meant a positive change in him. Still, Lucifer had no interest in giving anyone from Cronus's bloodline the benefit of the doubt.

"Though we're not each other's fan, I'll follow him dutifully," said Poseidon.

"Watch over him. Many others covet the throne, and only a few of those today have been banished." Lucifer's father was referring to the expulsion of the traitors to another dimension nicknamed Hell, sometimes called the Inferno, as it had no official name. As the centuries flowed by, the story of this place was shared with younglings at bedtime to scare them into being good or else they would end up in a horrible place called Hell, where a very bad monster ruled over the land. And now Hell had such a monster by the name of Cronus.

"My son has few friends," Lucifer's father continued. "You two are more alike than you think." He laughed. "Maybe that is why you don't get along.

You are too much alike in stubbornness and ambition."

"I don't have much ambition, my Lord."

"For the females you do." He playfully shoved at Poseidon's bent arm on the table as they laughed.

It was unexpected to see his father kidding around like this. It burned him inside to see that. Lucifer wished he could have experienced such happy moments during his youngling days. Even now, he longed for such memories.

"In honour of your kinship to me, I'll watch over him like my own brother."

Zeus's brother watching over him. It was like an impending dagger in the back. The ambitions of Cronus's bloodline amounted to no more than seeing their own lineage to rule. Nothing less.

"It may be one of your brothers you will be protecting him from."

"We're all aware of Zeus's aspirations, my Lord, but I assure you, his loud thoughts never come to fruition. I'll leave you now to your rest and alleviate their fears of your health." Before flying off, Poseidon looked back. "Thank you for the invitation to your table, but I must politely decline. I fear Posedia has blackened my heart and may cloud my judgement when at this table. Michael is a better fit. Two Calliopes at the table is better than one."

"If only you could see how wise you are, Poseidon, you would achieve greater things. Know this, the dark path you are going down will see light again."

"You speak in another language sometimes, my Lord. There's nothing special about me."

Poseidon's dark blue wings spread out and he dove from sight, returning to view, shadowed, unsteady, clumsily nosediving from sight.

"You can step out from the shadows, Lucifer," said the Almighty.

Lucifer smirked. His father was sly like that.

"How long will you be gone, Father?"

"How long do you want to rule?"

Lucifer trudged to the other side of the table where Poseidon had sat. "Being your seat warmer isn't my idea of fun."

"How long I am gone will have everything to do with how well you govern."

What game was he playing? Was he even truly sick? He looked barely able to keep his aged face within view like he was dozing off. It seemed exaggerated. It was hard to believe his father could suddenly look so old.

"You're having fun with me. With all of us."

"Follow all commandments, make decisions according to them. Other than that, rule as Lucifer wishes. Poseidon will watch your back."

"I prefer Michael as my guardian angel."

"Poseidon will do. He needs something serious to put him on the right path. Besides, Michael will be busy taking command of the Seraphim."

"Michael is more than capable of double duty. And nowhere does it say on that" — Lucifer motioned up at the Great Tablet — "anything about who watches my back."

His father let out a raspy breath, as if he were frustrated with Lucifer's persistence.

"I will not have Cronus's bloodline breathing down my back, Father."

"So be it."

His father's starlight eyes dimmed within his wintry hair like he was going blind or had cataracts.

"Tomorrow I will personally thank the heroes of today's battle, then pass the throne to you."

"I assume you will return as your youthful self?"

"Some things will regenerate. Hopefully my memory comes back. Already I have forgotten which planet I interred him on." The sight of Lucifer's father in such a state was humbling. "Was it one of the planets he drained of life? Or one of the planets still terraforming? To forget something that just happened, yet I remember your first breath . . ." He smiled fondly at that, then the grave look returned.

"You'll heal up, Father, and be your usual self soon enough."

"Lucifer, most internal wounds will heal, but this is my new form."

"Does this mean you can die?"

Was that what he was going off to do? Had the Tentacle King won even in his own defeat? Was the throne being handed to him before his time?

A Darkness Spreads

Zeus

Brother to Zeus and Poseidon, Hades was the least ambitious of the three. He simply wanted his own planet to rule over, nothing more, nothing less. And that was fine by Zeus. His other brother was the unknown factor. Poseidon being good friends with the Almighty Ego? Now that might be a problem. Or it might be to their advantage. Zeus was still working it out. Now that he was leader of his bloodline's House, he had much to think about.

Zeus and Hades caught Poseidon before he fell to his knees. All brothers were still in their similar crimson armour, weathered from yesterday's battle.

"Stubborn like Mother," Zeus said to Poseidon.

"We all are, Zeus," Hades said from the other side of Poseidon. A stretch of greased black hair fell between his eyes and dropped just below his chin. The rest of it was tied in a ponytail. The hooded black cloak hanging over his crimson armour flapped to a sudden breeze. Red and black feathers created a fiery motif on the inside of his wings, while they were mostly dark red on the topside.

Poseidon staggered like a drunk, sometimes using both of his brothers for support. The line was long to the steps of the throne. Their Lord wanted to personally acknowledge those who impressed him the most and rumour had it that he was going to bestow upon them gifts and new titles with greater responsibilities. But Zeus hadn't seen any of that yet. Just the names of angels mentioned and a quick compliment and off they went flying back up to their living quarters, more than happy with simple commendations.

"You're a walking wreckage, Poseidon," Hades said.

"You were always one for stating the obvious."

"Cheer up, Poseidon." Hades patted Poseidon's back. "We are now living legends."

Zeus looked up at the angels whistling and clapping from their living quarters as the three brothers approached their turn. Sunlight reflected off Zeus's armoured gauntlet as he waved to those all around and above them. The younglings watched from the crown of the Nest where the different warrior castes should be. Duty had them presently hunting down the traitors who had abandoned the battlefield once the fight was lost.

"Barely able to move on your own, Hades said to Poseidon, "yet they cheer your name the most."

"Fame isn't important to me, you know that."

Not even the divine nectar and ambrosia hastened Poseidon's recovery. It was the matter of the heart then, weakening his immune system. What a sorry sight. To see his younger brother like this was almost unbearable. *Chin up, grow a set*, were things he wanted to say but didn't.

"Your sudden popularity does our family crest honour," Zeus said to Poseidon. "It gives us more pull with the masses but turning down a seat at the Twelve was unwise."

"I don't have your ambitions."

"We lost a seat after Father's betrayal. Reconsider accepting his offer. The line is still long enough for you to change your mind before Lucifer takes over."

It was important to Zeus that both brothers were on the same page. Especially Poseidon. The Almighty trusted him, and now suddenly everyone loved him. Zeus knew better. They pitied Poseidon more than anything. He was that sad violin story angels were a sucker for. Unfortunately, it looked like Poseidon would cling to Posedia's betrayal forever. He took things too personally. Posedia was just a *nashiym*, a temptress, there were always others to bed. To see Poseidon stretch out this pity ride sickened Zeus. Nonetheless, his brother's wretched state was another opportunity to heighten their popularity with the masses.

"I have no interest in ruling over anything," Poseidon said. "That path is yours."

"It would be nice to have friendly company walking side-by-side on that path."

"Poseidon walks with us now, brother." Hades waved to those around as they briefly cheered his name. "No need to politic. He's never failed us. Let's not forget he was the first to declare the arrival of the House of Zeus, on the battlefield, of all places."

Poseidon didn't say anything. Didn't look at the crowd. He looked straight ahead, up at the throne. What was going on in that scrambled mind of his? Was he struggling with his allegiances between family and friend?

"Well, Poseidon, it appears the females have their ambitions for you," Hades said from the other side of Poseidon.

"I have my eye on one." He kept staring at the throne.

"You aim your head too high, Poseidon." Hades patted him on the back of his armour. "Remember how early life goals had you planning on impregnating as many females as possible in the universe, mortal and immortal? A much better and safer ambition than Calliope."

"I hear she stood up to Cthulhu. Who would have thought? And I have our Lord's favour."

"True," Zeus said. "But not for long if you don't unfix that stare from her. There are others to occupy your mind and help you forget that traitorous bitch. Safer for you to build an army one impregnation at a time."

"For you to command?" Poseidon's eyes had a wolf-like nature to them. When he had enough of ribbing, he had enough. Zeus would back off. "It's you who dreams too big."

Zeus made no bones about it, he imagined being an overseer over more than one planet. If not that, then command over the Furies. He could make that despicable lot into the most feared division in Heaven's army. It was one of the things he expected their Lord to bestow upon him—if not today, then soon. They were the last in line, meaning something big was coming their way. He was confident after today that the House of Zeus would be stronger in power than the House of Cronus had ever been. And all in less than a day, at that.

And someday, the throne would be his.

"You two expect too much," Poseidon said. "Others fought well and regained their honour after avenging the betrayal of siblings, parents, cousins. We are no more special."

"But none have his friendship like you do. And none have your story." Zeus looked to the crowd. "Again, it's your name they mostly chant."

Poseidon's eyes seemed to grow wilder the more they cheered, like it was poison to his soul, somehow, like he genuinely believed he didn't deserve applause while in this pitiful state.

"But enough teasing." Zeus put an arm around Poseidon's neck in a brotherly way. "Today is going to be a good day. Can't you feel it, brothers?"

Neither brother said anything. Both were deep in thought.

"No Seraphim or Death Dealers," Hades said, as the line grew shorter. "For such a glorious day of celebration, where are they? They fought well and deserve praise. Their work is never done."

"Michael and Gabriel's forces are hunting for stragglers who escaped punishment," Zeus said. "It's unlike our Lord to leave himself so exposed. Well, he still has Lucifer at his side."

"Planning a coup, are you?"

"Not at all, Poseidon. It's just an observation."

They stepped ahead.

"And look at our Lord." Hades nodded up at the throne. "Sickly, aged, and bearded more than you, Zeus. Open wounds still on him. Look there, look at his neck. Did you see his unsteady balance when he landed? Did you see? His house is ripe for attack."

"Watch your words, Hades." Zeus watched for Poseidon's reaction.

"Just an observation," Hades said.

"Someone close by may overhear and repeat them," Zeus warned.

Poseidon's expression didn't change. He remained fixated on Calliope, who was now whispering something into her father's ear, bringing a huge smile to his face.

"He doesn't need the Seraphim," said Poseidon, who started walking without using his brothers for leverage. "He has Lucifer, Lilith, Calliope—and me at his side. That is more than enough for today. The war is over." He looked at Zeus. "Nobody will be challenging for the throne today, or anytime soon."

"You put too much imagination into Calliope," Zeus said. "Only trouble can come from it."

Poseidon squinted, clasping his chest.

Was he embellishing for attention? Not like Poseidon. But he healed at miraculous speeds. It was one of his gifts. Over the years, Poseidon would leave deep cuts in his leg or chest or stab himself as a cheap parlor trick to the amazement of younglings. Nothing left a mark for more than ten seconds. Zeus wondered if his brother truly did love Posedia, that his immune system was on shutdown because of it.

"Truly, she's a warrior, a credit to her father's bloodline," Poseidon said, staring up at Calliope. "Indeed, I would like to taste her mind, inhale her—"

"Now who has insane ambitions?" Zeus laughed.

Calliope stood at the left of her father, closer than usual, guarding him, her long hair branched down her tunic that barely hid her fertility parts. Rumour had it, she could twist the mind of any angel to her favour, for her entertainment, and Zeus wondered if she was messing with Poseidon's head for some harmless fun, having picked up on his sudden juvenile crush on her. A silly notion. Still, it was an easier reality to swallow than accepting Poseidon's pity party. But what a weapon she would make. There may be a part for her in Zeus's plan yet. He smirked at that. Yes, things were coming together nicely.

"They don't deserve his counsel before us," Hades said. "We made great sacrifices, yet here we are last in line, paraded in front of everybody."

"You forget about our sisters in bed unable to roll over to their sides," Poseidon said, still looking up at the throne area. "I think their sacrifice is worthy of equal accolades, yes?"

"Of course." Hades nodded in agreement. "I was getting to them, but they did make it clear they wanted nothing to do with these festivities."

"Without them distracting our father," Poseidon said, "without them sacrificing their bodies, we may not be standing here."

"Yes, yes, I agree. Further proof our family has made the greatest sacrifice," Hades said in a voice many heard in front and around them. "We should have been first in line."

"Keep your thoughts to yourself," Zeus said. "We're last because we shall get the loudest praise and awards."

"No, this is an insult. We're being punished for Father's betrayal."

"Hades, enough." Zeus jerked at his arm.

Hades shrugged his grip away, stepping closer to the steps, passing the archaic Gaia and hulking Quetzalcoatl.

"What kind of treatment is this?" Hades shouted up at their Lord on his throne, the red glow within the dark crystal pulsating at half speed.

The Almighty glared down at Hades.

"We didn't join our father." Hades walked with immense pride towards the steps. "We chose you over the source of our bloodline."

"I am the source of all bloodlines," the wounded king calmly said. His daughter Calliope pushed off the side of the throne with him reaching over and gently urging her back to his side before she confronted Hades—at least that's what it appeared she was about to do. That wasn't like her. A change overnight.

Interesting, thought Zeus.

Lucifer hadn't moved an inch, as if he didn't consider Hades a threat. Such arrogance would be his undoing.

"We defied our father," Hades said. "Paint whatever picture you like. We fought him in battle and as much as it pained us, we beat him down, strengthening the will of your army again." He continued, shouting: "You all saw it. Our sisters are still broken."

"Forgive his outburst," Poseidon said, hobbling to their brother's side. "He's still drunk with—"

"Admirable to come to your brother's defense," the Almighty said. "But he's right, the three of you and your sisters livened up the spirits of my army, infusing them with great strength when it was needed. Now please, Hades, let things take their natural course. I have saved you three for last for a reason."

"We each deserve a planet to rule over," Hades said. "At the very least." He gave a slight bow, then returned to his brothers.

"Really?" The heartbeat of the throne picked up. "I can do better than that, Hades."

"My Lord," Zeus said. "My brother sometimes lets his fiery temper get the better of him. Poseidon and I will take him aside and talk some sense into him."

Poseidon leaned to one side, as if he were ready to collapse from exhaustion.

"You make me sick," Hades said to Zeus. "My Lord this. My Lord that. He's mocking us, he has no intention of rewarding us with anything worth having. He keeps us beneath his thumbs because he feels threatened by our line. He places his own son, his unworthy son, as the leader of the Seraphim when you, Zeus, deserve that honour. Yet here you are, groveling before him."

"I will stomp you to the heart of this planet," Lucifer shouted, stepping forwards, guarding his father.

Zeus's hands balled up. He did his best to resist the burning urge buzzing down his arms, doing everything in his power to keep thunderbolts from stretching from his fists. His brother spoke in blind rage, that was all. He meant nothing by it. If Lucifer attacked Hades, the House of El would be at war with the House of Zeus. Not something Zeus wanted. They were not ready.

The Ancient Wreck stood up from his throne, and the red glow within the dark crystal faded to black. He tucked Calliope behind him, and stepped to Lucifer's side, nodding at him. Lucifer's hand moved from the hilt of his sword.

"I'll do better than a planet." The Almighty staggered back with Calliope steadying him. "How about your own dimension, Hades, if you can defeat the others already banished there? I imagine your father has staked claim to it by now. Time is different there. Many days have passed."

"Please," Poseidon said. "He's drunk from battle. He's not thinking straight."

"No, Poseidon. Your brother speaks from his heart."

"What can we do to right this?" Zeus asked. Their father's wrath would be hard on Hades, he would be paying for all five of them standing up to him. "I'll do anything to have this decree lifted."

"Fair enough." The Almighty squinted, as if he were thinking something over very carefully. "Zeus and Hades will draw lots. Whoever draws the shortest straw will be the one banished to Hell. Do you agree, Zeus? Is your love for him stronger than your own ambitions?"

"You see, brothers," Hades said, "he keeps us firmly beneath his thumb. He fears the House of Zeus more than he did when it was the House of Cronus. Brothers, I would never allow either one of you to make such a sacrifice. I love you both. Pass on my love to Demeter and Hestia. But remember my words today." He looked around and upwards at those watching. "As much as my words have stung or have incurred his wrath upon the House of Zeus" — he looked fondly at Zeus when saying this — "remember this day, his true colours have surfaced."

A flaming portal opened behind the three brothers. Its flames lashed out along its outer rim, then filled the tunnel.

"My Lord" — Poseidon stumbled closer to the throne steps — "you're tired and irritable from battle. Please reconsider this, or let it settle for a day before it's made official? The sight of this is enough to humble anyone."

"In time he can return, Poseidon. You have my word."

"It's detention for me." Hades laughed. He hugged each of his brothers and stepped away from them. "How bad can it be? I get my own dimension to explore while you all suffer this old fool's absurdity. He'll be the death of our Order." Hades turned to the portal to willingly enter it. His wings lowered as he looked over his shoulder. "By the looks of those grey hairs, he may croak soon anyway."

The Almighty's eyes widened. The blazing portal closed before Hades could enter.

"Did I touch a nerve?" Hades asked.

The ground opened beneath Hades, dropping him from view. Smoke billowed up from fiery lava pits.

Zeus pounced at the opening, but it wasn't big enough for him to fly into. He fell on the chest of his armour, reaching to Hades who descended into the lava pits.

Bloodcurdling screams came from Hades, his skin melting away, his wings failing him as he sank from sight. The ground closed abruptly with Zeus pulling his arm out just in time. He looked back to see Poseidon still leaning to one side, dismayed.

The whole Nest had gone silent.

"Where did you send him?" Zeus pushed himself up. Other angels gave him room as he marched towards the throne, brushing by Poseidon, who made a weak attempt to stand in his way. "Such a horrid sight to live in my heart forever. You burned him. What kind of heat would that take? He has withstood dragon fire longer than any other. You—"

"He has fallen into your father's lap."

"In such a wretched state our father will finish him off."

"Why, my Lord?" Poseidon stumbled back to Zeus as if he suddenly feared their king. "Why such a horrible fate? Blood lust sticks to some of us longer than others. The pain he just experienced surely is enough punishment. Zeus is right, our father will give no clemency."

"I admit it was dramatic, Poseidon. Perhaps you are right, that I am drained and short-tempered, but that doesn't justify your brother's harsh words. He insulted not only me, but everyone in this court. We all fought well and kept the honour of each of our lineages, not just yours. I hope this message was loud and clear to anyone else who —"

"Message received loud and clear." Zeus's vast, white-feathered wings spread out. "I want nothing from you."

That day Zeus lost all respect for their king.

"I will rescue you, Hades," he said under his breath. He turned away from the throne, then sprung to the sky. "Then together our House will overthrow his tyrannical rule. I swear on it."

JAMES PYNE

BAIAME

JAMES PYNE

The Forbidden Zone

Lucifer

Baiame's wrinkles ran deep in his dark skin. His long, frizzy grey hair hung loose down his back. He wore nothing but a loincloth. No one besides Lucifer's father knew how old he was. The thing about Baiame's appearance of age was that he had no offspring that anyone knew about who would have greyed him. Not even Baiame's wife, Yhi, who had gone back on assignment on a distant planet. She wasn't here to greet Lucifer and give him a heads up on Baiame's mood.

Baiame wasn't eternally irritable like most Elders, but he had his moments, surprising considering the brats he had tutored over the years, Lucifer being one of them. He missed those days of watching Baiame

149

lose his shit in frustration with Lucifer's tenacity to do things his way.

"You smile wide, Lucifer. Has the weight of the universe already made you crack, my favourite pupil?"

"You exaggerate. About both things. I'm nothing more than a seat warmer."

"If you see yourself as a seat warmer, then you are a seat warmer." Baiame took his time, slowing Lucifer's pace. "But I see opportunity."

"I'm bound by rules, Teacher." That's what he always called Baiame. Teacher. Never his real name. Not until he had nothing left to teach him.

They strolled through a rock garden with very little vegetation, past the toppled and broken statues of unknown heroes and heroines strewn throughout the desert, past still-standing columns, and there, not far from a sand tornado was Teacher's stone house with its thatched roof. The Forbidden Zone stretched for miles with the sand tornado marking the beginning of the no-go zone. If anyone dared enter the sand tornado, the silt grated away their flesh. Whatever was hidden in there, no angel would ever find out. Not even armour could withstand the force of the sands for long—and many had tried to face it.

"This is a cold, empty place," Lucifer said. "Why stay here?"

"Someone has to keep an eye on the younglings playing back there in the ruins. You'd be surprised how many have tried venturing into that." Teacher motioned at the sand tornado, dark in comparison to the light tan-coloured sandstorms in the distance. "These days the scary fairytales only heighten their curiosity. The arrogance of youth is timeless and knows no bounds, but it doesn't compare to the arrogance of the greatly seasoned who never seem to learn."

"Yet at your apparent old age you've maintained your humility." He smiled affectionately down at Teacher, who didn't look his way, but kept his eyes on the ground as if making sure he didn't trip over one of the embedded rocks. "And you're not fooling me, Teacher. What's the real reason you cast yourself out here in these cold, desolate lands? What secrets are you guarding? Or do you hate the company of others that much?"

"It's home."

"My father doesn't just let anyone live off the grid, especially here. You don't even have to attend his meetings. What secrets do you guilt him with to be spared his ramblings?"

"He and I go back a long way, you know this. Insufferable those speeches, aren't they?" He winked up at Lucifer.

"How far back do you two go?" He had never received an answer to this question and didn't expect to get one today. "During the times of these ruins?" Similar remnants of a past existed throughout the planet. "What happened here? Why is it such a secret? Did you exist during these times?

151

"I'm afraid those are questions I can't answer."

"I'm in charge now. I need to know these things. What if I make the same mistakes that led to this wreckage of the past?"

"You might."

"You enjoy your secrets too much."

"You see what you want to see. Stop looking for the worst in people, Lucifer. Not everyone is a Zeus. Now, there was an impossible student."

They stopped just before the howling wind of sand.

"Do you fear death, Lucifer?" inquired Baiame.

"You've asked me this before in this very spot."

When he was a youngling under the tutelage of Baiame, to be exact.

"And what did you say?"

"I said 'no.' and remember being quite haughty about it."

"And?"

"That I have royal blood in me, that nothing can hurt me."

"And then what did you do?"

Lucifer clasped his hands behind his back.

"Well?"

"I stuck my hand in there. The skin sanded away into bone. Something tried to pull me in, and you pulled me out. Took me weeks to heal. The unbearable pain was something I'd never felt before and haven't since."

"And now? Do you dare to stick your hand in there?"

"Of course not." He kept his hands firmly clutched behind him. "Stop with these games."

"That day, you discovered that you weren't impregnable. You finally felt alive for the first time through your affliction. You had discovered what fear was and appreciated life more after that day, didn't you? You also questioned your immortality. Everything to you had a deeper meaning after that painful moment." He stared at Lucifer, as if waiting for an answer, a rebuttal, something, but Lucifer had nothing. "You don't dare stick your hand in there again, even now, in your maturity. But what if that's what it takes to rule?"

JAMES PYNE

The Sketchbook and Magical Pencil

Calliope

S haggy Back, the tallest conifer forest in the lands, shadowed the upper part of the rolling fields of Musical Meadows, called this by poets due to its surrounding scenery being music to the eyes. The steps of grasslands descended into the Serene Sea; a multi-blue ocean that swelled darker the further out one looked.

At about the middle of the casual drop, Calliope faced the Serene Sea, the coolness of a mossy boulder against her back while she sketched a new species into existence. Centuries ago, her father had given her this magical pencil that never dulled. Whatever she drew came to life after she autographed the drawing, tore the page from the sketchbook and tossed it to the wind. She never knew what colour her original creation would be. The main rule was to make

154

nothing that would be harmful. Her father had made that clear. Nothing that would offset the ecosystem of any planet, otherwise he would erase it from existence.

She shaded in the plumage of the second bird that had longer whiskers than its male counterpart, curving up from each eye like exaggerated eyelashes. The tails of the lover birds coiled each other, the name of the new species written below them: Cupidia, after her good friend, Cupid. She signed her own name. Pinching the upper corner of the page, she tore it from the sketchbook and flung life to the wind.

A great shadow moved up her body and she heard the sound of paper crumpling against something.

"Nice drawing," the voice of Poseidon said, his body silhouetted against the two suns.

"Poseidon, you might want to—"

"Amazingly lifelike. The detail is—"

Two black smudges spurted from the paper, causing Poseidon to flail backwards. She laughed at his reaction. The two new creations took shape, pigment slowly spreading throughout the shadowed birds. They hovered in front of her face, chirping, now white-whiskered, filling into streaks of red and black plumage, their beaks turning a sharp yellow.

"Delightful," she said of them.

Their fluttering wings warmed her face before they each bolted to either side of her. She stood up, and leaned over the boulder, smiling like a cherub seeing the sky for the first time. Her birds soared up the rolling hills and into the conifer forest, where she imagined them mating for their first time to the view of Musical Meadows and the Serene Sea. The perfect honeymoon for birds, surely. She wished they would spurt out into view, letting her get one more look. That was okay, she would see the blue sky full of them soon enough.

"Hello, I'm still here," Poseidon reminded her.

"How unfortunate."

"Sassy brat."

She pushed herself up onto the boulder, sitting with legs closed, the wind bubbling her toga. Her sketchpad and pencil were left in the shade.

"What are you smirking at it?" Poseidon looked at her with a curious expression.

"The great Poseidon is terrified of birds."

She felt a surge of darkness emanating from him, then it tempered when she smiled warmly at him. She had to remember that he still had open wounds, even if the topical ones had healed. The nagging betrayal by his betrothed, the shame of his traitorous father, and what she strongly felt was a wrongful exile of his brother to the Inferno—carrying all that would make anyone irritable.

"I was flying over with a mutual friend and saw you down here."

A shadow passed over. She looked up to see a winged horse of pure whiteness set against the azure-blue sky, ploughing through a sky wraith that put itself back together and enjoyed its final minutes of life.

"Pegasus!" she shouted up at the sky. "How did you tame his stubborn mind?"

She hadn't seen Poseidon ride Pegasus. He could be lying. Or kidding around. This winged horse was anything but easy to win over. She was the only angel Pegasus let ride him.

"He suddenly adopted me in the oddest way. He blindsided me, sending me hard to the ground, then landed next to me and for a time, stared into my soul. It sounds crazy, I know, but it's how it felt. He then licked my face and what a noxious smell his breath had. It still clings to me."

Calliope smiled at that. She knew that rotten egg stink well. Pegasus was the first sketch she autographed into existence with the magic pencil. He had started off quite small in life, then his wings quickly grew wide, although the rest of him took its time developing into the muscular stallion he was today.

Poseidon pinched his thumb and forefinger together and whistled and within a blink of an eye Pegasus landed, kicking up grass and dirt as he galloped up towards them.

Calliope slid off the boulder and greeted her old friend, pressing her face against his soft silky nose.

"I haven't seen you in over a year. What have you been up to, boy?"

The coldness of Pegasus's nose touched her forehead. He snorted, then emitted a long neigh, like he was trying to tell her about his adventures. She couldn't pick up feelings from animals or magical creatures like Pegasus, but she knew enough of their mannerisms to understand them. She kissed the end of his wet nose. He bowed his head to her and blew softly in her hair.

"I missed you too, big sook." She looked back at Poseidon. "What are your plans for him? Make him into a warhorse?"

What else would someone of the House of Zeus do with a potential weapon like Pegasus?

"I've had enough of war."

He scratched between Pegasus's ears as the winged horse licked the side of his face leaving a streak of glistening saliva along his cheek that he wiped away, making an exaggerated expression of disgust.

"He indeed has taken a liking to you."

"Now to get him out of that habit." Poseidon wiped his face of drool, only to have Pegasus lick him again.

"I think he might be in love with you." Calliope laughed.

"I suspect he's lonely." Poseidon looked over at Calliope, and a warm feeling came from him, something she hadn't felt coming off him since his love for Posedia. "Lonely like myself." He looked away from her, shyly, and that was amusing to Calliope, as much as curious. "Tell me, why haven't you made a mate for him?"

"No one ever asked me that before. They just want to be the one who tames the fire in Pegasus. To have bragging rights. I admit, you would be the last I'd expect him to choose." She giggled. "But now that I think about it, it makes perfect sense he chose you."

"What does that mean?"

"I guess I have time for a story."

APOLLO DESCENDING

JAMES PYNE

The Planet Sweeper

Apollo

On the surface of the green planet existed reptilian beings who hadn't yet reached the stars, so when a second sun appeared in their skies, they were sure it was doomsday. But far above the emerald clouds, way up there in space, was the angel Apollo, that mistaken the second sun.

He was Big Cranky's Planet Sweeper, as his sister Aphrodite had nicknamed the Almighty and when in a mood, playful or irritated, she would call him that much to his annoyance. Poseidon could think of a lot of other unkind names to associate him with.

Fully nude, with arms outstretched, one foot over the other, toes pointing down, he slowly descended to the surface of the planet. His wild shoulder-length hair, darkened parts of his sight. He didn't feel good about this. He never did, no matter how many times he carried out the Almighty's orders.

The lizard planet was one intelligent being over its quota for evil. The Almighty had given strict orders to Apollo that the very moment when evil outnumbered good, he was to harness the powers of the sun of that solar system and incinerate all living things on it. He could not risk their wickedness spreading to nearby planets.

Most back home didn't know what Apollo did. They figured the planets had it coming, that there was no hope for the inhabitants. It wasn't just those who warred who were slapped on the tipping scale for evil, it was those who cheated on their significant others. The more he thought about it, the more hypocritical it seemed. Angels cheated. Angels warred. Angels had slaughtered countless mortals over the ages. There was the Harvest, not seen in centuries. Not since Apollo started this crappy gig. He tried telling himself that they didn't feel anything, that the incineration was quick. If they felt the burn for just a few seconds that was too much, as far as Apollo was concerned, and it sounded like many did, like he was hearing billions of souls scream as one on every condemned planet.

The sun's power charged Apollo with the extreme heat raging inside him to the point where he would become desperate to expel it before he went up in flames. That's what he was told would happen if he didn't carry out the mission. He figured he looked like a glowing cross to them down there, the way other doomed races spoke of him when he touched ground before they became puffs of smoke. He wasn't a threat, he was here to enlighten them, so they always thought, bowing to him, addressing him as their sun god. This time he descended to a barren area lost to war centuries ago with no life nearby. First his toes touched the surface of cracked clay, then his heels.

His insides were roasting. It was the worst kind of punishment, all because of one petty day when Lucifer had landed in the courtyard in a sour mood. Apollo was plucking a tune on his lyre, reciting a new poem for the Almighty from a folding chair in front of the throne steps.

"Leech," Lucifer said of Apollo, passing him to walk up the steps and report to his father on whatever mission he was returning from.

Apollo had enough. It wasn't the first time Lucifer had publicly questioned his usefulness. He didn't see the point of Apollo's role in things. Musician, poet, songwriter, and musical instrument maker. A waste of time.

"It is not I who leeches off his father's legacy."

Lucifer stopped climbing the steps and turned partway around to glare at Apollo who remained seated.

"Mind your place, string picker."

"Everyone speaks of it. You wouldn't be where you are without your father."

Apollo laid his lyre down, stood up, hand on the hilt of his sword.

"Are you challenging me to a duel?"

"Not at all. But it's my experience that once the likes of you have lost the war of words, you turn to the sword."

Lucifer turned with his hand on his sword. "I'll leave a scar on the side of your face if you don't sit back down like the dog you are."

"Always jealous of my looks, never more apparent than now."

With his chiseled face and perfectly sunken-in cheekbones, it was as if the Almighty had spent more time on the idea of Apollo's conception than any other male angel, even his own son. That's what other angels said. Not that Apollo believed it, or cared, but he would play on with the intent to vex Lucifer.

"That is enough, Apollo," the Almighty said calmly from his throne.

"Seriously, my Lord?" A rush of anger came over Apollo. "I was minding my business, entertaining you, and he attacks my character, and you tell me to be silent?"

Lucifer smirked and started up the steps, as Apollo said, "It is not my fault you're a bad parent and raised an entitled cherub who comes back from a botched mission, pouting, taking temper tantrums like his father."

Lucifer stopped his ascension. The Almighty's eyes widened.

And here Apollo was with a new job.

"I'm sorry," he said to the inhabitants of this planet. His tears of guilt sizzled into steam, his hair flamed up and scattered into ashes. It would grow back when he cooled down. He didn't want this, but it was them, or him. He loathed himself for not doing the right thing and standing up to the unjust sentencing because no matter how one looked at it, his punishment came from the bruising of two insurmountable egos. One still held a grudge after all these years.

Apollo's feet sank into the dry soil. Arms still out, skin now blackened with cracks of lava breaking open all over him, he bowed his head, mourning the coming genocide. The dead soil began to smolder. It would be a mere hour before everything was scorched earth.

"Stand down," a commanding voice said from above.

Apollo looked up to see Lucifer in full battle armour, along with Archangel Michael.

A portal closed behind them.

"How strange. You were just on my mind. Come here to mock me?" Apollo said. "Hasn't your father done enough—and you bring that?" He motioned at a golden lyre held against Lucifer's armoured chest, the same one Lucifer had snatched from Apollo's hand when he was banished to his new duties. He wouldn't be needing it anymore now that he had real duties, was how Lucifer put it. "Come to break it in front of me, no doubt a message that the idea of Apollo is dead? You don't need to be symbolic about it. I died inside long ago."

"There's that dramatic fire I've missed." Lucifer landed with Michael, placing a gauntleted hand on Apollo's shoulder, sparking contempt in Apollo. "I'm here to free you of this burden my father wrongly put on you and that I wrongly sanctioned with my silence."

Michael stood there, silent, in his armour that blinded mortal and immortal alike with its approaching shine, if he willed it. He didn't look like he wanted to be there and in fact, he looked as confused as Apollo imagined he surely did right now.

"Free me?" Apollo said. "Then do it. I prefer death over this burning pain inside me. I should just let it light me up. All those dead souls are on me. I let them burn so I may live. I'm the champion of 'cowardly' things. So yes, end me. Free me."

Smirking, Lucifer slowly looked over his shoulder at Michael, then turned back to Apollo.

"And free you are," he said. "Father's left me in charge, he's away on other business." His face was mere inches from Apollo's. "I miss your poems, your songs. I have an appreciation for the arts these days. I'll give you credit for that. I wanted to understand what made someone of your ilk defy my father and me in the manner you did."

"What game are you playing?" The molten earth around Apollo bubbled, waiting to spread. "You thought I was a waste of space."

"That was centuries ago. I've grown out of my snootiness. I miss your wild ways, your honest mouth. Does that surprise you? I've always been a prisoner under my father's shadow. But you, Apollo, rose in defiance of him and me both. How could I not be moved? It was your right, and I was wrong to have instigated it. Honourable Apollo, please accept the apologies of an *entitled cherub* so I may bury that part of me forever."

"If I was so honourable, I would have let myself go up in flames long ago."

"What if I told you he lied to you, that you won't burn up in flames if you defy his decree and allow this planet to live another day? Yes, there you are, I see you now."

"He lied?" Such emotion raged inside him. "All those deaths, all those innocent—No, you're lying. It can't be true."

But what if it was? Was it a test of Apollo's character? What a horrible notion, to think his failure to stay true to himself had led to countless deaths these last six hundred years. Even if that were the case, the Almighty would have destroyed life on those planets another way. His resolve was unbreakable.

"You must take a leap of faith, Apollo." Lucifer stepped back. "Choose *you*." He held out Apollo's golden lyre to him. "Or continue to live this lie."

How could he trust Lucifer? There was no way that accepting the lyre would lift the Almighty's curse. It was either continue to be the Destroyer of Worlds or blaze up. Yet there was a genuine honesty in Lucifer's words, and with the most virtuous Michael present, he wouldn't allow such a cat and mouse game to unfold before his eyes. He was much too honourable for that.

"It's too much," Apollo said.

When he first inherited this hellish job, the temptation was there to let himself burn up, but it never got that far. He always gave in to the fire inside, bending under the will to live.

"This is wrong," Michael said to Lucifer. "Your father won't approve of you editing his decrees."

"Apollo's unjust punishment has nothing to do with my father's commandments." Lucifer looked at Apollo. "Trust in me. I will remedy my father's mistakes. I know where he's gone wrong. His ego refuses to admit his failures, so we all suffer because of it. No more. Return home. We've missed you and your beautiful music, your moving poetry, your heartfelt songs. The place has grown stale without you."

"The pain is unbearable."

Apollo clenched his fists in front of his face, resisting the persistent burn, swelling inside his belly, his chest. How much more could he take before exploding?

"All these deaths are by my father's hands," Lucifer said. "Not yours."

Everyone knew Lucifer had been groomed for the throne, and everyone had their theories on how it would happen, but no one really believed it would come into fruition due to their Lord being indestructible.

"Why help me?"

Lucifer stepped closer to Apollo and whispered into his ear. "Because I agree, you are more beautiful than me."

Apollo's eyes expanded from the shock of hearing this. He, himself, had never really believed those words he had shouted that day.

"I'm a monster, but will have to be, to make things right," Lucifer said. "You don't need to be. Let me carry that burden, Apollo, while you fill the hearts of mortals and immortals with songful bliss."

And Apollo took his leap of faith and accepted his golden lyre, holding it close to his heart. He was finally home.

JAMES PYNE

PEGASUS

The Story of Pegasus

Calliope

I admit, it was amusing to me, the House of Cronus getting their asses handed to them by a winged horse. So determined you all were to the point of absurdity. We all watched from our rooms as each of you tried everything possible. Remember how Cronus was the only one to take flight by forcing himself onto dear Pegasus only to be flipped into a mountain, making a new cave in it. And Zeus, after countless failed attempts, playfully bribed Pegasus with wild oats, much to the laughter of all ages.

And you, Poseidon, getting batted aside by one of his wings for pulling his tail in hopes of distracting him long enough for Zeus to mount his back. And Hades jokingly glaring into Pegasus's eyes, hoping to stare the steed down, only to have Pegasus raise his front legs and uppercut Hades, knocking him out for hours. And how comical Cronus was when pleading with your sisters to help, offering them all manner of gifts, but Demeter and Hestia only laughed and waved all of you away for being so ridiculous.

I'm sorry if bringing up your father and brother saddens you, but these were good memories, Poseidon. Keep them close to your heart.

I give you all credit, though. Once realizing there was no winning Pegasus over, you were good sports about it and continued the comedy a little longer for the sake of the crowd. Yes, the House of Cronus was determined to be the one that had bragging rights of ownership of Pegasus, but you gained something much more important that day: the hearts of everyone.

It didn't stop with you guys. Others for months after tried to ambush Pegasus, only to have their mighty egos crushed. He would only let me ride him, maybe because I was his creator, or because he looked at me as his mother. I guess I'll never know the answer, but his love is genuine. I don't take it for granted.

There's nothing like riding him, nothing in all the universe. He's magical. With each step, he can make water spurt up like fountains while stomping through the waves. I didn't even imagine that into his creation, it just came out of nowhere. His wings can blow clouds away or make the ocean part with his passing over. He was my first sketch with this pencil and something that should have occurred to me sooner, didn't. Sadly, it took my father being turned down by Pegasus for me to discover what that was.

"He's fiercely independent, like you," my father said. "But something's missing. I've learned over the eons that most things want to be in love, want to procreate. You paired off all your other creations but not him? Why is that?"

I had no answer. I felt horrible for not even considering that. I thought about it, finally concluding that I wanted him to myself and not have him go off parenting foals. But that was wrong of me.

I set to it, sketching Pegasus a mate, right here against this very boulder. Pegasus watched over my shoulder. He sometimes snorted and neighed, or pranced around the rock. I didn't know if it was to get my attention or if he was having second thoughts. He slapped a round full hoof on the sketchbook, tearing away the sketch before I could autograph it into creation.

He galloped off into flight over the Scenic Sea, leaving me there, struggling with the idea of sketching a female companion for him without his blessing. I was his creator and should know what's best for him. Or did I respect his wishes? I don't know why I didn't autograph one into life. I confess, I hope someday he motions for me to draw him a mate, but I doubt he will. Poseidon, you asked what I meant by not being surprised he picked you to ride him. You're both stubborn to the point of absurdity.

Snort all you want, Pegasus, you know it's true.

The Harvest

Lucifer

Apollo didn't burn up from the raging fire inside him when accepting his golden lyre from Lucifer. He did, however, fall to his knees the moment he accepted it from the relief of his boiling guts and for a split second, Lucifer considered he was getting to his knees to pay respects to the one who had liberated him. That wasn't the case, of course. Distrust for Lucifer was heavy in Apollo's eyes.

He offered to help a staggering Apollo into the portal.

"I'll walk by my own freewill." Apollo glared back at Lucifer and Michael. "A political stunt to garner support from others, that's what this is, right?"

Partially, yes. Lucifer also wanted to liberate Apollo because it was the right thing to do. Not one member of the Council of Twelve disagreed with Lucifer. The vote was unanimous to unchain Apollo from this appalling duty.

"I'm not my father, Apollo. All will understand this soon enough. With Michael as my witness, I encourage you to call me out on anything and everything with no fear of retribution. Apollo, the glory days of art have returned. Myself, I've taken up a liking for violin playing, much to Lilith's annoyance. You know how she likes her peace and quiet. Soon, we shall play together, entertain family and friends . . . as friends."

"We'll see."

Apollo entered the portal, looking over his shoulder one more time, then disappeared.

"Your father won't be impressed that—"

"You keep saying that." Lucifer interrupted Michael, who now stood by his side. "Like a parrot. Do you enjoy being his parrot? Everyone's his parrot." He looked over to Michael, whose armour blended in with the colour of the boulders and desert ground and emerald sky. "Say something new. Something profound. Use that mind of yours. I know there's something independent in there."

"Do you think when your father returns, he'll just slap you on the hand?" Michael's hand rested on the knob of his sheathed sword, like it always did when he was standing still.

"Do you truly believe Apollo deserved this fate?"

"There's a reason for everything your father does. Just because you don't understand, it doesn't mean he's wrong."

"My father made Apollo a reflection of himself a monster."

"Harsh words against your father."

"What did my father say to you before he left for a new project?"

It was tempting to tell Michael the truth about the real reason his father left. Tell him all the dirty secrets. He didn't want to win Michael's support like that. House of Zeus tactics were unworthy of him.

"Well, what did he say?"

It was killing him to repeat it. He grinded his teeth. "Obey your every command."

"Ignore that order," Lucifer said.

"What?"

"I need honest ears and mouths if I'm to rule fairly. Now tell me, what point is there in their evolution?" Lucifer spoke of the reptilians of this planet. "If they're not given a chance? The thing about darkness, Michael, is that beautiful things are born from it. Tulips bloom from darkness. There would be no beautiful sunrise or sunset without darkness. And they, too, will rise from darkness and flourish with a little guidance."

"There's a reason why —"

"Yes, yes, there's a method to his madness." Far away, vehicles approached, throwing up dust. "I've heard it many times."

"Who will replace Apollo?"

Lucifer looked sternly at Michael. "We'll finish what Apollo almost started, with a change in script."

"And that is?"

"Hephaestus!" Lucifer shouted, though there was no need to because whenever Hephaestus's name was uttered, even whispered, he would be able to hear it inside his head. "Open the sky up into beautiful colours." He looked at his protégé. "There's art in war, Michael. Someday you will see this."

Thousands of portals opened in the emerald sky. First came the Death Dealers in their doom armour, led by Gabriel and Muerte, then came the Seraphim soaring into view. Their armour sparkled despite the dull green of the atmosphere. Their swords were already drawn, pointing down to Lucifer in allegiance. Their armour turned to fiery red, signaling their upcoming bloodlust.

"With the help of the Death Dealers, we will seek out all evil on this planet, Michael."

"You're bringing back the Harvest? It has been banned due to its cruelty."

Lucifer unsheathed his sword. "We'll skin them alive, do unspeakable things to them, and leave the rest to become whatever it is they are to become."

"And how will the rest react to the sight of such horrors? What will they become because of it? What will we become?"

"Their mortality will never have been so fearsome to them. This day of horrors will lead to their kind becoming something beautiful. We will do this with every planet. Unlike my father, I will carry this burden now, not Apollo. Am I not fair?"

"You're drunk with power," Michael said. "I'll take no part in this. I'll have your back, nothing more. Have your bloodlust." His dove-white wings spread, stretching quite a distance, the ends curling at either side of Lucifer. "He will send you to Hell for this."

Best Friends

Calliope

"Sassy brat." Poseidon playfully nudged her after she finished off her story with a dig at him and Pegasus, who snorted, as if trying to blow snot on her. Poseidon had sat next to her against the boulder with Pegasus standing at their side.

Calliope didn't mind Poseidon's company. The gloom in him softened in her presence and that made her warm inside, knowing he felt at ease with her.

"It's good to see you smile again, Poseidon." She was assessing him. No negative emotions spiked. He just radiated more sunlight from within. He was genuinely happy, nothing faked to impress her. The temptation was there to read his mind. How could anyone from the line of Cronus have any redeeming qualities?

"When's the last time you rode him?" he asked.

"Sometime last year." Calliope remembered that day like it was mere seconds ago, a memory between just them. "We rode for days. I saw sights on this planet I may never see again, not in the way I saw them those days."

"What do you mean?"

"Every day, every hour, every minute, every second, we're changing. Everything we saw yesterday will be a little different next time we see it, though we might not notice because we see those things every day. But if we see something we haven't seen in a year or a century, it'll appear fresh to us again, but not in the same way. Because we ourselves have changed and we may have more of an appreciation for things. One year, the Bellowing Mountain was a pleasant memory where romance was sparked, the following year the sight of that summit was sickening due to a broken heart."

A wave of negative emotion left him, then faded as quickly as it appeared. How tempting it was to explore his thoughts.

"Some of us immortals have seen it all," Poseidon said, arms resting on his bent knees, "making everything stale to our senses."

It was tempting to ask him how betrayal felt after each time, the same, or worse, because she couldn't imagine it getting better. But that would be a heartless thing to do.

"You rode Pegasus for the first time through familiar sights, yet it was all a new experience, yes?"

"Point taken," Poseidon said. "Go for a ride, will you? It's a reunion, act like it. I'll watch from here."

"You know, I've never ridden Pegasus with company. Care to join me?"

He jumped up, beaming.

"You first. He may not even let me on him now, after all this time."

"He will, if knows what's good for him." Pegasus nickered. "Easy fella, just teasing." Poseidon mounted Pegasus, then held his hand down to Calliope. She accepted. He pulled her up. "Hold on."

Pegasus suddenly galloped forwards, almost flipping her off. "Might want to grab on to something—or someone."

"Don't get any ideas." She wrapped her arms around Poseidon, who, at the buckling of her hands just beneath his chest, emanated such a lively feeling that it spread through her too.

Pegasus pounded the ground with his hooves as he picked up speed during their ascension towards the Serene Sea.

Calliope hooted and screamed with pleasure, as ocean water sprayed her face and hair, her entire body, like she was being cleansed of all the vile things witnessed the last while—that's how it felt to her, all of the bad washed away. She would cherish this moment for all eternity. She looked back to the forest backgrounding Musical Meadows, where songbirds scattered to the clear blue sky. She turned back in time to feel herself rising with Pegasus, his wings flapping with such power the water parted into a trough, even ahead of them.

"Lower, Pegasus," Poseidon said, his fingers entwined in Pegasus's thick mane. Shades of blue whipped by them. The water parted deeper. "Keep going. Faster—faster!" The closer to the ocean Pegasus took them, the deeper the parting of the sea became. Even in front of them, Pegasus's power pushed the water apart at such low depths. They descended until the walls of the ocean were at either side of them, roaring like coming thunder, collapsing at their passing, water splashing up from behind, tickling her back and wings.

"It's amazing." She inhaled the scent of salt, seaweed, and marine life. "How did you know he could do this?"

"I didn't. But you were right about everyday things seeming different. Even the suns have a wondrous glow from down here."

She clasped her hands tighter around him.

Poseidon would make a good friend. A best friend.

The Politician

Zeus

Since the battle with the Tentacles, Zeus had been his brother's keeper. No one argued that Poseidon wasn't himself, that much was evident. He still had an attachment to the Almighty and he was madly infatuated with Calliope, and all of this was a problem, because with Hades in Hell, this left Zeus needing Poseidon at his side more than ever.

Zeus's sisters, Hestia and Demeter, wouldn't shut up about Lucifer being the one to change things for the better. Zeus's children bore a mix of good and bad feelings toward him. Athena had adopted Lucifer and Lilith as her parents centuries ago, becoming a pain in the ass once Hera and he briefly broke up. Hephaestus had a hate on for Zeus, one he understood, but he had no idea how to fix their estranged relationship. The others, like Aphrodite and Persephone, were on board. As for Apollo, he seemed content returning as a musician. In time, Zeus would whisper revenge in his son's ear. Zeus had never believed the official story of Apollo's promotion. All had been done to keep the House of Cronus fractured, the Almighty's way of showing who was boss.

Zeus was having strong thoughts of challenging Lucifer for the throne but then there was always the possibility of their king returning. Zeus was no fool. He knew he couldn't defeat the Supreme One on his own. Now Lucifer, yes, but why waste the effort when he had the support of others, like the House of Odin, ready to install him as king? The problem was, Michael and the Seraphim would cancel them out.

It came down to Poseidon. He had the ears of the court.

The Death Dealers were the X factor. He sometimes had Gabriel's ear, and it was no secret Lucifer and he were divided on many things, but the recent changes involving the Death Dealers playing a big part in the return of the Harvest made Gabriel chummier these days with his new king. Some of his followers suggested an alliance with Lucifer to overthrow the Almighty permanently, but Zeus had no desire to share leadership. Why would Lucifer join him when he was preordained to be the next ruler? Besides, when Zeus had asked Lucifer to free Hades,

Lucifer made it clear that by freeing one he would have to free them all, as every relative of the banished would call out favouritism.

No, Zeus would have to take it by force or keep it political.

The latter for now.

Lucifer was seated on the throne with Lilith on his lap, while Apollo recited poetry, strumming a tune on his golden lyre. Most of the angels had been assigned to new, more fulfilling duties, at least according to Lucifer. He bragged about putting an end to planets darkened of life, declaring that such actions were no better than Cthulhu's ways. Lucifer was a pompous fool and messing with their king's decrees would bring his father's wrath upon him. When it did, Zeus would be there to make his move.

"All hail, Lucifer!" Zeus shouted. Those here vacationing from assignments looked his way, stunned. "I admit, I was faithless, convinced you would be nothing more than a mirror reflection of your father. I have never been so glad to be wrong."

Lucifer gave Zeus a courteous nod while he leaned into Lilith, who whispered something, bringing a smirk to his face. He would encourage Lucifer's arrogance, making his impending punishment that much worse, while he worked in other ways to bring shame to the House of El.

An Underwater Secret Revealed

Poseidon

Poseidon had never felt anything like this before when around a female. The way she clung to him, wasn't in desperation to hold on. Rather, it seemed natural, like this was how things should be between them. She smelled of the best flowers found in the Hanging Gardens, her floral notes changing every few seconds.

The waves roared, crashing behind them, the force of Pegasus's wings splitting the ocean. The power behind them would knock down an entire mortal army with minimal effort. Send the entire fleet of Seraphim spiralling out of control. Wipe cities clean from existence. The possibilities were endless with Pegasus, a one of a kind weapon of mass destruction. What could an entire squadron of winged warhorses do?

"I'm glad you asked me to tag along," Poseidon shouted back at Calliope. "I wouldn't have appreciated any of this by myself."

"It's amazing! I had no idea Pegasus could do this."

Shades of blue rippled throughout the walls of water at either side of them. Below, yawned a dark blue chasm, and in front of them it felt like they were chasing a tidal wave while retreating from an endless one collapsing behind them.

"What else can you do, boy?"

Pegasus tilted and descended into the Serene Sea, his wings flapping with such impact, they pushed the water away at even greater distances, leading to a bubble forming around them. Poseidon's hair felt like it was pulling away from the quick descent. Above them, the sunlight dimmed, but not into complete darkness, for an angel could see in the murkiest of depths, however grainy in quality their surroundings might be. Beyond the watery walls, sea life spun out of control.

"An underground city," shouted Calliope, pointing downwards.

How could something at these depths ever have existed above the surface? They flew over columned and domed buildings, much of the city ruins shadowed outside the air bubble, coming into plain view at their passing. Lone columns suddenly cracked, toppling over from the gush of wind from Pegasus's wings.

"It can't be," Calliope said of a statue of a monster every angel now knew.

There, standing in the middle of a giant square, was a towering statue of a bat-winged figure, with one closed fist raised high, its tentacles raised like cobras ready to strike. With a proud, chiseled angelic face, the statue of the Tentacle King held a tablet close to its chest bearing writing in the Ancient Language that very few could read. The stonework of the city had intricate tentacle patterns winding around each other, forming humongous structures.

Pegasus lifted them back to surface, so carefully not one wave collapsed on them. It wouldn't have mattered, though, as angels had hidden gills that opened into sharp slits once underwater. The same gills opened in outer space. They pushed out of the water and the ocean swallowed its secrets once again.

So Cthulhu was king of an amphibian race of angels. Why had he become a destroyer of all living things? What set the hero of his kind on such a dark path? The accusations of the Almighty massacring Cthulhu's race appeared true. Had they served him for a time, until they became a threat in numbers and he obliterated them?

Pegasus returned them to Musical Meadows, which wasn't that far off and still in sight from this location. Calliope slid off Pegasus's broad back. Then Poseidon dismounted.

Calliope turned. "Wait until the others hear about this."

He didn't say anything.

"Poseidon, you're looking at me very strangely."

"You know," Poseidon said, "we stand where Pegasus was written into existence, where thousands of other species have been born from your heart. And why not one more thing born here?" Poseidon gently held her chin, tilting his face to kiss her. Her glowing sapphire eyes pulled away before his lips touched hers. "Wasn't the moment, right?"

"Don't be offended, Poseidon."

She picked up her sketchbook and pencil in the shade of the boulder. Her giant dove wings spread.

"It's not you. It's not me. It's just how things work out sometimes. You're great. And you'll make a good friend if you can handle that. If you can't, I understand." She whistled to Pegasus, as if to get his attention. "Keep Poseidon out of trouble, you hear?"

She looked back at Poseidon, and a sudden worry came over her face as she forced a smile, then she turned away and flew off toward Rainbow Ridge to cross over to the other side, heading for the Nest.

Calliope had rejected him as if it were no big deal, like it was just routine for her to decline the love of an angel. She left him there embarrassed, breathing heavily with discontent. After all that had happened, this stung the most. He would choose sides then. The bitch daughter of the Almighty had driven him to it. Their love could have bridged their two families together.

Now, one House would fall.

Declaration

Zeus

No one had seen Poseidon in weeks, so when he landed at the foot of the throne steps riding Pegasus, Lilith slid off her husband's lap, withdrawing her sword.

Lucifer stood up, ready to withdraw his. He had been giving a speech, updating everyone on how the universe was doing under his rule.

Calliope dropped into view from Mount Titan, where she liked to gather her thoughts, she had told Zeus when he inquired.

Zeus knew differently. Just like her father, she hadn't been the same since her run in with Cthulhu. Less sociable. Muerte and Poseidon also had changed since their encounter with the Tentacle King.

"My apologies," Poseidon said.

Pegasus, festooned with gleaming silver body armour, snorted.

"Still learning how to ride him. I assure you, nothing was meant by my abrupt landing."

Lucifer would not withdraw his sword. It was just for show. Lilith, on the other hand, looked more than willing for combat when it came to protecting her husband. Calliope now stood at the other side of her brother, with no clean intention to withdraw her weapon. She was scanning everybody's feelings, though. That was clear.

"The rumours are true," Zeus said. "You have tamed this beast."

Pegasus snorted at Zeus, glaring at him with those coal-black eyes.

"He's as sensitive as ever. Tell me, Poseidon, where have you been? We were worried about you."

"I was ruminating on things. Along the way, new discoveries have been made."

Poseidon looked up at Calliope, not with infatuation, but with a squint of anger in his eyes. Lucifer must have noticed, too, as big brother stepped ahead of Calliope, hand still ready to withdraw his sword.

"Don't keep us waiting, Poseidon." Zeus stepped ahead of Pegasus. "Any more underwater cities? That miraculous discovery has caused such a stir, angels suddenly have become archeologists, diving into the Serene Sea in hopes of finding secrets kept from us younger generations. Exciting times. Credit to Lucifer for allowing us such freedoms. Come on, what new things have you uncovered?"

"About myself."

"Oh?"

"I now know what matters most."

"That is?"

"Family." Poseidon smiled down at Zeus. "And I'll do anything for my family, as I would for a lover, but the latter is nothing more than the stuff of fairytales."

He glared up at Calliope, then Pegasus and he turned away from the throne and galloped off into flight, -leaving Zeus beaming inside.

The Return

Lucifer

Down there, Apollo plucked the strings of his golden lyre while reciting poetry in the courtyard of the Nest. On the pulsating throne of black crystal Lucifer sat beneath the sunrise sky, legs spread shoulder width. Lilith sat on one of the armrests, leaning into Lucifer with one arm around him. Both wore their light armour, and the tail of Lilith's black cape flowed down the steps.

The Death Dealers, Seraphim, and Furies had returned from their Harvest, along with other warrior castes, for this special day. Younglings sat on the ledges of their living quarters with one leg tucked beneath them while the other hung over the jagged stone ledges. Others leaned against their doorways.

All adults stood in the main part of the courtyard, stretching into the botanical gardens and in the arena where angels practiced swordplay or settled their disputes via weapons or fists.

The only missing one was Calliope. She remained at the round table way up there above the clouds on top of Mount Titan, which always reminded Lucifer of a giant tree stump, skinned of its branches long ago. She would remain up there until Lucifer finished with his declaration. She was the only one who had voted against Lucifer becoming the official king. Even Zeus had given his support, but Lucifer didn't buy into his fakeness.

Apollo's tragic poems had much of the court clearing their throats and wiping tears from their cheeks. Apollo's pain, the guilt for those he had murdered came out strongly in his music. Lucifer had similar remorse but never did during the act. It came easily the killing, an addictive high. The scent and taste of mortal blood were aphrodisiacs to a warrior, but days later he would hear every plea, see the horrified face of every being he had slain, leaving him wondering if he had done the right thing.

"Beautiful." Lucifer clapped. Everyone else did the same, although some reluctantly. "Truly, Apollo, you are the moralist among us. A true inspiration. Don't you agree, my dear?"

"It was a tad depressing," Lilith said.

"I can do better," Apollo said, seated in a folding chair at the front of the throne steps. "I'm just—"

"I disagree," Lucifer said to his wife, interrupting Apollo.

"Surprise, there." Lilith leaned back, her long, dark ponytail hanging down to her hips with a spearhead fastened to the end, the heavy scent of mortal blood still clinging from the last Harvest. "His poems are full of tragedy these days. We only have so many tears, Husband."

"Bah, you're impossible to please. What was that line? Ah yes, 'Black smoke gave way to new life.' Well put, Apollo." Lucifer smiled down at the House of Zeus huddled together behind Apollo, with others of the court behind them waiting for Lucifer's speech. "Zeus, what do you think of Apollo's latest poem?"

"Rings true to the ears," Zeus said, both gauntleted hands squeezing the backrest of Apollo's chair. "Especially the line, 'Someday the *sun* will fall from the sky.' I rather like that line. Anyway, I'm quite sure you didn't gather all of us here to critique Apollo's artistic talents?"

"Yes, yes. Let's get to it then." He made them wait a little longer. "As you all know, my father has been gone for exactly six blood moons. Things have changed since his departure. Some mistakes have been made, admitted, and corrected with the sound advice of the Twelve, who have honourably represented all your concerns. It was a rocky first few months, but we all kept it together and now we're all stronger for it. Each of you has taken a part in this." He motioned with his hand at the multitude below.

"Many of you whisper that my father was a tyrant. I disagree. The pressures of a throne, in time, will make anyone crack. With his long absence, my father admits he's not fit to lead. I am my father's devoted son, but it's been a long time. If anyone disagrees, arise, speak your mind."

Lucifer waited, looking around.

Zeus nodded his approval, along with the rest of the patriarchs and matriarchs.

Lilith's persistence had won Lucifer over. Six years were more than enough time. Father could have passed on. Not that he wished such things, but he always mentioned about someday moving on to see his mother and father and old friends again.

No one spoke up. Not surprising.

"With the support of the Twelve it's time to declare myself as —"

A blinding light flashed in front of Lucifer, then he was tackled through the throne by a great force knocking the wind out of him. His armour clanged hard on the ancient stone of the dais; pieces the throne sprinkled all over him. Lilith thudded next to him. The dust from the shattered throne settled slowly, revealing a hulking silhouette.

"Father?" Lucifer pushed himself up, then he helped Lilith to her feet. "You attack us?"

"You declare your allegiance to me." His father's hair and beard remained winter-grey, his face was still bearded and weatherworn, but the limp gone, his muscular frame returned. "Yet in the same sentence you are about to declare yourself king. The universe stinks of your treachery."

Lilith held Lucifer back.

"She is wise to restrain you. She wouldn't want to see her investment crumble."

Lilith hissed at him.

Lucifer's father looked around, as if expecting someone to make a move while his House was in disorder. "Apollo, why aren't you at your post? Traitor as well?"

"Leave him alone," Lucifer said, his three sets of wings spread out, casting a shadow on those closest to the steps. "I relieved Apollo of his draconian obligations, righting both our wrongs. But why am I trying to reason with someone who, when having his words questioned, scratches their arrogant nose with an uneasy smirk before he explodes into a laughable hissy fit?"

"You push me."

"I don't fear you, Father."

The Seraphim army clasped the hilts of their swords. Michael told them to stand down, but they didn't.

"Yet your army is about to do the fighting for you?"

"Not at all." Lucifer motioned at them to stand down. They obeyed, now standing at attention with right fists over the chests of their armour. "They're about to watch me put you in your place with my words. Forever you have bullied us. You speak of free will, but none of us have it. Up there . . ." He motioned up at Mount Titan, the top part hidden by passing clouds lit up in red by the flaming commandments on the Great Tablet. Was Calliope listening or had she fallen into a trance looking over at Rainbow Ridge? "You told me to rule according to the commandments, otherwise I could reign as I saw fit. And that I have. We now guide the mortals to the stars, saving them from making the mistakes of previous races, errors we've made by the looks of the ruins spaced throughout this planet." Lucifer didn't look away from his father. "I am steadfast to my convictions."

His father grinned. "Are you, now? I will allow your changes to remain, but you must agree on one thing."

Lucifer looked at Lilith. What was his father's game?

"Anything," Lucifer said.

"I won't hold you to that."

"Nothing you can say will deter me. Nothing."

"For the changes to remain"—his father turned his back to Lucifer, barely looking over his shoulder with the beginnings of a slight grin—"you must willingly rule Hell until I say otherwise." His father looked down at Apollo, who in return stared down between his legs. "Do you agree?"

Everybody in the courtyard waited for his answer, whispering to each other, shaking their heads in disbelief. Above, the Seraphim with their fists over their hearts, continued looking straight ahead. Michael, too, stood at attention, hand on his sheathed sword.

Lucifer looked at his wife—his fate was her future. He looked at Apollo, the once defiant angel, now fallen back to a beaten beast at the mere sight of Lucifer's father.

Apollo looked up at Lucifer. "Don't do it, Lucifer."

Why would he say that, knowing it meant him becoming a planet killer again?

"You can't," Lilith said. "Swallow your ego. Another day."

Every angel crowded down there waited on his words. Zeus with that damn smirk on his face. Poseidon with his arms folded, grinning as well. They would love for him to be out of the picture.

Calliope dropped into a crouch just before the crumbled throne and sprung up, rushing towards them. The sight of her sealed his decision.

Lucifer kept his head up. "You won't get rid of me that easily."

"As I thought." His father barely looked over his shoulder. "Go lick your wounds, boy."

Lucifer stepped forwards only to have Lilith stand in his way as his father turned to face him, one eye in a squint as if calculating his son's next move.

"Not now, Lucifer." Lilith meant it.

In the background was Calliope's voice. "Father. Lucifer. Stop this now."

There would come a day he would prove his father wrong. There would be a day Lucifer would right this universe. It was his destiny. He fully accepted that now without any second thoughts. Lilith had envisioned it and he felt it surging through him. But Lilith was right. Not now.

"Another time," Lilith said. Her ponytail whipped around from her turning away, the spearhead attached to the end of it stopping about an inch from his father's right eye, making it look accidental.

His father winced. Lucifer smirked at the sight of that. He slowly turned away with Lilith, her fiery-red wings unwrapped from her body as a second armour and spread out into their full glory.

As Lilith and he rose to the sky, he heard his father say, "Remain here, Apollo, and move us again with your music and gentle voice. I hope you can forgive me for the burden I put on you. I see things more clearly." A pause. "I now see I didn't punish my son enough that day."

That day had been the first and only time Lucifer was backhanded by his father and experienced excruciating pain. The physical wounds had taken weeks to heal, the mental anguish months, all for disrespecting Apollo. Lucifer hadn't seen anything beautiful about that until now, because it did lead him to studying the arts more seriously, to understand every aspect of the field, to understand his father better, and even Apollo, too. During that process he fell in love with the arts and if it hadn't been for that newfound adoration, he would not have freed Apollo. There was beauty in pain and suffering.

Wise old Teacher, wise Baiame indeed.

Falling into Place

Zeus

Zeus's allies had wanted him to make a move while son and father bickered. The chaos might have allowed them a quick victory. With enough swords in their returning king's back, Zeus would have been given the honour of beheading the Lord with one clean swipe, then there would only be Lucifer and his army to contend with.

They really believed that would have worked. Zeus didn't see it that way. He would stay the course, keep it political until left with no choice. He would let Poseidon do his thing and drive the wedge between father and son even deeper. He knew the perfect vessel to do just that.

Calliope confronted her father who politely waved her away and before she could tend to her brother, Lucifer flew off with Lilith. Yes, with Lucifer now estranged, Calliope was the key. Thanks to her, Poseidon was back onboard more than ever. Everything was falling into place.

Primal

Lucifer

In the Giant Forests at the backside of Rainbow Ridge, facing the Serene Sea, Lucifer landed on one of the fat mid-branches of a cedar tree overlooking a valley of cascades, water spray misting the air. Lilith landed next to him.

"He built me up to tear me down." Lucifer crouched on the branch, arms resting on his knees. Birds flocked by, briefly erasing the view below.

"He's not the same." Lilith crouched next to him.

"Another vision hidden from me?"

"Your father is mortified by his ageing. He might be able to hide his present thoughts and his fears from you, but his mind is more accessible to me, more than he realizes. He knows we're all questioning his impregnability. Surely he questions his own immortality? He returns to see he's been forgotten, written off. Then he hears you about to declare yourself king."

"How did he know? Was he watching us the entire time, like we're a game to him? Or was it — of course, he learned of it through Hephaestus."

"How would he know?"

"Zeus most likely told him after the vote by the Twelve, knowing Hephaestus would snitch."

The mere mention of his name would allow Hephaestus to hear their conversation for about a minute.

"That rat. He told my father. I won't forget this, Hephaestus."

Lilith simpered. She was on the same page. They both chewed up the reputation of Hephaestus, stretching the roasting of the portal maker by repeating his name, then moved on.

"I only get a taste of your father's emotions. Calliope would know best. You should seek her counsel."

"I won't get her involved in this. You're now defending his actions?"

"I'm at your side until the end, you know this. We need to be able to look at it through everyone's perspective. The coming days and months will be telling. They've had a taste of your leadership and many have spoken highly of it. The seeds of doubt have been planted. Your father's physical attack has only planted more doubt in their minds. Take the higher road and be patient, you will sit on a throne again soon enough."

"Your wisdom quells my anger," Lucifer said with a sigh. "I'm truly blessed to have you at my side. Otherwise, I would have done something impulsive and unfortunate."

"It seems you need to vent some anger."

She bit into his ear and licked the side of his face.

Lucifer needed no more encouragement. He shoved her against the trunk of the tree, and they shed each other of their light armour, flipping it to the lower forest, kissing, spurring in each other an uncontrollable passion. She bit into his chest, drawing blood, then licked it up as the wound healed. He burned off all that anger, pleasure numbing his bruised ego, grunting like a feral beast. They went primal, biting into each other, then they went to a place of ecstasy only Lilith could bring him to.

Message Loud and Clear

Poseidon

Poseidon sat on Pegasus within the shadows of Shaggy Back forest stretching across both sides of Musical Meadows. Every day he had hid in here since Calliope rejected him, autographing a new species of bird or insect or tiny animal into existence from that boulder down there. And after she flew off, he would hunt down every one of her new creations, squashing them in his hands. He hadn't seen her since her father's return six days ago. Word had it she was on hiatus on the planet Kolob, escaping all the drama between Lucifer and her father.

He leaned down and massaged Pegasus's neck with both hands. Then he sat up straight with full resolve.

"Hephaestus, open a portal to Calliope's location. I have a message for her."

Poseidon unsheathed his sword.

JAMES PYNE

ATHENA AND LUCIFER SWORDPLAYING

Lucifer the Father

Athena

When Athena's stepmother, Hera, left him due to his infidelity with Metis, another lover from back in the day and Athena's biological mother, Zeus could not manage the pressures of single parenting and put Athena up for adoption. It came as a shock to everyone, when Lucifer and Lilith adopted her, having no offspring themselves. This was fine by her, because she knew Hera would be back and she was the worst stepmother ever. Athena spent much of her time with Baiame, as she was only a few years from adulthood and Lucifer wanted her to have the best education possible. Baiame pronounced her the most difficult student he'd had to deal with since Lucifer, who would only smile at Baiame, then mess Athena's hair up and say how proud he was of her much to Baiame's annoyance.

Athena was grateful for everything Lilith and Lucifer did for her. Whenever formal events were held, she happily declared herself the daughter of the greatest warrior, Lucifer, and daughter to one of the wisest of angels, Lilith. She didn't care what anybody thought, especially Zeus. That included her adoptive parents because they were stuck with her forever.

"Show mercy to your enemy?" Lucifer asked her, while they sparred in the arena section of the courtyard, where the Botanical Gardens separated them from the throne area. Sparks flew from the collision of their swords. "Or do you crush them?"

"Pound them into bone powder," Athena shouted with glee, as Lucifer dodged another one of her crafty moves that got everyone else but him. Their wings wrapped around them as their only armour. This was a rule of Lucifer's when sparring. Dressing with little armour inspired more seriousness, because even if an angel healed quickly from most sword wounds, it still wasn't a pleasant experience.

"Why show such aggression when the enemy has already been defeated?" Lucifer sheathed his sword.

She sheathed hers as well. "To spare your enemy would be considered a weakness by other rivals." While his blond hair was bundled up in a tight ponytail, hers crept down her front and back in different lengths. She had the most muscle tone of any female angel, keeping her femininity, always sought after by the opposite gender. She had no interest in them. She had a higher duty: protecting the throne.

She and Lucifer headed back towards the throne area, both keeping quiet, passing through a fountained and flowered area, the scent of lilac heaviest in the air. The throne steps appeared at a distance through the stone arbour. They stepped inside the gazebo, where an arched bridge tongued from it, passing over transparent fish that sparkled like crystals, hopping about the stream that stretched beneath both sides of the Nest and out into the Wilderness.

"Yes, showing empathy would be considered a great weakness to some. However," Lucifer continued, clasping with both hands the railing of the arbour, staring over at his father sitting in his new throne that was identical to the last. "You will soften more hearts by showing clemency and acquire a friend in your enemy. Absoluteness is not the answer. The greatest of strengths is to let your enemy keep their dignity, resist the temptation to squash them from fear that they'll become a threat again. That is true strength."

"But won't they become a menace again?"

"Most become a lifelong friend."

"Long enough to get close enough to cut your throat. Evil is evil. It doesn't change."

"I've seen a planet suffer no wars, no killings, nothing malicious going on, everything and everybody truly at peace, then, poof, suddenly they're killing each other. If good can become evil, then evil can become saintly. But my father's absoluteness always surfaces, not giving them a chance. No mercy. None comes from my father. His draconian ways only anger others in this court."

The heartbeat of the Lord's throne pulsated slowly with a hint of speeding up as he pretended to pay no mind to their conversation by looking elsewhere. Athena knew better. That ear was listening in on their conversation.

"One cannot please everyone," she said. "There will always be someone who disagrees."

"Not everything's black and white. There are all manner of personalities one must contend with as the Supreme Leader, and by showing mercy and respect to those conquered, you will win most discontents in this court, at least short term, allowing you time to win them over the long term. My father has forgotten this. He taught me that lesson. It was why he was so tolerant with the House of Cronus for so long."

There, he almost turned his head, Athena was sure of it. The Almighty was listening. His throne pulsated more quickly, a silent warning to them to cease with this talk. Father must see, yet still rants.

"Has he forgotten?" Athena said. "I see it another way."

"That is?"

"What of Zeus?" she asked. "He considers mercy a weakness and would never cross your father knowing how absolute he is in his convictions. Yet I've heard whispers that he considers you anemic."

"Zeus will someday challenge for the throne, nothing new." They walked across the bridge and stepped into the throne area. "Zeus uses my father's brutal absoluteness to his advantage, as a tool to acquire favourable ears in this court. If my father started showing a measure of mercy in certain things, he'd win those ears back to his side. But ever since his return, he's more impulsive. This court is growing bored of the old ways and is ready for change."

"I love you and Lilith." Athena looked over at the new throne, its heartbeat a steady pulse. "But your words are borderline treason." She turned to Lucifer. "Tell me, are you planning on taking the throne?"

He said nothing.

"Well?"

"Only if offered."

A part of her believed him. The other part of her feared that someday they would face each other on the battlefield.

A Mirror of What He Should Have Been

Zeus

It killed Zeus inside to see Athena so happy as he watched from the door of his living quarters. He had just finished doing meditation, which every angel did every day for at least six hours unless on assignment. The clanking of swords spurred him to see if a domestic dispute was taking place. Such moments were no opportunities for allies. Always pick the loser, for they had the most agreeable ears.

It wasn't that he didn't want Athena to be happy; seeing her joy because of Lucifer and Lilith was the problem. Zeus simply wasn't ready to be a parent again. It could be argued, when was he ever? The rumour of him not wanting her because he felt she was a threat against him was asinine. He never saw it coming though. Lilith volunteering Lucifer and herself to be Athena's adoptive parents blew everyone out of the water. It was no secret Lilith had no desire to have any offspring any time soon, she valued her youthful looks too much, but who knew she had a secret affinity for motherhood?

Seeing Athena grown into the warrior princess he imagined her becoming, had him longing to be the one to take credit. But that ship had long passed into the realm of dreamland.

Athena looked over at Zeus before swinging at Lucifer, the impact of their swords throwing up sparks high in the air.

The wind carried a fragment of their conversation his way.

"You seem perturbed, Athena," Lucifer shouted over the clanging of their swords.

"The sight of someone sickens me."

Zeus accepted his own blood hating him. Seeing Lucifer smirk while looking his way gutted him.

JAMES PYNE

CALLIOPE'S PAINFUL TRANSFORMATION

Stabbing Madness

Poseidon

Calliope sketched and shaded in another species of bird to go with the hundred thousand plus already thriving on the planet Kolob. She sat cross-legged on the highest mountain-top, appreciating the planet's trademark scent of sweet honey. Since the return of her father, she had been on vacation here. She'd had enough drama to last her the rest of immortality. No wonder she wanted nothing to do with the throne, all it brought was backstabbing and childish bickering. There were days she wanted to step down from the Twelve. The problem with that, most on the Council didn't have the best intentions for the Order or the mortals, using their seat for political gain, nothing more.

The songbirds hiding within the patches of thicket copycatted the tunes she was humming, amusing her. She autographed the new species of bird into existence and with one clean tear, tossed the paper to the wind. The male and female spurted from the paper that burned up at their exit, black and red hues rapidly spread throughout their plumage. Each had a spiked mustard-yellow mohawk, blood-red eyes, a long tail tipped like an arrowhead.

Shadows passed from black-bellied songbirds flitting over. The newly introduced species darted towards them. Their arrowed tails spearheaded the songbirds, then curled over their heads and began stacking dead birds onto their spiked mohawks, action that went against anything she would create. Since her encounter with the Tentacle King, dark images sometimes crept up and now she wondered if they were affecting her art.

"What monstrous things."

It saddened her to think that she had given life to such a horrid species of bird when the planet itself knew no such violence. Their spiked mohawks now stacked full of dead birds, they flew to the closest ledge and shook the bird corpses from their heads, filling the area like the table of a great feast. They syphoned all blood from their kill via their jagged beaks, then swatted each drained corpse from the cliff with their tails. Finished, they whizzed by her and sought out more victims, their hunger insatiable.

She almost snatched them from midair with the intent to squash them in her hands and she still might do that. It went against her beliefs of allowing every species to take its natural course, but these two were treating the entire planet as their main course, and that just wouldn't do. Besides, they weren't natural inhabitants of the planet, making them fair game, right? Then again, she had created many species on Kolob. Should she play the part of her father and choose who lived and died? It would make her no better than him and the rest of the Twelve. She would think about it. Until then, she would sheath the magical pencil inside her sketchbook.

"Why stop? I like them," she heard Poseidon say behind her. "Excellent hunters. I won't kill them. The first thing you've created of worth. That horse of yours was of no use, had no desire in it to kill anything."

Before she turned, the severed head of Pegasus bounced, then rolled next to her, splashing blood. It teetered at the edge. She scrambled backwards from the horrible sight. Her heart thumped faster with a mix of emotions flooding her.

"Pegasus!"

Poseidon swaggered into view, stopping at Pegasus's head. "The sight of him greatly depressed me. All I could think about was that day that seemed so perfect, when everything old became new to these eyes. Until you soured it and made it familiar. Until you made hurt a whole new beastly thing. So, I killed part of that day, but the memory still lingers." He bunted Pegasus's head with his foot, sending it off the edge and out of sight. Poseidon turned to her, hand resting on his sheathed sword. "It's strongest at the sight of you."

She stood up with no blade, seeing no reason to carry her sword on a planet of birds and insects. Now she wished she lived by Lucifer's rule: always carry a weapon even if just a dagger.

"I killed them all. Everything you created. I hunted them down. The sight of them reminded me of you. Don't worry." His hand slid from the handle of his sword. "I'm not going to cut your head off."

He swayed towards her as if he were a predator. There was no light in him anymore, not even twilight. Only pure darkness in him. He had cracked. The last time such darkness had flooded her was from her father seeing her almost dead at the feet of the Tentacle King.

"Hephaestus," she shouted. "A portal."

Poseidon pounced at her.

"Poseidon, no, you're not thinking clearly."

"Things have never been so clear."

No portal opened. It happened from time to time, but now? Poseidon had portalled here. Hephaestus had to be at the helm. He never slept.

"Hephaestus. Help!"

"I'm going to make reality clear for you," Poseidon snarled.

"You're mad."

"And you're mine."

He stopped her attempt to stab his right eye with her pencil. Grabbed her wrist, yanked the pencil from her. With her free hand, she punched him with everything she had. He pushed his jaw back in place just in time to have it put out of place again. When she went for a third swing, he jabbed the pencil into her fist.

She didn't feel discomfort right away. Its sting crept into her knuckles, buzzed up through her entire arm to her left shoulder, and a sharp crippling pain spread through her without stop. A coldness flooded her. Was this pending death? She was too weak to even remove the pencil.

Poseidon tossed her to the rocky surface. The lead turned into liquid and wormed up her arm like dark, pulsating veins.

"Sister!" her brother shouted from above.

Hephaestus must have alerted Lucifer, concluding that a portal wasn't enough.

The shadow of three sets of wings passed over her and Poseidon.

The last of the magical lead melted into her veins. The pencil blew away into dust.

"Lucifer, I feel myself—"

It wasn't death coming over her. Something else crept to the surface of her mind, pushing out of her. Something hidden deep inside was darkening her soul. Something was adding itself to her, rewiring her.

Poseidon withdrew his sword, turning in time to have Lucifer slam him into the wall of a nearby mountain. Pieces of rock splashed out. Poseidon fell to the ground. He staggered back to his feet, still clasping his sword.

"I'll make clean work of you."

Calliope suddenly found herself inside her brother's head, seeing out of his eyes as he whacked Poseidon with his wings, sending him hard against the wall. Lucifer eagle-clawed Poseidon's face and bashed the back of his head against the mountain countless times. One side of his wings rose, coming down hard with the intent to axe Poseidon's face. A mere second from Poseidon's ugly mug, the downward force of Lucifer wings stopped.

"*Do it,*" Calliope whispered inside her brother's head.

He looked back at her own crumpled body, barely sitting up, staring, like something else was in there as she spoke aloud, "Calliope says, do it, Lucifer."

Her conscience hauled back into his body as their father portalled into view and yanked Lucifer from Poseidon, shoving him aside.

"Enough!"

"Look at Calliope!" Lucifer pointed over at her, the liquid lead swirling and shifting into various faces all over her skin, passing each other and sometimes snapping and tearing at each other's pencilled flesh. Her living tattoos matched her current mood swings, confused, disturbed, sudden grins. "And you stop me. You should be helping avenge her."

"You act too quickly with your blind rage." Father looked over at Calliope, as if he were disgusted at the sight of her, but that was crazy thinking. Why would he think badly of her? Where were these dark thoughts coming from?

"Excuses," Lucifer said, pushing off Poseidon.

Their father willed armour from his flesh, ripping away his tunic, still looking her way. An act of aggression? It couldn't be. He sensed it in her too. She felt herself falling deeper inside herself as darkness, somehow jumpstarted by the magic of her pencil, took her over.

"You've always favoured him, ignoring his debauchery. He tried to rape your daughter."

"It's already set in, Lucifer." Their father looked down at her helpless. "Nothing can be done. That pencil was your mother's, before that my mother's. Impossible to know what it will do to her."

Grandmother's pencil? Why hadn't he told her? What did he mean, nothing could be done? The Almighty could wave things into and out of existence. How hard could this be for him? Why did he look at Poseidon with such concern when she was the one in need?

Calliope became lost in what felt like every thought slamming into her, none hers, like she was taking in the emotions of everybody in the universe. She was going mad from it. She whined, howled in agony, and clamping her head with both hands, she tried standing only to fall. The words of her brother and father cut in and out. Her wings tried to lift her, but she was too disorientated.

"Look at her, Lucifer said. That agony. Undo her pain, erase that mess on her skin."

"The lead of that pencil is permanent inside her. She's now its vessel as the wood was before her."

"Calliope says, shut that egotistical trap of yours, Old Fool." Calliope looked up at Lucifer and their father, both clearly in shock from her words. "Calliope will deal her own justice upon the wretched residue from Cronus's loins." She looked over at a hunched over Poseidon, one hand on the mountain to keep himself upright. "That day plaguing you, Poseidon, will be erased by the horrors of today."

Calliope's wings armoured her; devilish grinning faces shaded all over her body. A stabbing madness took over. She approached her brother and father. The latter grabbed her by the arm, only to be willed from her. She didn't look to see how far as she roundhouse kicked Poseidon back into the mountain. She gripped his throat with one hand. Never had she possessed such strength. It felt like she could crush his neck with little effort. It was a liberating feeling. An invincible feeling.

"Let Calliope be your muse," she whispered in his ear, playfully nibbling it. She licked one side of his face, tasting fear. Then she looked down at her shoulder, where a shaded image of Pegasus's head appeared, gritting its teeth at Poseidon in anger. "Let Calliope inspire you." She slammed into Poseidon's mind. Her gifts heightened to unknown levels.

Poseidon tried fighting off the images, the suggestions she was inserting in his head, but she willed them in with such relentless fury. In the end, he obeyed and dragged his fingernails down the sides of his face, screaming as she willed him to pull at both corners of his mouth, stretching them until the skin split at both ends, widening his mouth into a slasher smile. Blood poured down his chin and chest armour. She licked a stream of it from his face. It was like nectar. His flesh was like ambrosia.

"Calliope!" her father shouted. "Stop!"

Poseidon tore open his nostrils, then went for his own eyes.

She pushed deeper into his mind, was about to plant an addiction in there, one that would have him tearing apart his body all over again after it finished healing, over and over for the rest of eternity, but Calliope was forcefully yanked from Poseidon.

"Father's stuck his nose where it doesn't belong." She entered her father's mind, mixing up his thoughts, disorientating him. She exited. "Let Calliope finish this, or it will be worse next time."

"Don't make me do this, Calliope."

"Calliope does what she wants."

Lucifer didn't try stopping her. Didn't get involved at all. She read Lucifer's thoughts, to hell with the covenant she made with the Order, she was going to do whatever she wanted from now on. A part of Lucifer wanted to stop her while the rest of him wanted only to stop her before severe punishment came her way. He was still deciding at what point to intervene.

"Brother, it's time for us siblings to take over." Calliope turned to Poseidon. "Time for Calliope to finish what we started with you."

"I said *stop!*" Father shouted.

Poseidon tried resisting the urge to gouge out his own eyes to Calliope's amusement.

"Daughter, my patience fades—out of my head. Now."

"Watch him," Calliope said. "Watch him go blind."

Poseidon dug into his eyes, scooped them out, screaming in such agony as he held them out. They rolled from his hands and plopped to the ground.

"Now step on them," Calliope said. "Aw, what's wrong hon, don't like feeling so helpless. Calliope's loving your thoughts of frustration, screaming at your body to resist when your eternal fate is about to be sealed."

A red glow appeared on the mountain and Poseidon's eviscerated face. She looked back to see a flaming portal.

"Calliope's your daughter. You wouldn't."

"You're sick, Calliope. A danger to everyone."

"Calliope's going to make you pay for this."

Their father stepped aside from the portal. It pulled at her and she lost control, spinning towards it, calling out to Lucifer for help. She righted herself and flew toward her father, burrowing herself inside his mind, her fury roaring into him, tearing at his thoughts and memories, stealing whatever secrets she could before he waved her away in obvious distress — a horrified look coming over his face. A powerful wind pushed her into the portal, fanning the circle of flames that lashed out at her at all sides.

"Lucifer." She reached out to him. The tattoo faces all over her silently screamed for help.

Lucifer reached in for her, as the flaming walls started to shrink, started to burn them both but her dearest brother wouldn't give up, his brotherly love true.

To Calliope's shock he pulled away, vanishing from sight, like he had been taunting her, glad to get rid of her, all this time pretending to be a loving brother. He now got what he wanted. No challenge to the throne.

As the portal closed, a burnt Calliope screamed her hate for her father, for all males of any species, especially one angel.

"Brother, Calliope will hunt you down for this betrayal!"

Coal Black Eyes

Lucifer

Calliope reached out to Lucifer, but before their burning hands interlocked, a force yanked him out of the flaming portal as it shrank from view. His last sight of her was her face lit up, the living tattoos silently screaming in agony. She cursed with such venom at their father, the loudest hatred aimed at Lucifer. Why was she mad at him? He had tried to pull her back.

"She's your daughter." He got in his father's face.

"It pained me to do that."

"At a snap of a finger," Lucifer said, "you could've fixed her."

"That's not how this plays out. That pencil was my mother's, unknown magic to me."

"Bring her back now."

"Don't push it."

"We're just a game to you," Lucifer said. "Even your own offspring. Are we such a disappointment? Did Mother stand up to you, is that it?"

"Another time, Lucifer."

"This is just an appropriate time as any."

He wouldn't say much about their mother and when they pressed for information, their father would shut them down with an annoyed look, from which a youngling knew to back off. It felt like that when it came to Calliope.

A spray of moths and birds filled the area.

"They come to pay their respects to your sister." The moths and birds circled where Calliope had sketched. "As for him . . ." He glared down at a silent Poseidon, then his eyes softened. "Let everyone witness the distorted mess he has become and let them know why."

Lucifer grabbed the blind Poseidon, whose hands shook like those of a scared old mortal, head turning about in panic, reacting to all the noises around him. He would heal soon, even if his injuries would have been permanent to most angels. That was one of his gifts. Sever his limb, it would grow back.

Lucifer whispered into Poseidon's ear, "No matter how long it takes." He leaned closer still. "I will castrate you, and the cuts from my wings are permanent, even on you."

Father opened a portal to his throne area.

"Calliope can be helped," Lucifer said.

"Such things must take their natural course," his father replied, squinting from apparent discomfort. "Even in me."

Lucifer tossed Poseidon into the portal and into the throne area of the courtyard. Before he followed, a deafening scream of pain sent shivers down his back because someone he had always thought impregnable to everything was presently in a state of immense calamity.

"She left her mark on me, the visions, the things she tried to inspire me to do." His mouth opened like he was going to cry. He bit into his lip and turned away from Lucifer. "Leave now. I must sort this out. The darkness in there feels undying. I need to cleanse it. Cut it out if I have to."

"I'll stay with you."

"I said leave."

He whipped his head around, coal-black eyes piercing Lucifer.

Lucifer backed into the portal, stunned into silence at the contorted, monstrous face, however brief. The wretched sight of his father emptied all hope of saving Calliope. Their father was a staggering wreckage, barely able to keep himself together. No one could know of this. The House of El was prime for attack. Lucifer turned into the courtyard where Poseidon stumbled around with his sisters, Hestia and Demeter tending to him.

The portal closed.

"What did you do to our brother?" Zeus shouted. A thunderbolt stretched from his fist.

Lucifer turned all the way, clasping his sheathed sword.

"Nothing—yet."

The Challenge

Athena

The House of Zeus and the House of El were both in disorder. Athena wanted to rip what remained of Poseidon apart. She and Calliope had become like sisters.

Their Lord returned irritable. No surprise there considering he had just banished his daughter to Hell. His conscience had to be tearing him apart. Calling him out on that unspeakable act would only risk banishment to the Inferno. But how could she just stand by and say nothing? The only one speaking out was Lucifer.

"Poseidon needs to be punished!" Lucifer shouted. Athena stood next to him, Lilith on the other side in black armour. "If he's not to be banished to

Hell, then once fully recovered he must face me in battle."

The Almighty sat there in silence, the heartbeat of his throne a deep red pulse not seen before. Zeus was in crimson armour while his sisters, Hestia and Demeter, held up Poseidon in front of his living quarters. His eyes were gouged out, lipstick-red gouges streaked his face, his nostrils looked like they had blown apart, and his mouth was torn open into a disturbing smile. He shook like he was terrified or cold; the pain he was feeling almost made Athena feel bad for him and that sickened her.

Everyone vacationing from assignments on other planets, along with the younglings and military, watched from the doorways of their living quarters or from the top of the Nest along the parapet walk. Angels defended Poseidon, saying he was a war hero who hadn't been himself since the Great Battle and couldn't have known the lead of that enchanted pencil would cause Calliope such grief. Others sided with Lucifer, shouting that it was his sibling right to avenge his wronged sister, for Poseidon's intentions had been anything but friendly.

Athena held her golden winged helmet to her side. Her wild hair flowed down the black cloak over her armour. She and Lilith were dressed for battle to symbolically support Lucifer. They were prepared to interrupt him if he got too lippy, as they had discussed. But if things got physical, they both would fight at his side. They expected the House of Zeus to make a move.

"Will justice prevail? It is my blood right."

Their Lord sat slumped like a pile of boulders, chin on fist. The heartbeat of his black crystal throne softened its pulse, like the calm before the storm. He looked so conflicted up there.

"He tried to rape Calliope!" Athena hollered. Lilith gave her a look that warned her to tread carefully, while Lucifer kept his eyes on his father. "Yes, he got a beat down for his troubles. Under normal circumstances that would be enough, but his actions have led to Calliope being cast into Hell, leaving the hearts of a brother, a father, and many friends aching. Let us not forget Poseidon's barbaric slaughter of Pegasus to get back at Calliope for rejecting him. It was a cold, calculative mind that did that."

The Seraphim and other warrior castes watched from the top levels, in full battle armour. Michael stood out among them, in his shimmering armour.

"Your rebuttal?" Their Lord was addressing Poseidon. "What were your intentions for Calliope? Rape? Bodily harm?"

"She flirted with me, played with my emotions many months ago." Poseidon's speech was slurred from his mangled mouth. He tried standing on his own. "Made advances—invited me into her arms. When I decided to oblige, she slapped me—spat in my face. It festered inside me for months, ate me alive. I finally snapped and killed Pegasus in a blind rage. She lost her mind at what I had done and punched me a few times. Tried stabbing my eye with the pencil—I blacked out with anger and did the unforgivable thing I did."

Poseidon, though blinded, with signs of his eyes slowly growing back, looked upwards at the others. He finished with, "It was a pencil. How was I supposed to know it would have such consequences?"

"He lies as much as he lies with all manners of beasts. The dog," Lucifer shouted.

Zeus was barely able to hide his smirk within his beard, one Athena wanted to wipe away with a quick, spinning kick.

"A proposal to both houses." Lucifer didn't look away from Zeus; obviously, he saw what Athena had seen. "When fully healed, he and I must do battle. If Poseidon defeats me, I'll willingly walk into Hell. If I defeat Poseidon, I get to throw him in there at Calliope's feet. And she returns home under my watch."

Zeus squinted at Lucifer, who had turned away from him. If he made a move for Lucifer's back, Athena would introduce him to centuries of pent up anger against him.

"Fully healed, Poseidon's no match for your skills," the Almighty said.

"Then let him choose a champion if he's too much of a coward to face me. And if I defeat his champion"—Lucifer looked back at Zeus, then back to the throne—"Calliope returns. And Poseidon can remain here."

Whatever the decision, it would be political. Poseidon still had pull with one third of the court, with enough of the Twelve longing for the kind of change someone like Zeus promised.

"For the sake of peace . . ." The Almighty sat back in the throne. "Poseidon, choose your champion from anyone in this court so we may get this finished today."

"I choose Athena," Poseidon said without hesitation.

"What?" Athena couldn't believe her ears. "I will not fight my father."

Zeus frowned at her.

Angels shouted that it was wrong for family to do battle under these circumstances. Others reminded the court that Athena was not of Lucifer's blood.

The Almighty raised his hand. Everyone fell into a silence.

"Father," Lucifer said. "First, he tries to rape your daughter, leading to her madness and banishment. And now this? Why can't you see the House of Zeus is doing everything it can to make ours fall? I'll not fight my daughter. I'll not forsake her as you have forsaken Calliope."

"What would this court think if I hadn't exiled her? You saw the condition she was in. I would have kept her here, even for the bodily harm done to

Poseidon. But she was going to kill him, and you know it. Favouritism is what everyone would have shouted, and they would have been right." The Almighty sat up. "You suggested this, Lucifer. Now stand by your word. Or is that waning like your allegiance to me?"

"She's my daughter—"

"If you don't, you will be relieved of your command, stripped of all titles, and stricken from this House for you will no longer bring shame to it."

"You've gone mad."

"Father." Athena placed a hand on the chest area of Lucifer's armour. "I'm fine with it." She put on her feathered gold helmet. "It will be like our sparring, no different, only one of us will have to concede defeat. We could cut each other for eternity and our flesh would heal before our next breath."

Was she trying to convince him or herself because it really wasn't okay? Lucifer had done nothing wrong. He had defended the honour of their House, avenging a sister wronged. Why couldn't the Almighty see that? What had gotten into him? What Lucifer was not saying was that he was there at the end, he saw what happened between Calliope and their father, but was keeping it from everyone, even now. Whatever happened, it had brought about a sudden urgency on his part.

"My Lord," Michael shouted down from atop of the Nest. "Allow me to take Lucifer's place! Poseidon gets to choose his champion."

"Lucifer asked for this," the Almighty said.

"Then let me replace Athena and fight on behalf of Poseidon. I promise, I'll show no quarter."

"Michael, your intentions are honourable and move me and this court. But the combatants have been chosen."

Lucifer nodded up at Michael.

Athena willed her wings around her first layer of armour.

Lucifer's remained in full view.

"The stakes," the Almighty said, "If Athena wins, Poseidon remains here, Lucifer loses his command of the Seraphim and is disowned by my House. If Lucifer wins, Poseidon will be banished from the kingdom of angels for a thousand years."

"That's it?" Lilith shouted. "This is what they're fighting for? It seems Lucifer has more to lose out of this."

"Mind your mouth."

"He's my husband, my love, something you know nothing about."

The Almighty's eyes widened.

"I will not fight Athena," Lucifer said.

"Then you forfeit your command."

"What are you doing?" Athena shouted at Lucifer.

"I will not fight you. Unlike you, Father, my love for my daughter is unconditional."

The Almighty sat up. Both of his hands squeezed the ends of the armrests of the throne that pulsated the quickest Athena had ever seen. "I forfeit my army to Athena's command as she is the victor."

The court awed in disbelief and angels mumbled to each other at the shock of it.

Lucifer unsheathed his sword and pointed it at his father.

The entire court went silent.

"And I challenge you for the throne."

JAMES PYNE

LUCIFER VERSUS HIS FATHER

JAMES PYNE

Father and Son Clash

Lucifer

"Father" — Athena tugged at him — "emotions cloud your judgement. This is exactly what the House of Zeus wants."

"Listen to her, Lucifer," Lilith said at the other side of him. "You're acting on emotion. You haven't thought this out."

Lucifer kept his sword steady and level with his chin, pointing at his father who leaned over one side of his throne, speechless, like he hadn't predicted this happening at this very moment.

"It is done," Lucifer said to both. "The madness in the universe ends today." He nodded at his father. "Come now, you ancient wreck, and face me. I'll see you coming this time. Today you fall. Today old friends and family banished to Hell return to our loving eyes and embrace. When I'm done with you, I'll give Poseidon to Calliope in her present state and I will relish every second of her tearing him apart."

He pointed his sword at Poseidon.

Zeus smirked.

Lucifer's father stood up, slowly, and the throne's heartbeat faded away.

"It is the Almighty, no one dares," Athena said to Lucifer. "It could be to the death."

"I dare, my daughter. I dare to right everything."

"You can still back out of this, Lucifer," Lilith said. "You're emotional from Calliope's fate, everyone will understand."

"Are you coming to face me?" Lucifer looked past Lilith at his father. "Or did you shit yourself from the thought of inevitable defeat?"

Lilith stepped in front of him. "If you think my vision involved this day, you have never been so wrong. I stand with you, nonetheless. I know that look in your eyes, there's no changing your mind."

"This is my battle, Lilith." Lucifer pressed his forehead against hers, then pushed off and turned his back to his father with sword resting on his shoulder, returning the insult given to him not so long ago. He had lost some respect with the other angels, he saw it in their eyes, their brief acknowledgements of his presence as if he were a plague to avoid, something shameful.

Lilith walked to the side with Athena, opposite of the House of Zeus.

"Lilith will suffer the same fate as you, Lucifer," his father said. "Think twice about this."

"I welcome it." Lilith spat on the ancient stone ground. "I will enjoy seeing my husband drag you defeated across this courtyard and through the heavens, announcing to the universe that it's free of your psychosis." She walked in a circle as she shouted, "Freedom!" to all those now standing in the doorways.

Lucifer's army, the Seraphim at the top of the Nest, stood with heads bowed, fists over their armoured hearts. Michael remained emotionless, clasping the hilt of his sword.

Lilith continued to rev up support for Lucifer.

"Be silent!" the Almighty shouted.

Lucifer turned to see his father land in front of Lilith, backhanding her aside. She slammed hard against one of the walls of the Nest, bits of rock sprinkling on her. Staggering forward, she drew her sword, dizzied, bleeding from her nose.

"You'll pay for that," Lucifer said, motioning for Lilith to back off.

She sheathed her sword with authority.

Athena stepped in front of Lucifer's father.

"You too? Sworn defender of this throne?"

"Stop, all of you," she said. "Madness rules the day."

"Are you with him or me?"

"He's your son," Athena continued. "He's emotional and not thinking, like you aren't. Are you both really going to fight because of the actions of that monster?" She pointed at Poseidon. "Only the House of Zeus benefits. What common sense is there in that?"

"Out of my way."

"No."

The Almighty's wings expanded, and one side batted Athena aside.

She landed in a crouch, sliding backwards to a stop. Athena stood up with Lucifer motioning for her to stay out of this.

His father's armour pushed out of his flesh, dark red, like molten lava spreading all over his body, cooling into impregnable armour. He raised his right fist and from it protruded a crystal sword.

"I'll spank you over my knee, then flip you into Hell."

"I'll drag you there," Lucifer said. "And all Banished will have their fun with you before returning with me."

"Is that so? Come then, youngling." His father motioned with his free hand for Lucifer to make the first move and from that hand protruded dark claws—a fresh look for his father, one out of character.

With purpose, Lucifer marched towards his father.

A great wind came down upon the entire planet. His father scratched an exaggerated itch along the side of his head with the point of his crystal sword. He waved Lucifer forward with his clawed hand and the most condescending smirk Lucifer had ever seen.

"You don't take me seriously," Lucifer said. "But you will." He lunged at his father, who blocked Lucifer's first swing with his sword, almost giving way to the impact. "What's wrong, Father?"

With their swords still connected, Lucifer leaned into his father's face.

"Why surprised? I'm of your blood and much more mature than the days when we sparred."

His father pushed Lucifer off sending him towards the sky, part of the Nest still above him.

"And ashamed I am of that!" his father shouted up.

Lucifer's six wings shadowed much of the courtyard and lower living quarters below. He dove towards his father and at the last second, curled his impregnable wings in front of him and like a battering ram collided with his father, sending him onto his back. Lucifer stood over him and raised his sword, driving it downwards, to have it blocked at the last second.

His father pushed up with his sword sending Lucifer to the sky again.

"You see it," Lucifer shouted to those standing at their doorways, hope in their eyes. "He's not unwavering. He's no better. Just older and wiser to what life brings. The old ways die today. You will yield to me, Father."

The Almighty's wings rose into view, while his bearded cheeks grew blood red. No doubt he wanted to simply imagine Lucifer straight to Hell, but there were rules when it came to settling disputes. An angel must be defeated via swordplay or by fists or by other means, excluding magic.

His father launched himself at Lucifer.

The sky rumbled with each collision of their bodies and the clang of their swords, sending shockwaves ripping through clouds, dispersing sky wraiths into nothingness. Lightning branched throughout the sky. Mountains rumbled, sending pieces of rock tumbling down, bowling over forests. The planet had gone mad, eating itself alive.

Lucifer shouted, "I will beat you without this."

He tossed his sword back to the courtyard, where Lilith caught it by its handle and held it high, declaring her husband braver than his father, and the inevitable victor.

The crystal sword sank back into his father's fist and those same knuckles slammed into Lucifer's jawbone, sending him twirling out of control. He shook off the dizziness, and turned to a fist coming at him, smashing into his nose, spattering blood. Lucifer punched back, to the sound of bone cracking, a look of disbelief on his father's face. He took a swipe with his clawed hand at the stomach of Lucifer's armour, drawing blood.

Lucifer looked down at the torn away armour as his stomach healed . . . and looked up. "My turn."

He drove one of his six wings downwards, cutting away a piece of his father's armour and skinning his shoulder. Cthulhu had been the first and last in Lucifer's lifetime to do any damage to his father until now. He could beat him. Humble him. Lucifer spun again with his wings slicing through his father's chest armour, and thick blood oozed from the slash. The armour didn't close. The wound didn't heal quickly.

Blood dripped onto the courtyard for all to see.

The Almighty's eyes deepened into black pearls. He clawed at Lucifer, whose wings shielded him but were beginning to give way to his father's onslaught.

Lucifer twirled, releasing his bladed feathers, denting armour, the rest blocked by his father's wings before they could tear away flesh. His bladed feathers returned and as his wings rose to release them again, his father tackled him, powering him into the courtyard, stomping him, raging in an unknown language.

"Admit defeat!" the Almighty shouted down. Lucifer released bladed feathers, one spearing through the side of his father's neck.

He howled with anger. "Stubborn."

"Like my mother," Lucifer said, his bruised face slowly healing to its glowing tan. "Did you kill her? Is that the big secret?" The court aahed at that accusation as one of Lucifer's wings swiped at his father, who swatted it away.

"Do not speak of her!" He stomped Lucifer deeper into the ground. "No one speaks of her!" The Almighty looked up at the others. "No one!"

Lucifer's father raged more on his son, leaving Lucifer's armour dented, torn away in places. The planet seemed to howl and ache because of it. His father shouted things in a language not understood by any angel, including Lucifer, only spoken one other time, during his battle with Cthulhu before they portalled from sight.

He ceased his assault on Lucifer.

"I allow things as they are for a reason." The Almighty bent over for Lucifer to hear, but no one else. "Until you understand why, through your own trials and tribulations, you are not ready to be king. When you are, it will be during what will seem the end of everything and at that moment with all the fallen around you, your friends and family no more, and with all that horrible pain, then and only then will you truly understand your purpose and who you are keeper to." He leaned closer. "This is your destiny. As it was mine."

Soundly defeated. What seemed assured victory had become a nightmare.

"But you are not ready. You are nothing but a spoiled brat. But someday." He avoided Lilith's attempt to stab him through the back with Lucifer's sword. He eagle-clawed her throat and threw her into an opening portal, its flames swallowing her screams. "Someday you will understand. Until then, Lucifer, my son, reign in Hell."

He dragged Lucifer's beaten body along the courtyard for all to see. They looked down at him, the hope they had now gone. Others, like Zeus, smirked. Even Poseidon's battered face managed to produce a noticeable smile of his own with one side of his mouth almost healed. Others whispered to each other while gaping at Lucifer. His father stopped at the portal, looking over his shoulder, barely down at Lucifer. Was he reconsidering what he was about to do?

"There's no other way," he said.

He bowed his head and dragged Lucifer into the fiery portal.

The side of Lucifer's face started to flame. What kind of heat was this? He had withstood dragon flame, but this fire stung deep. He screamed in agony as his father remained stoic, the flames having no effect on him.

Lilith waited for them on the other side of the portal, still clenching Lucifer's sword, ready to use it. Others, long ago banished, hurried toward Lucifer's father, begging him for clemency.

"Here is Hell's throne," the Almighty shouted.

Molten lava pushed up through the magma of the ground and settled into a fire-cracked throne, its spiked backrest stretching to the dark sky.

"He who sits on this throne has dominion over all here, including its creatures, discovered and undiscovered. Now fight over it like the scavengers you are."

He backed into the flames of the portal and it slowly closed behind him.

"Father!" Lucifer bellowed; his partially burned hair already starting to regenerate. "I never surrendered — remember that!"

The banished, unable to escape through the portal, turned their attention on Lucifer. Lilith stepped over him in protective mode as he staggered to his feet to fight alongside his wife if it came down to that.

"Did he say *he?*" a familiar voice said.

Lucifer looked up to see Calliope, wearing metallic armour of unknown origin, looking like it may have come from this realm, but how? She had not been here for a full day.

"*He* who sits on that throne, Father said — Calliope sees Father still looks at females as the inferior sex."

The other angels surrounded Lucifer and Lilith. In the background, volcanoes took turns erupting rivers of lava; glittering stars in the dark sky and a huge moon lava-fissured like it was breaking apart. Dragons in the distance exhaled flames as if they were terraforming an area to their liking. The place smelled of sulfur. The air had enough moisture to sustain them, nothing more.

"Welcome Lucifer, welcome to the beating Calliope's been waiting to give you. You did nothing to stop Father from banishing Calliope to this desolate place and he will do nothing to stop the beating about to be put on you and your darling wife."

Stripped and Shamed

Zeus

The Almighty stepped out of the flaming portal in a rage. No one said anything as the portal shrank behind their king, the voice of Lucifer faintly heard from a distance, "I never surrendered — remember — " His voice cut off and Zeus could only wonder what else Lucifer would have said.

Their Lord breathed heavily, and the clouds above darkened into a mix of angry red and soot black. The sky wraiths blackened into wood smoke with blazing orange eyes, and puffs of smoke left the furnaces of their nostrils.

"We cannot imagine the heartache you're feeling, my Lord." Zeus decided he would be the first to speak. "To make such a sacrifice is moving to the court."

Their king bled from the nose and corners of his lips. His face was bruised and swollen. Lucifer had left his mark. Zeus would make note of how long it took the Supreme One to heal this time. He could make a move for the throne now, sure, and his supporters looked down at him to do so.

"Yes, a great sacrifice was made by my House today." He stared at Zeus for a time. "Now it's your House's turn."

The Almighty glared at a broken Poseidon, hunched over to one side.

"You look too comfortable," the Almighty said.

Poseidon screamed in horror as flames ate away his kaftan, his hair, and parts of his skin before dying out.

The Almighty pounced at Poseidon and held him by the throat, like he wanted to crush it.

"Please, my Lord." Poseidon's eyes still hadn't fully grown back. One was white, the other hollowed flesh. "I'm sick, you said it yourself."

"The things I want to do."

"You're letting anger get the better of you," Zeus said. A part of him felt like intervening, but he wasn't ready yet. "You're not thinking straight. He has suffered enough."

"You said nothing as I dragged my son from sight. You said nothing about Calliope's banishment. You cried no mercy for them. Yet now you speak. There are other kinds of woe he will experience from this day forwards." He pressed his forehead against Poseidon's. "This is for your own good."

"My Lord, what are you going to do to him?"

Thunder shook the Nest and lightning lit up a monstrous face, however briefly.

The Almighty pushed Poseidon into the wall.

"My Lord, please forgive me." Poseidon's fists shook beneath his chin. "Bring them back, we will not judge you. It will not be favouritism shouted by any of us."

A downpour of rain soaked everything in seconds.

"From this day forth . . . " The ground in front of Zeus burst open, shooting out a neck collar attached to a golden chain that clamped to Poseidon's neck, and blood trickled down his chest. "You shall remain here shackled and nude. No shelter. No comfortable bed. Your wounds will no longer heal until that collar falls from you."

Zeus hated himself for just standing there while all this happened. But what could he have done to prevent this punishment? Nothing. The result would be him chained to his brother.

"How long must my brother suffer this shame?" Zeus asked.

"Until the day my daughter and son are ready to return."

Slap in the Face

Athena

She stood before the throne in full battle armour, red cape blowing in a light breeze, helmet held against her side.

"The leadership of the Seraphim is now yours, Athena," the Almighty said from his throne. "Use them wisely and defend this throne as you always have."

He fell back in his throne, its rhythms irregular, as if his heart were skipping beats. Signs of his battle with Lucifer had returned, the wounds raising eyebrows.

Athena looked up at the upper levels of the Nest, where the armoured Seraphim stood at attention. Michael leaned on his sword, as was the custom of the second in command during ceremonies.

She thought of her adoptive parents, both lit up in flames. It was an image she couldn't shake.

"I accept the promotion only to hand leadership over to Michael." Instant rumblings came from all around and above. "He's a more seasoned warrior and most faithful to your word. I do this because I might do something with such power I would regret."

Rage surfaced in her. She needed to leave before she said something that would land her in the Inferno. The expression on his face was of disbelief.

"You slap me in the face?"

"I honour the throne by doing this."

She gave a slight bow, then descended the thirty-three steps, not once looking back, expecting to be portalled to Hell. She spat at the nude, shackled Poseidon, broken, eyeless. She flew off to her parents' favourite place, the Lake of Souls, to work things out.

That Way Madness Lies

Calliope

"Calliope thinks her brother's not done being dragged around. Calliope thinks her brother needs another beating to make things clear to him."

Calliope unsheathed her new sword. Its steel glowed orangish red, its handle had been constructed from the black bone of one of the demonic, primitive things diseasing the planet. She rested the sword on the shoulder of her rock armour, sashaying towards the two new residents of Hell.

Lucifer leaned to one side, bloodied, and bruised, breathing heavily with parts of him burnt, his hair growing back, deep dents in his armour with parts of it torn away. Father had given him a solid beating. Too bad he had another one coming.

The other exiles stood behind Calliope, beaten down by her mentally and physically, seeing things her way now. So would Lucifer and Lilith. She wouldn't kill her brother, there was still a use for him against father dearest.

"Once Calliope finishes with you two, you will kneel before her. Your minds are strong. Calliope could rip through them, but she has a use for both of you." She smirked. "An old-fashioned beating, it is."

Lilith stepped in front of a lopsided Lucifer. "We're here because of you." She held Lucifer's sword firm.

Calliope kept hers to her side. Lilith's ponytail swung back and forth from her movements; the arrowhead fastened at the end of it gleamed. Calliope was ready for it to lash out at her.

"Lucifer fought your father with the intent of gifting you Poseidon and freeing you from Hell." Lilith looked at the others. "To free all of you." She looked back to Calliope. "Your father has lost his mind. But I see you have, too, Calliope. It's in your eyes. You're truly broken."

"Calliope's never felt better." She took a swipe at Lucifer.

Lilith blocked it with Lucifer's sword.

Calliope smiled. "Through you then."

"As you wish." Lilith whipped her head forwards, and the ponytail flew into view with its arrowhead whizzing towards Calliope's face.

"Enough!" Lucifer shouted, snatching Lilith's ponytail back, stepping in front of her. "Calliope, I tried pulling you out of the portal. Look at me. Does it look like our father and I are getting along?"

"He does seem a little mad at you." Calliope sheathed her sword, smirking. "Calliope believes you. Welcome to Hell, little brother, where we can do whatever the fuck we want."

Something inside her was trying to overcome the new her, drag her back to the old way of looking at things. Take her back to the Calliope everyone loved and didn't fear. No, she didn't want that. Why would she? She was much stronger now.

She glanced at her hand where Poseidon had jabbed her with the pencil. She felt the living tattoos moving beneath her rock armour, swirling into different emotions.

"You're wrong, Lucifer, Calliope is much stronger now. No one will ever hurt Calliope again." She nodded at Lucifer, then turned away. She looked at the palm of her hand to see a living tattoo form into the face of a youngling, of Lucifer, the one who had cried in her arms so many nights. "Calliope believes you. You were the one groomed to lead. Here's your new army, subdued, prepped, a common hatred for our father. Calliope has yet to contend with Hades and his crew, and Cronus has retreated into the shadows of this bleak dimension, unable to cope with Calliope's mind. Would you like Calliope to hunt them down? As for these ones, I'll erase their revulsion for you. Unless of course you'd prefer to beat allegiance into them?"

"Leave them with their freewill. I will not be my father ruling by fear."

"Have it your way." She looked back to Lucifer. "Now when do we dethrone the Old Fool?"

"When we find a way out of here." Lilith passed Lucifer's sword to him, and he sheathed it. "We'll all take turns dragging him beaten around the courtyard."

"Calliope likes the sound of that."

"You've only been gone from Heaven not even a day," Lilith said to Calliope. "How is it you have new armour already? Not even Hephaestus could ornate such military decor so quickly. A sword too. And they are with cherubs and younglings. How's this possible? None of you have been gone that long."

"It's been many suns since Calliope was banished. Centuries for them."

Old Friends

Baiame

El landed with regal mastery, but Baiame detected a slight limp before the king of angels regained his imperial strut, still in the spiked and craggy armour he had been wearing since his fight with Lucifer. Baiame had just finished today's lesson with his latest student.

"Old Friend, how are you doing?" Baiame held his arms out, the sleeves of his tunic hanging deep. They embraced. "You're almost a reflection of me these days."

"If I could be so lucky."

They walked towards the stone ruins. The eternal sand tornado whirled at their right.

"How's your latest student doing?" the Almighty asked.

"He's proving to be more of a pain in the ass than his father."

"More than Odin? That says something."

"Those are new cracks in that face." Baiame motioned at a severed statue head, deep fissures in it like it was ready to crumble. "Young Thor got a hold of my old war hammer and who knew he had an itch for smashing things."

"Amusing."

"Speaking of younglings, I heard you grounded yours the other day. Like the old days then? And you seem so casual about it."

"Don't mistake my front for callousness. My heart is heavy with it."

"You're also burdened with heavy wounds, externally and internally."

"Some feel permanent. He hits like me." He gave Baiame a rueful grin. "And Calliope gets in the head like her mother." He looked at the blowing sandstorm, then back to the Land of Grouchy Heads, as the younglings had nicknamed this section of ruins due to the lack of sunny expressions.

"Both were diligent students. It's a tragedy what happened."

They entered the area once called the Hallway of Heroes, now mere remnants of giant statues half-buried in sand. What a sight it was to walk through.

The city ruins stretched for miles either way, with the sand tornado not taking up much space.

"I have never been a fan of the House of Cronus," Baiame started up the conversation again. "His bloodline has always been trouble. I hear Poseidon is still here. I can only think of one reason. Political?"

Nothing was spoken for a while. Baiame was accustomed to this kind of reaction when asking Old Friend a question he preferred not answering. Tiny shadows passed over while the squawking of crows grew loud, then faded into abrupt silence.

"What brings you here, Old Friend?"

"To hear from an honest mouth."

It was in Old Friend's eyes, a father struggling with decisions that might seem haphazard, or too quick to most, but had been carefully thought out in that mind that worked a lot faster than everyone else's. He would have worked out every scenario within seconds. What seemed horrible to everyone else was the best chance for the happy conclusion he so desperately wanted for the universe.

"So, it was your wife filling you in on things?"

"They think you're all-knowing." He chuckled at that. "I'm sure you could knock on my head a little harder and get your answer."

"A superior intellect as yours so easily amused."

"Those nails are sharp. And it was Young Thor who told me. My wife is away on the assignment you sent her on. Your memory fails you these days, I see."

"I've been too emotional and irrational lately."

"Bound to happen, thinking mostly with your brain for eons with only glimpses of emotion, which were mostly shown to your younglings, especially your sweet Calliope." And there was the reaction he hoped for, eyes glistening in the sunlight at the mention of his beloved daughter. "Younglings are a delight but can only do so much for someone who's been around as long as you. And even your offspring frustratingly remind you of their mother, yes? Both have her sense of honour to friend and family. Lucifer is stubborn like his mother, vindictive, speaks with such conviction like her, has her swagger, and most annoying to you, has her tough questions."

Old Friend nodded in agreement, not looking his way.

"Calliope inherited her mother's grace," Baiame continued, "her intuition, her love for nature, for all things to have a chance to exist, to thrive. She has her mother's timeless beauty, her creativity, the yearning to be a mother which you quelled by gifting her that pencil and sketchpad. And now she has that biting wrath of her dear mother that stains a mind for eternity." Baiame kept looking at Old Friend's eyes. "And what new trait will Lucifer show of his mother during his mental affliction? Or more worrisome, what part of you will surface?"

Eyes widened, and for a frightening second Baiame was convinced punishment was coming his way.

"You obviously have it all worked out," Old Friend replied. "Did I do the right thing?"

Baiame hadn't seen that coming. Usually when it came to such things, he either wouldn't say anything, or get a little ornery.

"It seems when we get to this part, neither of us has the answer." Baiame turned back to the whirling sandstorm. "At least not the right one."

A God is Born

Lucifer

The magma-fissured throne with its spiked backrest was three times the height of Lucifer's seated position. He leaned back into the surprisingly cool stone. A surge of energy buzzed through him and with it, feelings that overwhelmed him. Thoughts came at him, too, with no prying. Even the arcane Elders gave up glimpses of their ancient minds, things he didn't have time to sort out before they were replaced by other thoughts flooding him. His abilities were stronger here. Was it the throne's doing?

Lilith's love was never in question. It still warmed him to feel it. Calliope's rattled mind sent anxiety his way, and she wasn't giving up much. He wanted to know what the others really felt, everything he was getting were of trapped minds wanting independence from Calliope's grip. She had not freed them as promised.

"Release them, Calliope."

"Calliope thinks you don't trust her. She has your best interest at heart."

"I don't want slaves. We all have experienced this under Father's rule. If they wish to leave, then they're free with no consequences."

"Rethink this, Husband. They betrayed all of us for that beastly thing." Lilith sat on the left arm of his throne. "They'll do the same to you with their ambitions to rule."

"They followed Cthulhu of their own free will. They followed him because they lost faith in my father. We all harbour a common contempt for him now."

"I won't be so trusting," Lilith said.

"Have it your way, Lucifer," Calliope retorted.

A wave of feelings and brief images slammed into him. His grip tightened on the armrests, then he relaxed it, keeping an outside appearance of being in control. It felt like his head was going to explode. The common thought was winning the allegiance of most angels just for freeing them from Calliope's control.

The twin sisters, Styx and Nyx, had a longing for family and friends back home. The Elder, Nemesis, longed to ride alongside his Death Dealer comrades. Hyperion simply wanted to be under a beautiful blue sky again while looking out to the Serene Sea. They all wanted something of home, hardly any vengeance in their hearts. Cronus, the most bitter of the lot, where was he? Calliope said he had gone into hiding, yet Lucifer could pick up images of him watching them from a distance, from one of those reddish-orange areas of scattered boulders. Cronus and Hades had no doubt made amends. Better to be allies than enemies in an inhospitable place like this. Thinking of Hades led to Lucifer briefly seeing out of his eyes. He was flying after a brood of winged creatures not much bigger than angels.

How far off was Hades? How far did Lucifer's newfound powers reach? And how often and for how long? The further away, the less time it lasted, but the more he saw. He was getting fewer images and more feelings from those closer to him, as if his mind could only manage so much at a time. With fewer minds further out, he could focus solely on them.

He could learn to love this place for a while. The sulfuric air and sudden waves of heat would take some getting used to, but those cool gusts carrying every scent of home, would become a cruel addiction.

He needed to bring more home to this infernal place.

"Nemesis, we need a leader for our own army of Death Dealers. Interested?"

"Most honoured to serve." He bowed to Lucifer.

"Nyx and Styx, will you be the first under his command? And fear not, someday we'll look into the eyes of our friends and families again, under kinder skies. But we need to be prepared for anything, nonetheless."

The twin sisters nodded at Lucifer, amazed at how his words matched their thoughts.

"Hyperion, Oceanus, Chaos, and Cronus, if we can find the latter, will you sit at my Table of Thirteen?" He added the thirteenth seat not to outdo his father's Twelve, but because there had been incidents where a tiebreaker was needed, leading to nothing getting done, leading to billions of lifeforms dying when it could have been prevented.

"Calliope and Lilith will sit at either side of me in the Council. Hades would make an excellent addition to our Thirteen." An image of Hades took over Lucifer's mind, of Hades striking down one of those demonic things. The beast looked terrified, hardly a threat. His vision returned to the throne area. "We just need to find father and son."

"Calliope will assist you in finding Hades, but you won't like what you find."

"You're generous today," Lilith said, squeezing Lucifer's hand.

"And you, my love, will sit next to me as my equal."

"Look there!" shouted the red-bearded Hyperion, motioning to the side of the throne, one of his younglings clinging to him.

Lava bubbled from the ground, shaping into another throne, stone spikes stretching from it stopping at the same height as Lucifer's throne. It kept its glow while cooling down.

Lilith slid from the armrest. "Beautiful. Thank you."

She bent over and turned his face to her, and gave him a deep kiss, then pulled away.

"I think she's happy." They laughed as Lucifer winked up at her.

"You lived in those?" Lucifer motioned down at the stone houses with roofs arched with baby dragon rib bones clustered within a red desert.

Lilith walked through his view towards her throne. He imagined a huge, black tower reaching to the stars, unsure how they would build it, but he would not have his kind live in such primitive conditions. All angels under his command would live in it, with huge living quarters for each, not the humble ones of the Nest. It would take time to build, to find the right stone.

"Another sight to behold." Hyperion pointed to the right of Lucifer's throne, resting one arm on the shoulder of his youngling, smiling down at him. "Look at the godly power of Lucifer, sisters and brothers. Is he not worthy of our allegiance?"

A sudden exhaustion came over Lucifer as rock bubbled out of the ground, piling into a tower of crystal-black stone cut in odd shapes, all fitting perfectly into a haphazard design. Dragons glided over, looking down, diving deeper. Lucifer glared up at them and though he couldn't control them or read their thoughts, they seemed to be able to read his. Turning belly up, they flew around the mounting tower as if defying him.

"It seems they've claimed it as their new home." Lilith chuckled, sitting back, crossing her legs.

"They will have their own."

When his energy returned, he would imagine a home into existence for them, too, eventually winning their allegiance, giving him an aerial advantage over his father's army. Dragon fire damaged a good percentage of angels for weeks, with one of the worst pains ever experienced. A last option, but he would give such a command if anyone stood in his path to Heaven's throne.

Running Out of Time

Baiame

"I have come for advice, not to leave with more questions. It is like you get personal enjoyment tormenting me."

"Now you know how we feel." Baiame gave a big- toothed grin. The sound of the sandstorm shifted from a billion bees buzzing to howling winds. "What's done is done, Old Friend."

They continued through the ruins of the Hallway of Heroes. Over there once stood the library where a pupil of Baiame's had spent much of his time. The thought of his old pupil, Thoth, almost brought him to tears even after all these centuries. How he had ever won the heart of Baiame's daughter, Nut, he would never know.

"Are you okay?" Old Friend asked.

"It is hard to stomach even after all this time."

"A century is but a day to us immortals. We lost many good friends and family that day." Old Friend rested his hand on Baiame's shoulder urging him along. "I will never understand why you torment yourself like this."

They walked on. The scents of a million flowers from the Hanging Gardens that sometimes found their way here, making him long for civilization, but then the ruins reminded him where civilization always ended.

"How long will you keep them there?"

"Until they are seasoned."

"Or until the House of Zeus and their supporters are satisfied?"

"They had no real influence on my decisions."

"Yet Poseidon hasn't been cast to the Inferno."

"What do you think Calliope and Lucifer would do to Poseidon? They would kill him. I could never allow them back then."

"There are other places. And you were not concerned when banishing Hades to an angry father."

He didn't acknowledge that as they walked back towards Baiame's modest stone hut.

"There's one more thing Calliope and Lucifer have in common with their mother."

"And that is?" Old Friend briefly looked at the sandstorm.

"Like you did with her, you have now hidden them from your sight but no matter how hard you try to forget Asherah—"

"Never speak that name again."

His eyes meant it.

"You cannot avoid that day." Baiame stood his ground. "Something will always remind you of her."

"The end is always the same no matter the path traveled."

"Instead of trying to forget the past, how about honouring all three of them by thinking about them every day? Create things inspired by them." Baiame stepped in front of Old Friend and looked up at him. "Stop finding ways to make the same mistakes, El. You are running out of time. You got what, one last run in you to make things right?"

HADES

JAMES PYNE

King Lucifer Tours Hell

Lucifer

Calliope said Hades had built his throne of bones in a nearby province he named Tartarus. Lucifer rather liked that name but why just call a small section of the planet that, when it was a fitting designation for an entire world, one he declared his throne planet? Lucifer had no issues with Hades ruling over one of the landmasses amongst the lava oceans. He simply wanted to visit Hades and see where his head was, and see if he could arrange a meeting with his father Cronus.

Lilith and Lucifer flew side by side. Calliope remained behind to keep an eye on the others. Lilith still seemed unsteady in flight after minutes ago falling helpless as one of her visions came out of nowhere. When they slammed into her like that, they

289

left her with no motor skills. Lucifer had caught her before she splashed into a river of molten lava.

"My visions don't lie," Lilith said.

"Yet here I am in this infernal place instead of the ruler of Heaven."

"There's no expiry date on my visions. That day will come."

"And you've had other visions involving it?"

"One other."

"And?"

"You sit alone in your father's throne next to an empty one that is cracked and seeping blood."

"Where are you in this vision?"

She said nothing.

An image of that cracked throne oozing blood popped into his mind. It was the only image shared by her. Away from his throne, thoughts from others were rarer. Lilith insisted it had more to do about honing his new skills, than anything to do with the throne.

Who knew? One thing he was sure about, visions could sometimes be ambiguous symbolic things, nothing concrete, and though hers were sounder than most, usually dead on with what was shown, he didn't see himself seated next to a cracked throne dripping blood.

"Any more visions of my sister?"

"Just the one. She cannot be trusted."

She shared with him a vision that rang true with him. Calliope's splintered mind would betray him.

When? Lilith wasn't sure, but it was his sister's booted foot coming down at his face, then the vision cut off. At least that was all he got from Lilith.

"You're hiding something from me. I feel it."

"That cracked and bloodied throne, it's my death. What else could it be?"

"No angel dies, that rule rings true in Hell. The consequences of such an act would be far worse than in Heaven. You have nothing to fear."

"You can't control everything, and you can't be everywhere at the same time."

He got an eerie feeling from that. She was hiding something. There was more to her vision., he was sure of it.

"You're holding back."

"Another sits down in my throne. Her upper body is shadowed, but I see enough to know it's not me."

"I would never dump you for another."

"That's how I know I'm dead."

What could he say to that? Again, who would sit in a bleeding throne? It was symbolic of something else.

"Look there, Lucifer. All those crucified."

Calliope called these creatures demon; dark red with spots of black, tattered bat wings, curly goat horns, and rows of uneven jagged teeth. At the sight of Lucifer's landing, then Lilith's, a feeling of mass fear came from the demons.

"Barbaric," Lilith said of their appearance. Some had limbs torn away, were missing an eye, or both. Others had stomachs torn open where crow-like birds nested — and somehow those demons were still breathing.

"Surely, a message being sent to others for some unforgivable act?"

"Left to die slow, agonizing deaths like this? You can read them as well as me. They're helpless beings."

Lilith was right. They were terrified. Even now in their excruciating pain, they were more frightened than hateful at the sight of other angels. Their tongues had been torn out. Even Harvests didn't stretch out death this long and these creatures were not deserving of this fate. The images Lucifer was getting from them were of creatures living day by day in fear of dragons and angels, never the aggressor.

"There!" Lilith pointed up at silhouetted figures against the orange sky descending in their direction.

"It can't be," said Hades who landed into a walk, stopping at Lucifer's side. He took off his horned helmet fashioned from one of demons. "First his daughter, now he banishes his only son. Or have you come to free us? Is Zeus here? Poseidon?"

"Your brothers remain home."

"What could the Almighty's beloved son have done to be exiled here?"

"It doesn't matter."

"Oh, but it does. With you and Lilith here, and Calliope, it's only a matter of time before Zeus and his supporters make a move. We'll be free of this damn place soon enough."

"You place too much confidence in Zeus. Tell me, where's Cronus?"

"Ran him off the planet. He tried avenging himself." Hades motioned at his compatriots. "They came to my rescue. My new family, whom I've adopted into the House of Hades."

"Fair enough. But we must find Cronus and make amends. We all have a common foe now."

"As you wish. But he's untrustworthy."

"I can bring him back to the light. And who are these unfortunate creatures?"

"The slow-witted locals. They're on nearby moons and planets too."

"What have they done to deserve this?"

"I don't want their kind in my district," Hades said. "They won't leave. I would think after all this they'd get the hint and move on, but they speak of a savior coming to rescue them. Why is it every world we've ever cleansed had the savior bug in their ear? Simpletons." He spat at the crucified. "So we amuse ourselves by hunting them."

"You're killing them for sport?" Lilith said.

"You two are welcome to join," Hades said. "Surely you have an appetite for killing, to burn off some of that anger seething in both of you due to the Supreme Asshole."

"We're in agreement there; my father is an asshole."

"I'm glad you're not offended, Lucifer."

"And you're no better than my father with all this needless killing."

"Just to satisfy your superiority complex," Lilith said, glaring at Hades and the others with such legitimate disgust that the feeling coming off her moved Lucifer. "They're of no threat and were here first. You're all nothing but cowards, hunting such weak and defenseless beasts for entertainment's sake. And you wear the head of one of them like a crown. Pathetic."

"Mind your mouth, Lilith." Hades readied to draw his sword.

"She speaks for both of us. You've admitted they've done nothing wrong, haven't shown any evil towards you and I sense no ill intent in them. Cut the living ones down and bury the others. And if I find out the hunt continues, the predators will become the hunted."

Lucifer turned away to fly off with Lilith.

"Who made you ruler?" demanded Hades. "If you think I'll follow you and your crazy wife, think again. We'll do what we want. This is my planet. They'll be hunted until they get the hint to leave. Even then, we'll keep the sport going, make it a tradition."

Lucifer didn't turn. "Don't try my patience."

"Here's what I think of your orders."

The sound of a sword unsheathed compelled Lucifer to quickly turn while withdrawing his, but Hades was not coming at him as he expected. Instead.

he gouged the stomach of the nearest demon with his sword. Its innards plopped out. The horrible wails from the other crucified demons, the fear emanating from these helpless creatures, moved Lucifer deeply.

"No more."

Lucifer cut Hades' sword in half with a powerful swing, then stuck his sword into the sooty ground. Hades' fists lit up into flame. Lucifer willed two bladed feathers from his wings, and each speared one of Hades' hands. Lucifer pounced on him and pummeled him with bare fists, doing to Hades what he wanted to do to his father.

"Neither one of you is any better than the one who banished us here."

That wasn't Lilith's voice. It was one he had heard in passing in Heaven. Lucifer looked up to see Persephone in nothing more than a tunic. After Aphrodite, she was the most beautiful female the House of Zeus had to offer. She was rumoured to still be untouched.

"How is it you're here?" Lilith shouted from behind her. "You were standing behind Zeus before we were banished here."

Lucifer stood up, keeping his eyes on Hades, willing his two bladed feathers back into his wings. He turned to Persephone.

"I called him out for banishing you two, I even slapped him. You'll be happy to know Poseidon has been collared in the courtyard, forever to be in a broken state until Calliope and you return home."

"It seems we should expect more company, a lot more, if my father is casting such innocents into Hell."

He smirked at the brief surge of jealousy coming from Lilith. He would never cheat on her. Just the same, it was nice knowing she cared that much.

"Anyone else want to question my rule?"

The other angels bowed before Lucifer, except Lilith.

Persephone only nodded slightly.

A wave of reverence toward Lucifers came from the demons, a tinge of fear remained when it came to the other angels. He would remedy that.

"I promise, I'll get us back home. Now free them. They're like helpless cherubs, treat them as such, and Hades, you will be crucified here until further notice."

"You're no better than your father," Persephone said, turning away and flying off.

"Want me to deal with her?" Lilith asked.

"No, Lilith, she's here because she stood up for us."

"Something smells rotten."

"Jealousy is a nice colour on you, my dear. Now to try your theory about me not needing the throne anymore."

To his joy, molten lava bubbled from the ground, rising high, solidifying into a crystal-black cross. Flaming vines sprouted and lashed out from the thicker magma-fissures, twining around a beaten Hades, pulling him toward and up the cross, tight against it. His skin burned, then healed, burned again, over and over, keeping him too weak to get loose. Hades' screams of pain disheartened Lucifer who almost took back his decree, but it had to stick, to send a message to everyone else, that such inhumane acts would not be tolerated and would be met with equal punishment.

Because he was not his father.

A Rare Smile

Baiame

"I would like you to come home," Old Friend said, "to keep me in line. I miss the days when I had your counsel daily."

"I am home." They stood with their backs to Baiame's humble abode, facing the sandstorm. "It is you who is not."

"You hang on to another time."

"I appreciate the friendship, but we both know only she could keep you in your place."

"She would never forgive me for what I have done."

"Is that what you fear? A slap in the face?"

"It would be more than that. All of creation would be at stake. However, your words have not fallen on deaf ears. She once spoke of creating a race in our image. Remember the pushback from the others in those days when she suggested such a thing?"

Old Friend smirked at that, and it made Baiame smile. It was the first time Old Friend had ever smiled at the thought of his wife since before that nightmarish day. He would work on him more and soften El's heart to make things right with the only love he had ever known. For now, Baiame would play along.

"Caused quite the stir." Baiame beamed back; it was a pleasing memory of the good times. "A great insult, they cried, to have inferior beings in our image."

"I still have the sketchbook she drew in. She called this new race: *humanity maximus*. Wingless, with magical powers. Not like the ones we tried in the past. But these ones, I know just the blue planet for them. They will have long lifespans to give them time to mature and become enlightened beings, as she hoped for. So, let it be done."

JAMES PYNE

The Sunset Moth

The Golden Years of Humanity

Humanity was born with higher knowledge than any other mortal race in the universe, with some born possessing extraordinary abilities. Like Iris.

Iris, wife to Adan, was the self-proclaimed protector of all insects—and guppies, too—dressed in rainbow colours, and she danced to her favourite music. Synthesizers blared from outside speakers, sometimes playing older electronic compositions, most times creating new sounds. When in an exceptional mood, like Iris was today, her positive energy would give power to those speakers to create new life.

From the speakers, a species of orange and black-spotted butterflies fluttered and bounced into existence, mimicking musical notes as they sprayed

300

from the craggy cliff where the House of Iris and Adan sat.

Below that cliff was the calm ocean where yesterday's creation, rainbow cockatoos, circled and conversed with each other in their bird language on what exactly was their purpose and where would they live and why they had a taste for something called crackers, something that hadn't even been invented yet?

Adan's ability was that he was in the mind of every living thing. It was nothing he could control. It just happened and he really hated this gift. He didn't care what a porcupine was thinking or the philosophies of a long-toothed walrus.

Iris twirled with the new butterflies, her soaked crimson hair splashing out. Adan stopped cutting logs into firewood. He watched her and the butterflies spin in harmonious precision. It got to the point where he couldn't see his wife through the tornado of butterflies. What a remarkable sight, beauty complementing beauty. Parts of her appeared within brief breaks of the whirlwind of butterflies, her face beaming with joy — then she dropped from sight.

"Iris!"

The butterflies scattered to all ends of the planet. Adan rushed to where she had fallen, collapsing to his knees. There was no sign of her. Her mind was cut off from his. The ocean slammed into the base of the cliff. Foamy water splashed over rocks. Minutes later, the waves coughed up rainbow clothes with no sight of her body.

He covered his face and sobbed. The sky cried with him.

Adan wept for six days at the edge of the cliff, and just before sunset, the clouds dispersed, giving way to a huge rainbow on the horizon that lasted into the night sky.

Adan, during the sunset of the seventh day shouted up to the heavens, "Why her? Why rob the world of such splendor, such benevolence? What kind of god are you?"

He remained on his bruised and bloodied knees.

"I miss you, my love, I'm nothing without you."

El was moved by the tragic events and gave life to Iris's clothes within the crashing waves below. The fabric tore apart into a new species of moth that proudly wore the rainbow colours of her clothes, with the bottom part of the moths resembling teardrops, symbolic of Iris's husband's unending sorrow.

"Rejoice, Iris's beauty is now eternal," Adan announced to the young world.

And El whispered into the hearts of humanity the name of this species, the Sunset Moth, as Calliope had named it in her sketchbook of drawings that for whatever reason hadn't been autographed into the light of day until now.

King Brahmeid

The Golden Years of Humanity

As the centuries dragged by, one of the bloodiest wars was taking place after one kingdom assassinated the queen of another monarchy. King Brahmeid had become unhinged over the murder of his beloved wife. His armour was made of the rarest metals of his time, various shades of gold, black, and silver. Blood splashed on his armour, fading into it, disappearing into his soul, blackening it. Into the night the battle raged. Moonlight splayed over the silhouetted piles of corpses outside the walls of the enemies' castle.

There, the Enemy King slew every one of King Brahmeid's warriors challenging him. Brahmeid cut down one, then another. He would get his revenge soon enough and put an end to this war. A tiny soldier King Brahmeid didn't remember seeing amongst his ranks jumped in front of the Enemy King, who waved the miniature soldier away as one of his high ranked took his place.

"Unworthy of my sword." The Enemy King smirked. "But your head, King Brahmeid, will look nice mounted in my dining chamber." He waved for Brahmeid to hurry up.

The Enemy King's warrior made quick work of the tiny soldier, sending them flying onto their back, and their helmet rolled away from their youthful face. It was a girl barely into womanhood, a shine to her face like Brahmeid's beloved Estonia had. He didn't know whose child she was, but she screamed revenge at the Enemy King for the death of her parents. Such bravery despite the face of death looking down at her.

Brahmeid neared the Enemy King. Their swords almost collided until Brahmeid veered his course and stopped the warrior's sword with his from decapitating the girl. He slayed the warrior with one slice down his frontside, and blood poured out of the long slit in his leather armour.

"Behind you!" the girl shouted, reaching for her sword.

A sharp pain surfaced in Brahmeid's back, coldness slid through his insides, and the point of a blade pushed out of his chest armour. One more thrust into him, then the blade wriggled about inside him before slowly exiting. His sword dropped from his weakening grip, as a sudden coldness rushed through him. So this was creeping death then. The girl now stood with sword at ready.

"Face me, coward!" she shouted at the Enemy King.

"Such bravery for a small thing. I shall place your skull with the others who have fallen at my sword. You should feel honoured by that. But first I have a head to collect."

The girl charged at the Enemy King with an admirable war cry.

Brahmeid, on one knee now, pushed her down. He staggered back up, unsheathing his long knife, and turned quickly to see the Enemy King's sword raised high to behead him. He jabbed the Enemy King's throat, crumpling on top of him as he watched the battlefield slowly dim.

El, seeing this great sacrifice, tore and flung a piece of paper from Calliope's sketchbook to the wind. From it, two tiny shadings flew out with long, forked tails, a puff of smoke leaving one of them as colour filled them both, black and green scales. They would be called the Brahmeid dragon. Their home, along with that of any other magical creatures created during the era of humanity, would be known as the Forbidden Zone, which someday would become known as the Arctic Ocean.

The Burnt Man

The Golden Years of Humanity

In a faraway land, on an island that someday would become Atlantis, there lived a certain Princess Cordelia. Today she was dressed in the jazziest rainbow-spotted/bell-bottomed pants that the world had ever seen. Of course the world was still incredibly young, but that's beside the point. Today she would choose a mate amongst the men as was the custom of her kingdom. Some were transparent, others bright as the sun, some small, some tall, some muscular, some not so defined. Princess Cordelia's royal march of chihuahuas circled her, with every one of them leashed to her belt buckle. They were very loud barkers, especially if someone dared to step within ten feet of their princess. They would also bark at someone with food, and if one were wise, they would give up their meal and starve for a day or risk becoming a fire hydrant twenty times over.

Following exactly eleven feet behind the princess was her main servant, holding the train of her dress, his bare ankles dog-bitten.

"Not you," Princess Cordelia said of the freckled man. "No," to the one with long, spiked hair, though she thought he had a cute butt and rad tattoos.

She passed over every man, until coming to an abomination.

"Who is this? Why is he here? Is this a joke?" She angrily asked her advisor of the man with one eye, the other patched, parts of his body long ago burnt although, obviously, he had survived the ordeal. As a child, she had almost died in the palace fire of a forgotten year, so she felt instant pity for this scorched man.

Her advisor answered back, "We found him in the dark alleyways of your kingdom and give you the honour of making an example of such ugliness. Surely he is of despicable character deserving of your harshest punishment?"

"By the looks of him, he's already suffered greatly."

She motioned for her chihuahuas to collapse behind her and they did. As she approached Burnt Man, each of her pets took turns growling.

"Who are you?" she asked Burnt Man.

"No one important, my princess."

"Your princess wishes to know."

"I have no name."

"Everyone has a name," Princess Cordelia said.

"It burned up in smoke that day, that horrible day. Nobody recognizes me. Everybody's forgotten me. Not even you remember me, Cordy."

The princess stomped her feet. Only one male had ever dared call her Cordy and he was dead.

"WHO ARE YOU?" The princess stared into Burnt Man's lone eye, the prettiest blue eye in all the land she so decreed that day. "Answer me. Your name, the one that is forgotten, tell me."

Burnt Man looked away. "It was I who carried you out of the fire that night. I was the first that was out, for I was always the fastest, and when I heard you were still missing, I soaked a blanket in water and hurried back inside. When I found you, I wrapped you in the blanket. I caught fire while carrying you out. You had passed out from smoke inhalation. I managed to get you into the secret tunnel that took us to the river out back, which I fell into in hopes of stopping the burning pain, and was carried away in the rapids. When I returned to the kingdom no one recognized me, no one believed I was who I said I was."

The princess stepped back.

"Edmund? It cannot be! He died in the fire. You're an imposter, that's what you are."

Burnt Man's gnarled hands opened to reveal a gold necklace with a blue butterfly pendant that upon the sunlight's touch would undulate like the ocean was swishing back and forth inside it.

The princess had thought it lost in the fire, along with Prince Edmund of the Second Kingdom. That day, when Edmund died, she turned dark inside, for they were the best of friends and had sworn to marry each other.

"Edmund, it is you."

She hugged him, much to the awe of the onlooking citizens of the kingdom, who were sure this was a ploy and that any second, the princess would make an example of this horrid excuse for a man.

Instead, she decreed, "A promise is a promise, one I'm most happy to keep."

"No, you're right, I died that day," Edmund said, and turned away.

The princess turned his face back to hers, holding his chin up. "And today I have been reborn. I've always loved you, it's why I could never choose a husband . . . until now."

El was moved by the princess's unconditional love and by the new prince's relief, and as a reminder of his great sacrifice, flipped through Calliope's sketchbook and ripped from it a drawing of two horse-like animals named unicorns and tossed the paper to the wind.

THE KINGDOM OF TOWERS

JAMES PYNE

The Kingdom of Towers

The Golden Years of Humanity

The Kingdom of Towers was just that, a city of small and tall stone towers. Inside each of these towers could be found everything needed to live: vegetables grew on the turret, located in the basement chamber were animal stables that stank to high heaven, a noisy bazaar was situated on the main floor, and other things of entertainment filled the remaining levels.

Princess Isadora ruled here. Her father had just passed on, leaving her the kingdom. Preparations were under way for the most epic of royal weddings. That is, before Isadora discovered her fiancé in bed with a male dwarf, his personal servant to be exact, as they were literally rolling in several types of powdery drugs. The infidelity was bad enough, but another male, and an ugly one at that? It was too much to bear.

Now Princess Isadora, with her beauty, who could bring two opposing armies to their knees was as sweet as they came. But anger her, look out, that red hair of hers literally flamed up. She had dominion over the ocean bordering one side of her kingdom. That wasn't such a good thing for Prince Eldrick and his dwarf lover who were presently boarding a ship destined to take them to the Kingdom of Oddities.

Isadora leaned out her chamber window, her hair in flames, her face an angry red, eyes pure black, not a sight of white in them. She glared down at the ship with its tall masts and huge sails, at all the people scrambling about on the deck. Her heart cracked. Hate surged in her and she willed the ocean to rise into waves at all four sides of the ship. Like four great hands the waves came down hard, crushing the masts and sails, obliterating everything wood and human.

She screamed in torment, realizing what she had done, killing well over two hundred passengers for the sake of revenge, and that guilt, coupled with her broken heart, darkened her soul. She shouted down to the kingdom for all the servants and citizens to abandon the towers and flee, that none of it, including herself, deserved to exist.

The residents of the kingdom obeyed, running to the high hills with whatever belongings they had time to grab. They heard stories of her attending war campaigns alongside her now deceased father, single-handedly crushing opposing naval fleets with her power over the ocean.

She called upon the waves to crash into the Kingdom of Towers. Some edifices quickly fell over, but hers was ancient and solid, made to withstand tsunamis, as if her father had suspected that someday her ability would test the kingdom's resolve. The day grew dark, and tidal wave after tidal wave chipped away at the circular stone walls. It was only a matter of time before the last remaining tower crumbled with her inside it.

"Fall, damn you!" she shouted. "Harder!"

The waves roared and smashed into the walls. Water splashed up into her chamber window and sprayed her, the droplets turning into steam once they touched her flaming hair.

"Your royal highness," someone said from behind her.

She turned; the waves continued blasting the wall hard. Before her stood the son of the kingdom's head metal worker. His fate was now tied with hers.

"Pray to whatever you worship," she said, turning back to the rising ocean of emerald green.

"I'm here to save you."

"Save me?" She looked back. "Who are you to save me? And who said I needed saving?"

"We need you."

"I trusted him. Trusted him with my heart. I see no point in any of this existing. It will only remind me of him."

"Were you in love?"

"What kind of question is that?"

"Well, were you truly?"

She was amazed by his arrogance, by his relentlessness. "Yes. Why else would I be like this?"

"I believe you."

"And what makes you so special that I should feel honoured that you believe me?"

The metal worker's son bowed his head, not from respect for her royal blood, but as if hurt by her words, and with all of the hate in her churning, his sadness bothered her.

"I love someone," he said. "But she doesn't love me, or cannot, due to who I am."

"And who is she?"

"I can't give her the world. I can only give her my heart. My spirit. My devotion. My faithfulness. But because of my social statue, she doesn't see me."

"You test my patience. Tell me, who is this woman?"

"I would stay by her side, even die by her side, for living without her, unable to see her ever again, would be worse than death. Even if I can never touch her lips with mine."

"Then why are you here with me. Go be by her side."

"I am."

The tidal waves ceased smashing, leaving the last tower standing.

The Silver Age of Humanity

Baiame

There weren't many moments during humanity's early existence that gave Old Friend much hope. It confounded him. Why was there so much sorrow in the New World when he gave them all special abilities or heavenly knowledge? Gave them everything they needed. Yet they killed each other over land, over lovers, over the colour of their skin. The strongest of them grew god complexes and instead of helping their weaker but smarter compatriots, they subjugated them.

"How do you live in such a confined space?" Baiame had agreed to meet El on top of Mount Titan where he was sitting at the Table of Twelve, the rusty-looking Great Tablet shadowing them. He hadn't been here in centuries, and even the last time he hadn't stuck around long. It was just them up here, so he agreed to visit, making it clear that else, especially that jerk, Zeus, should come. "Everyone's in such close quarters to each other. No privacy. And all that flatulence going off. Is Odin still having issues controlling his gift of stench while sleeping?"

"On occasion."

"One of these nights all that farting, and his fire, is going to make you all go *BOOM*."

"That crude imagination of yours is quite refreshing. But no one's complained."

"There's the illusion of it. They have freedom to go anywhere, but they aren't free. Bound by a code of honour, chained to the holy commandments."

"And what does this have to do with the humans? What do you suggest I do with them?"

"You're giving them too much freedom."

"You just finished saying I am playing too much the warden. Having fun with me, are you?"

"Letting some have greater powers than others make for too much temptation. It was all too quick. They had no instruction manual."

"Their mortality should have quieted their dictatorial ambitions."

"To be ruler of all things is a hard drug to kick, yes?"

The Almighty El had nothing to say to that.

Two sky wraiths smashed into each other, exploding into black smoke and balls of flame above them.

"The mutant gene for this new batch has been shut off from their DNA. The question is, will they be too vulnerable?"

"Is it ever enough?" Baiame kept his back to Old Friend. "You sit in your chair that is the same as everyone else's to give the illusion that all at this table are equal, but we all know that is not the case. Seriously, what are we all striving for? To be as powerful as you? To be your replacement? The other day I asked Young Thor why he wants to smash things into pieces? His reply was interesting."

"What did the little firecracker say?" Old Friend sounded amused.

"He said that things need to be smashed so there can be new life. Even Young Thor likes playing god."

"Well, then, it's good he has you guiding him."

"But who is guiding the humans? I'm not talking about anything too parental. Really, how can you be so strict when even you are looking for answers? Rules are made to be smashed by the Young Thors out there. It is a rite of passage for all living things. You have to bend or break the rules sometimes to survive, to evolve, to truly live."

"They will need something that reminds them of their mortality. I know just the two for that job."

A Looming Presence

Muerte and Gabriel

Gabriel smirked down at Poseidon, whose chain slithered into his living quarters, allowing him privacy half of the day. The other half, the chain shortened and dragged him back out into the courtyard, naked and screaming for clemency. Gabriel never got sick of hearing him beg.

Gabriel and Muerte stopped at the bottom steps of Big Guy's throne, black cloaks over their onyx armour, the tips of their wings touching each other.

"You called for us, my Lord?" Gabriel said.

They had been training new adults chosen as Death Dealers.

"A new assignment." Even in his present appearance the Big Guy was still imposing. "Humans."

"What's so special about them?" Muerte asked, giving Gabriel a look of bafflement on why they were there.

"Must you Muerte?"

"I'm sorry my Lord. It's just that we're warriors. This assignment is more suited to Cupid and his brother, Eros."

"Are you kidding me? There would be hybrids up to my neck. No, Muerte, I need a looming presence of death to keep them in line. That does not mean kill them. Set them on the straight with my rules, then be a presence."

"You could send Thanatos for that," Gabriel said. "A giant lug like him will keep them straight and narrow."

"No, no, I want a familiar face. They look like us, you see. They have our ambitions. They are much more curious, comes with being mortal, I suppose. Like I said, be a presence after first contact. Nothing more. Until further notice."

"Are you serious?" Muerte almost turned her back to him, then thought better of it. "We're doing better here than we will there. Being demoted from warriors to teachers is one thing, now we're downgraded to nothing more than harbingers of death? Are you still mad about us calling you out on banishing your own children and not letting you forget it?"

"Shh. We'll be sent to Hell if you keep it up," Gabriel reminded her.

"Your absolute devotion cripples your honest opinions most days, Husband."

They had married on the spot of their first kiss, during the evening, when Rainbow Ridge was at its peak of breathtaking beauty.

"Nothing you say will change my decision so why keep provoking me?"

"Your Lord, she speaks from the heart."

Poseidon's shackles rattled behind them as he listened to the conversation with mouth hanging open in amusement. What a pitiful sight he had become.

"There are no wars Muerte to send you to."

They bowed and Muerte turned her back before the Almighty finished nodding at them. She was still relatively young for an angel. It would be a couple more centuries before she simmered down. Gabriel did agree, this was beneath them. He would miss training the recruits.

A portal spiralled opened.

"Guess we get to spend some quality time together," Gabriel said, winking.

"There's no need for threats," Muerte retorted with a smile.

The Living Word

Michael

Archangel Michael's upbringing had hardly been an environment inspiring a military career. His father was a painter of respectable art and his mother was a teacher. It wasn't the killing part he enjoyed. He had never understood the point in slaying mortals, only to have them recycled back into the universe to be slain all over again but that wasn't for him to question. What he did enjoy was being the living word of the Almighty's commandments. It was a great honour bestowed upon him and now here he was leader of the Seraphim. Michael would have preferred not having it handed to him, but he did deserve it over Athena. He would be forever grateful to her. It wouldn't have been easy to turn down such a promotion.

Michael would watch over Athena on behalf of Lucifer. The other angels believed he hated Lucifer when in fact he looked at him like an older brother.

As a youngling, he had watched Lucifer become a living legend. The early duels between Zeus and him for leadership of the Seraphim were the stuff of legend. It was Lucifer who gifted him his first sword, which had happened to be Lucifer's first. All he had asked was that when Michael outgrew it, he would pass it down to another youngling full of learning and fight. He had never come across such a youngling until recently. Young Thor was now the keeper of Suncracker, named so due to the legend that if swung fast enough, the sword could split sunrays in half.

Michael had been eavesdropping from above. He and the Seraphim were on the lookout for dragons. They were in season, always looking for a new nesting ground. He waited for Muerte and Gabriel to portal from sight before landing in the courtyard. His wings lowered a little as he knelt before the throne steps.

"Stand up, Michael. Always faithful to the old ways even when I free you of them."

Michael stood up; head slightly bowed. "I couldn't help but overhear — well, to be blunt. Why send them?"

"They will do fine. We all need new challenges to grow."

"Gabriel is faithful to your decrees. But Muerte is young and impulsive."

"Like Aphrodite?"

"Please, my Lord. I'd rather forget those years."

Aphrodite had once been his protégé. The hope was that Michael's stoic and dutiful nature would quell the mischievous daughter of Zeus. How wrong everyone had been about that.

"I see only trouble with Muerte," Michael continued. "It has been noted by the Twelve that she has not been the same since her encounter with Cthulhu."

"She's not right in the head is what you want to say, yes?"

"That's an understatement."

The Almighty fell into a jolly laughter. "Don't ever change, Michael. Don't ever change."

Mount Morg

Muerte

Fifty plus years had passed since Muerte and Gabriel's assignment to this forsaken planet. Muerte never thought a year could drag on so much until cast to this mundane existence. The humans were the greatest insult to the eyes, a mirror image of angels. Muerte was surprised Big Dummy hadn't blessed them with wings.

They had done what Big Dummy asked: installed his commandments, then shadowed the lands with their eerie presence. The issue was—and it was a big one— that scent of mortal carnage awakened a bloodlust in angels, and when humans got a simple cut, or nosebleed, Muerte's nostrils flared up. She tried resisting at first but temptation came on strong.

Muerte made her own fun up there on Mount Morg where she had a bird's-eye view of all the villages of the land. It was the perfect playground to sate her darkest urges with its network of caves and dead ends. She started with twisted art on the cave and tunnel walls, painting the death of villagers in the cruelest manner. She only picked the grossly lame, or someone dying—she supposed it was her way of justifying breaking Big Dummy's orders. Within months, murals of the dead covered the torchlit walls, ceilings, and floors of every passageway and cavern. With no room left for her prophetic art, she decided on a more personal kind of amusement.

Gabriel never visited her haven. Their relationship had become stale by the repetitiveness of their duties to this damn planet. He was more than happy to be the boogeyman of the mortals' bedtime stories and myths. So when he showed up in the middle of her fun she was caught by surprise.

"Muerte?" Gabriel hollered, his footsteps drawing closer.

She was in her blood chamber, where she impaled humans on stalagmites and stalactites, their mouths laced shut by strands of her living hair. She couldn't stand it when they begged for clemency. Wasn't it obvious to them by the gory surroundings that pity didn't exist here?

Gabriel continued, "What's with all these paintings? I recognize these mortals. Their deaths were your doing? I should've known such fatalities could only come from your demented mind."

Muerte said nothing, sitting cross legged, head tilted up as blood dripped into her mouth from a woman's body slowly sliding down a stalactite. This addiction was therapeutic, putting her in a state of bliss, helping the days fly by.

"I was just talking to Michael." Gabriel neared her location.

She couldn't stand Michael. Always Big Dummy's lapdog. Always a pain in the butt of anything fun. When he walked into any joyful celebration, he soured it with his fussiness. Gabriel reminding her of Michael sickened her.

Gabriel's voice neared. "He says the Lake is missing a considerable number of souls. They've just vanished without a trace. Just gone like that. And all from this planet. Strange, isn't it?"

"More like they're in limbo," she said, catching another droplet of blood as Gabriel entered the chamber.

A long silence followed as he looked around. It wasn't the reaction she had hoped for. Muerte had never invited him up here, but she had never told him to stay away. She supposed he kept his distance knowing how tired she was with this assignment. Or was he bored with her?

"What have the humans done to deserve this?"

"You don't look right without armour."

In nothing more than a black cloak, he might appear ominous to the humans but meh to Muerte.

"And you in your armour. It looks like you've declared war on the humans."

"They're here because they crossed my path, that's the truth."

She caught another droplet of rich, red blood on her tongue as she stood up to face her husband.

"You're five miles up with no walking ledge," he said. "You've flown them up here, haven't you?"

"So, what if I did?" She goaded him with a smirk.

"You find this funny?" he shouted, getting in her face.

She hadn't seen passion in those eyes in a long time.

"It helps me get by." She put her hand on his chest and felt the beating of his heart speed up. Good to know she still excited him. "I understand now why you dragged out their deaths during the glory days. The scent of their blood invigorates me. The taste of it is divine, the gold standard of mortal blood. Have a taste."

"This is not what our Lord wanted."

"Relax, I'll return one of them to their village, so they speak of their time here. It will keep the humans in fear, like our king wants."

"Your logic is twisted. This isn't what he wanted."

"I've never felt so alive."

She spun with arms thrown out while looking up at the jagged ceiling, the horrified eyes of her victims spinning with her.

"We've lived so long we've forgotten what it's like to live. Being stuck on this damn planet has made us numb. Come now, Husband, inhale deeply. That's life you're smelling slowly leaving them. Intoxicating isn't it? Oh yes, I see in your eyes, that Harvester's gleam. Why resist?" She stood before him, clasping his hips with both hands. "The Death Dealers were once his plague, his pestilence, his war, his death bringers to many battlefields and entire planets. How can you not long for those days again? Join me and we'll—"

"He'll not tolerate this. End these atrocities. Give them their last kiss and make it quick."

"You've become spineless, Gabriel. There was a time you enjoyed ending the lives of mortals. I saw it firsthand, got a taste of what you were like back in the days of lore when the mortals were stronger and tougher. Those days when Lucifer was regent and sent us to cleanse all evil from every planet. You enjoyed it, even spoke of the olden days to me. Why so sentimental now? Because they look like us? Is that the problem?"

"We don't have the right to kill them unless commanded."

"What a bore you've become." She let out a forced yawn.

"Release them too." Gabriel motioned at the candlelit room across the hall. "All of them."

Strapped to a slab of stone a nude woman lay on her stomach with cross cuts all over her body. Shackled to the wall, a man with knitted lips, eyes wide from agony while he tried to shake loose. Along the shelves throughout the cave sat the beating hearts of mortals, their bodies long gone.

"I just moved those two in there, letting their fears ripen them before I peel away their skin." She crossed the hallway and strolled into the room of thumping hearts, the faint spirits attached to them moving about in a frenzy, trapped here until the last heartbeat. Gabriel followed. "By the time I'm done with them, he'll beg only for his life, not hers. Or vice versa."

"Release every soul now," Gabriel said, with such authority any other angel would have obeyed, but not this firecracker.

Muerte turned away from Gabriel and started carving up the woman's back with her fingernails. The woman screamed while her spouse's head thrashed about—whatever pain she inflicted on his wife, he felt.

"There's no point to this sadistic display."

"It amuses me."

"After this, no more humans, understand?"

"If one of them renounces their love for the other, their hearts end up there with the rest," Muerte said. "If their love prevails—well, I'm undecided about that, nobody has gotten that far. I might return them to their village, so they spread the legend of us Death Dealers."

She looked back at Gabriel, blood dripping from her fingernails. It was in his eyes, he hoped she would grow out of this addiction.

"Aren't you offended, Gabriel, by the humans looking so much like us? Nowhere else in the universe do mortals resemble us. Big Dummy's spitting in our faces. Mark my words, Husband, these are our replacements."

Missing Souls

Michael

How could the Almighty be surprised by Muerte's treachery? Yet he was. He had put too much faith in Gabriel to be able to tame the wild side of her. During her youngling years she was always in trouble for torturing animals and insects and when her abilities showed up before everyone else's, things got really bad. Selected students became subjected to her energy-draining and mind-messing abilities. Michael had been one of her victims. Younglings just didn't have the mental strength to resist such invasions and she plagued the student body relentlessly with what she called harmless fun.

Even with all of Muerte's flaws, Michael crushed on her back in those days. That was, until she stripped him of his dignity so that it took him years to mentally recover.

Michael was portalled to the foot of Mount Morg. He and Gabriel met annually to update each other.

"It's obvious Muerte named this mountain," Michael said, walking with Gabriel along a valley of orange rock. "When's the last time you've been up there?"

"Before she moved in. We found lots of caves and tunnels, a good place for privacy. Not sure what she does up there, but that's her business. If she doesn't want to participate, then so be it. I'm sure she'll come around."

"I don't think so, Gabriel."

"What do you mean?"

"Our Lord has noticed quite a few souls missing."

"Souls don't go missing."

"They do if they're being held in stasis by a Death Dealer."

"She wouldn't. For what purpose?"

"I leave it up to you, Gabriel. She's your business, not mine. Whatever she's up to, make it known to Muerte that it stops today. Otherwise, there will be severe consequences."

He knew what Gabriel would find, something that would challenge his love for Muerte. Or he would tolerate her sickness and that was fine by Michael, he would gladly throw them both into the Inferno.

Home Again

Gabriel

"I told you to stop months ago," Gabriel said, standing in the room of thumping hearts. The spirits passed through him, twirling around him, silently begging for him to free them. "Our Lord has made it clear. Make it right or —"

He couldn't finish the threat. He had shown up in his battle armour, more to add to the urgency of his message, than expecting confrontation but she wasn't backing down, dammit.

"Last chance," he said.

Why was she pushing it, forcing him to do something he didn't want to do? A portal was ready outside. He was to drag her out if need be and toss her into Hell. This was his wife. How could the

Almighty place such a burden on him? Just to show his allegiance? Or for some sick perversion?

"Isn't it beautiful?" She pointed at a panoramic painting of Gabriel and her that she had scratched into a woman's back via her fingernails. It was a picture of them dancing hand-to-hand amidst the corpses of an entire planet. The living canvas was splayed belly-down on the altar while her husband was shackled to the wall. Neither of the mortal lovers bellowed in pain, as if they had become immune to it, or refused to give Muerte the satisfaction.

"Renounce your love for each other and I'll end it quickly."

They ignored her as they stared into each other's glistening eyes, the kind love swam in. The kind of love Gabriel saw in Muerte's eyes when she looked up at him. But did she see it in his eyes?

"Frustrating. She looked back to her flesh canvas. "No two lovers have ever gotten this far."

She started etching birds just under the woman's shoulder blades.

"You're struggling," she said to Gabriel without looking back. "Your soul's conflicted. Your heart pounds for me as strongly as ever. Shed yourself of your sense of duty, then the things that truly matter will become clearer."

He didn't want to do this, but she was leaving him no choice.

"Muerte, please stop."

337

She yanked at the woman's hair. "I'll make you abandon your love for him. You won't have what I have lost."

That gutted Gabriel. He still loved her. He wanted to tell her that, but he had to separate personal feelings from duty.

One finger out, the rest bundled in a fist, she prepared to jab the woman's eyes. Even now the mortals refused to denounce their love, fighting through the pain, past their fear. It was moving to see such defiance.

"Muerte, stop this madness."

"And what will you do? Spank me over your knee?"

She drove her fingernail into the woman's eye and the woman howled in pain.

"I'll end it then."

Gabriel swiped the air with the scythe, touching nothing but changing everything.

Muerte collapsed to her knees and held onto the altar, keeping herself from falling backwards, gasping for air. Every mortal had gone silent in the caves of Mount Morg, not one whimpered, not one begged for death, every heartbeat silenced except Muerte's and his. He had released every tormented soul in one swipe, weakening Muerte in the process.

"I'm your wife. Traitor!"

One swipe wouldn't kill her, nor a second, nor third, but a fourth? He had never gone that far with an immortal.

"I'll acquire more." She pulled herself up, hunching over the dead woman. "Her peaceful face, the fun I would've had with her." Muerte looked over her shoulder. "I'll take ten times the humans next time."

"You'll never get better," he said. "I see that now."

Muerte turned to him as he raised the scythe high, ready for a clean sweep.

Gabriel bowed his head.

"Look at me," she shouted.

"Muerte." He paused. "I'll always love you."

"You won't do it. I'm your—"

He swiped the scythe one more time. She leaned back, the blade just missing her throat. It was his last warning. She fell on all fours, slowly looking up.

"You abandon me for that Old Fool?"

Gabriel raised his scythe but he hesitated, the most painful pause. He couldn't do it. He wouldn't. There was only one other way, even if it meant banishment.

"I love you, Gabriel," said Muerte. "It was supposed to be us versus the universe, even Big Dummy, if it came down to it. You said that. Not me."

Her anger sucked the moisture from everything, including Gabriel, who dropped the scythe as he fell to his knees. How had become so potent? She bent over and snatched up his scythe and held it close to her armoured body.

"You betrayed me, Gabriel."

"I couldn't go through with it." He was barely able to stay on his knees, head rolling back and forth as he tried to look up at her. "There's a portal outside waiting for you. If you have a backway out, use it. Michael is waiting with the Seraphim in case I fail."

It took everything he had to look up at her.

Tears streamed down her cheeks as she clenched the scythe, raising it like she was considering beheading him.

"I've failed you in so many ways, Muerte."

She searched his eyes, lowering the scythe.

"There you are," she said, pressing her forehead against his, then kissing him. She stared into his eyes and smiled. "Finally home again."

She dropped the scythe at Gabriel's knees.

"I won't sneak out of here. I'll face Michael myself."

"Muerte, no. There are too many of them."

"I'll drag Michael into Hell." She left the cavern and marched into the corridor. "A gift to Lucifer."

MUERTE EMERGES FROM MOUNT MORG

True Love

Muerte

She strutted down the tunnel lined with the murals of the dead. She would make quick work of Michael and his backup. Across from the entrance was a flaming portal. Wind blew her hair to one side as she stopped at the ledge of the tunnel.

"Michael, how nice of you to visit," she said, giving him a finger wiggle wave. "Care for a tour?"

"Where's Gabriel?" He hovered there, wings flapping. Six Seraphim hovered near him. "I said, where's Gabriel?"

"Taking a nap."

"He couldn't go through with it, as I expected."

"It's called love, something you should try sometime."

343

"Make it easy and willingly enter the portal and your cooperation will be noted for a lighter sentence. Or else."

"You're no Lucifer." She withdrew her sword.

"Your answer then?"

"Do you really need me to answer that? Big Dummy's rubbing off on you."

Michael unsheathed his sword. The Seraphim followed suit.

"I'll deal with her." Michael flew at her, sword out. She sprung from the ledge, dark wings spreading out as she blocked his swing. He blocked hers. That was fine, she only wanted him closer. She pierced his impregnable armour and helmet with her mind, messing with his thoughts, confusing him, while draining him of energy, turning him into a living corpse.

Michael dropped his sword from feebleness, his wings failing him.

"Some things don't change. Just like old days, Mikey."

She gave him another little finger wiggle wave as he tumbled into the clouds, toward the patches of orange and green below.

Two Seraphim came at her and she drained them. Hundreds of portals opened with Seraphim exiting, swords already drawn. They came at her in groups of six with her willing them into living corpses until she was out of energy. They pulled her toward the flaming portal, her wings propelling her in the opposite direction. With what little strength she had left, she drained three more Seraphim.

"To Hell with you!" she shouted up at the portals knowing Big Dummy was listening. "It will not be the last you see of me."

"Release her," a booming voice called. "Or I will make you."

Muerte looked through the moving mass of Seraphim to see Gabriel standing at the entrance in Mount Morg, leaning over his scythe.

"I said let her go."

They swooped down at him. With one swipe of his scythe they weakened and dropped from view. They kept coming at him and he held them off, long enough for her to regain enough energy to weaken the ones restraining her. They dropped from sight.

Gabriel collapsed to his knees from exhaustion. Flying them out of here wouldn't get them far; carrying Gabriel would slow their retreat.

"Go. Before more come."

"I won't leave you behind." She turned from Gabriel and stood to defend him. "Besides, why should you have all the fun?"

"Stubborn."

"True love does that."

There was a flash of light as the Almighty portalled into view, his vast wings darkening the ledge.

Muerte stood her ground. Gabriel staggered to his feet. The tips of their wings touched as side by side they fought their king.

Wounded Ego

Michael

The embarrassment of it. As a youngling he had suffered the same fate at her hands. She shuffled his thoughts, throwing a thousand memories at him. It was impossible to concentrate. She giggled and ran rabid in his mind, draining him to the point of nonexistence. He felt her struggle with the temptation to kill him, to see what it was like to be the first immortal to kill another immortal in the modern era.

Some things don't change. Just like old days, Mikey.

Those words haunted him. Over and over, they played in his head, as if she had burned them there for all eternity, her backdoor into his mind. She had always called him Mikey during their younger years. He hated the sound of it. Hated the fact that she got the better of him — again — even with him ready. How would he live this down?

347

He spiralled and tumbled until he slammed into a forest, causing a cloudburst of insignificant elevation or might, fueling his wounded ego.

Crucified

Gabriel

They were somewhere on the throne planet Elysium, a desolate place of mountains and sand dunes bordering a lush forest at the horizon, as if the desert were slowly overtaking the planet. By the looks of the area, it had been devastated by an explosion long ago.

Crucified on towering crosses, both of them still in their armour, Gabriel and Muerte tried to pull their wrists free from the spikes. Did the wood of their crosses have debilitating capabilities? Had the Almighty permanently taken their abilities from them?

Below, boulders within the sand rolled together, climbing over each other, rising just above the crucified couple. The head of the newly formed tower became a throne as the Almighty lowered into it. The tower of stone swayed back and forth, the rocks grinding and grating against each other.

"I don't understand why everybody has issues with me," the Almighty said, his armour sinking away into a blanket-sized robe.

"We're sick of stupid rules," Muerte shouted, her wintered hair crossed over her face from a steady wind. "And why aren't we in the court to receive our sentencing? Are you going to end our existence and not tell anyone, covering your tracks by telling everyone you cast us into Hell?"

"Your mouth is precisely the reason."

"Afraid others will be spurned to act against you?"

"If you had laid your weapons down at the sight of me, if you hadn't tried weakening me, we wouldn't be here."

"We never killed any of our kind," Gabriel said, "but you came at us with sword drawn and she reacted from blind rage."

"No, Gabriel," objected Muerte. "I was of sound mind when I tried cutting his head off."

"Will you shut up! What is wrong with you?"

"You admit it then." The Almighty's eyes widened. "I have always been patient with you, Muerte. I had high hopes for you. For you both. What must I do to win your hearts? All of you are turning on me."

"Are you asking a question?" Muerte smirked. "Will you have another temper tantrum if you don't like the answer?"

"Enough! You murdered countless mortals for no logical reason but to sate your boredom and to spit in my face."

"You spat in our faces by making the humans look like us. Admit it, they are our replacements."

"For eons you've had us genocide mortals," Gabriel said, and the Almighty glared his way. "What's so special about these ones? What's the point of their existence? They barely live six hundred years, hardly enough time to learn much of anything."

"To live," the Almighty said.

"What kind of life is there in an infant dying within seconds of its birth?" Muerte asked.

"There's beauty in such a death," the Almighty said.

"As long as their deaths are by your design, right?" Muerte shook her head. "Hypocrite, that's what you are."

"Something that takes mortals centuries to learn"—the Almighty looked Muerte's way—"some immortals never learn."

"And what's that?" Gabriel asked.

"How brief and important life truly is."

Heavier winds blustered in, blowing the ends of Muerte's hair towards him. The scent of apple blossom invigorated him.

"Tell me our Lord," Gabriel said. "What does a person learn from their death when accidentally jabbing their throat with their bow while fiddling the happiest, most beautiful of tunes?"

"That—"

"How humorous a death can be," Muerte said, interrupting the Almighty. "I imagine it went down like this. Big Dummy here was thinking about his traitorous son, Lucifer, and how he loved playing the fiddle during a full moon, and was so perturbed at the thought of his son that he decreed that any mortal in the universe playing a fiddle that very minute would die a ridiculous death for his sick amusement."

To have such sass in the face of severe punishment? Gabriel could hardly believe his ears.

The Almighty sprung from his throne and got in her face. "Be careful where you take this."

"We're not afraid of you," she said, trying to bite at his long nose.

"Impudent fool."

He flew back into the rocky tower, howling in anger. The tower collapsed into rubble sending up a mushroom cloud. The Almighty hovered in front of them.

"Hell is too good for you," he shouted at Muerte. The pile of rubble opened into a grave. "There you shall lay buried alive until I see fit to release you."

The Almighty tore the top of the cross off and powered her into the ground. Rock fell on top of her as she reached up to Gabriel, screaming for help.

"I'll tear you apart for that." Gabriel tried to wriggle loose, his wings flapping, in his attempt to raise his feet and hands from the spikes.

"And you shall remain here with her at your feet. The both of you will experience the feeling of every death conceivable. I might even try a few ideas out on you."

The Almighty flew off as Gabriel raged. He became so angry, so hateful, and full of such sorrow, that his ability to drain life from others turned on him, sucking away his skin, leaving mostly skull with patches of flesh here and there.

Gabriel looked down at Muerte's grave and in a brief moment of brief sanity, said, "Hon, you'll be the death of us."

Not Permitted

Michael

He would heal more quickly here within the warm glow of the rock, was what the Almighty had said when laying him here. He was somewhere within Rainbow Ridge, on the side facing Mount Titan. The flaming commandments on the Great Tablet against the twilight sky were easily read from here. The Nest was nothing more than a castle turret from this distance where sky wraiths spirited about blowing flames, eventually exploding into black clouds.

Michael squeezed his eyes shut, the colours of the mountains too intense, his head heavy, like a hangover from too much nectar. The Almighty had made it clear that any Seraphim seeing his quick defeat were not permitted to speak of this with others.

The Almighty vowed that Muerte and Gabriel would suffer the worst kind of punishment, with Michael being the only one privy to their location. No one would find them. Michael would keep his image intact.

"My image is greatly sullied," the Almighty had said before flying off., but yours can never be. You are all that exists of the image I once was."

An Eternity of Pleasures

Muerte

The heavy cold rock dug into Muerte. She was still nailed to the torn away cross, and the lack of freedom to move was the greatest punishment so far.

Pain scourged through her, flowing through her veins like a burning venom. She felt a numbing coming on, to the point she was sure mortality had found her, then she was yanked back to full life to suffer another kind of death.

How kind of Big Dummy to subject her to such a new addiction. Every time she reached inevitable death, she would burst into life again. It was orgasmic every time to almost die. An eternity of pleasures. The thrill of it never got old. Each death had its own distinct signature of pleasure. Was this how it was for Gabriel?

That was the only unbearable pain, to not be in his arms.

The Bronze Age of Humanity

Zeus

It looked like an invasion rather than a friendly union of mortals and immortals.

Zeus and his fiancé, Hera stood on the jagged crown of Mount Morg, the tallest mountain on this planet and Muerte's old playground. Below the peak, the lower clouds were sparse compared to the upper layer. They watched the last angel portal into District 1. The portal between this planet and its moon would remain open, leading back to the throne planet.

The Almighty had suggested at the last meeting of the Twelve to split the humans into twelve tribes, scattering them throughout the world. An example given by their Lord was the more apple tree varieties, the less chance of a disease wiping out all apples on the planet. The same went for the humans. Zeus saw it another way. Divided, the humans would progress so differently that when they met later on down the road, they would have forgotten that they had once been part of one tribe and would begin fighting over petty differences.

A designated leader would govern over each district with their own legion of angels assigned to them. A thirteenth district existed, a magical place of unicorns, dragons, and other fantastical beasts, but was off limits to all mortals and immortals. The purpose of the thirteenth district called the Forbidden District was unknown but Zeus had keen interest when it came to the dragons. A winged army was one thing, but one with fire-breathing dragons would be something terrifying and virtually unbeatable.

"I see an excellent opportunity, Zeus," Hera said, her perfume scent of lily, rose, and a hint of maple wafting off her.

"What do you mean?" Zeus folded his arms. Both his and Hera's hair were in ponytails weighted down by a blade fastened at the end.

"I see an army for the inheriting," Hera said.

"They are many," Zeus said of the angels assigned to him. "It seems our Lord is trying to make amends, entrusting me with so much firepower."

The Almighty included the Furies, but still not enough for Zeus to take the throne. Even Poseidon had been freed and given his own region to rule over. His last chance, or else, was the way the Almighty put it. This act of mercy had people whispering that it could only mean the imminent return of Calliope and Lucifer.

"Not many are happy with this assignment," Hera said. "They're offended that such a fragile race has been made in our image. Their ears are open to our thoughts."

"In time, Hera. Let them settle in. Let their bitterness fester, making them riper for our words."

"Don't wait too long, many will adapt to their new home and become complacent."

"A valid point. Would you be so kind, my dear, as to visit each district leader and get a feel for their politics?"

Her big eyes softened with her smirk. "Planting seeds is what I do best."

Her peacock-coloured wings spread into full view, eyes all over them that looked so real one expected them to blink. She sprung into the air and headed for what looked like the district ruled by Ra, who, during Zeus's youngling years, had been the Almighty's bodyguard during an era of unrest.

Below, angels picked which spots in the mountain to slumber, Zeus decided Mount Morg needed a facelift and name change. His wings slowly flapped him upwards as thunderbolts protruded from his fists. He slammed them into the peak, chipping away stone, forming a columned building, molding the pantheon into a pleasing image, hewing the rest of the peak into a flat surface. The mountain and its new structure were truly magnificent, reminding Zeus of Mount Titan, the tallest stone structure on Heaven's throne planet, and so he renamed Mount Morg, Mount Olympus.

Here, he and Hera would listen to grievances from their kind.

The moon was already faintly visible in the early evening sky. He had it all figured out, exactly when the moon would pass in sight of all of the pantheon's columned areas at some point in the year, a surprise for Hera while they sat in their thrones discussing the gossip of the day. He stared down at the clouds that briefly gave way to a flourishing city below. In the coming days he would introduce himself to the female humans. Only they could help him with his plan to free Hades from Hell.

JAMES PYNE

MEDUSA RISING

A Minute's Mirth to Wail a Week

Medusa

It was a time when the universe was healing, when there was an awkward peace in the usually chaotic macrocosm. A time when comets were suicidal, unable, while flaming through the galaxy, to get their rocks off, smashing into planets or moons and spraying out the beginnings of new life. They couldn't even slam into each other, no matter how hard they tried. It was a time when suns didn't expand and burn out galaxies. To most of the angels it was a boring period leading to unhealthy habits and mortal addictions.

Much to her distaste, Medusa had been assigned to District 1 under Zeus's command. She had no interest in guiding mortals to a higher learning. They were babying the humans too much, what good could come out of that? She wandered through the Angelic Gardens that for her were a reflection of the Garden of Eden back home. The gardens were the place where angels went to chill, to rediscover themselves.

The earthy coolness of the cobblestone path felt nice on the soles of her feet. A field of flowers at either side, the end of her tunic and long black hair sliding along tulips, buttercups, and young sunflowers, sometimes she would stop and sniff the ends of her locks with different areas smelling like whatever flower they had just grazed. Every bloom on this planet was represented here and she planned on sniffing all of them during her sabbatical, during her cleansing of recent drama. Her ex, whose name was unworthy of thought, had become of all things a raging drunkard. It was such a human thing to do. He was such a disappointment.

She inhaled a flower with blinking eyespots on its petals, a tribute to Hera's beauty, the Almighty had once declared, doing his usual politicking with the House of Zeus. When in full bloom, the petals would spread into wings and the flowerheads would fly off as butterflies.

With all this tranquility surrounding her, Medusa wasn't convinced that spending time here would alleviate the pain of another disappointing relationship. She was just taking advice from her old friend, Lucifer. He always insisted on a long walk through the flower gardens back home, especially when he got the urge to punch his protégé Michael, in the face. He would say that in a jolly form, but Medusa knew, along with everyone else, that someday they were going to seriously butt heads for reals. She hoped to witness such a prizefight.

That was still a long way off. Nobody expected Lucifer's banishment to be a short one. Truth be told, Medusa crushed hard when it came to the son of the Esteemed One. Lucifer also had feelings for her, even once declaring them to her, but she was still young, making him seem crusty and ancient to her in those oblivious days. How stupid that version of her had been. Centuries passed and he grew on her, but when one of them became single, the other would be in a relationship. Nothing ever lined up.

"That's life." She bent over and sniffed a black rose, taking in the scent of licorice. Her eyes closed in bliss.

It looked like a long wait for Lucifer to be single again. But he would be. He would tire of Lilith. Studs like him always did. Eventually every relationship became complacent to them, made them feel like a prisoner. The whole thing became stale to them, making them yearn for something fresh, someone challenging, not someone already conquered. Medusa would make the best of her chance when it presented itself. She wouldn't drape herself over him, wouldn't try to change him. She would call him out on things, keep him guessing, but she wouldn't be pushed around, that's for sure.

The cobblestone path led into the rosebush labyrinth speckled with multicoloured roses and leafy, arched doorways. These roses were the immortals' choice; the flowers lasted for months once picked, but their thorns could be pounded into wood like nails and could leave scars on weaker immortals. A large, daytime moth landed on the puffed-out area of her tunic, on her nipple to be exact, its wingspan covering a good chunk of her cleavage. In direct sunlight the flamed holographic wings appeared moving to the point where the creature looked on fire.

"Am I showing too much?" she asked the moth, having already walked through four doorways within the maze. "Are you offended?"

"Not me," a familiar voice said, as the moth flew off. "I would prefer nothing on you at all."

Her ex, Dionysus, stepped through one of the leafy doorways. Dressed in royal purple, drinking bottled plum wine, he appeared a little tipsy with each step. Alcohol wasn't something angels guzzled down often. It had quite the effect on an immortal, with the pleasures of sex heightened, making it dangerously addictive for that reason. Long term usage damaged an angel's divine intellect, turning their minds into *prime mortal*. Once having kicked one's drinking habit, it took years for the mental effects to wear off. Making it worse, this blue planet had the best ingredients in the universe for potent liquor.

The curly-haired brothers, Himeros and Pothos, staggered out of the same leafy doorway in matching crimson togas. Arms around each other, hands limp over their shoulders, they were singing in slurred voices. Their wings went up and down, out of sync.

"Seriously?" Medusa said. "Now you're stalking me. Get over it, we're done."

"Pure coincidence." A headband torn from the bottom of his toga kept Dionysus's long hair in place. He was such a wreck. She wanted to slap away that arrogant smirk. He was an embarrassment to the House of Zeus, a prime example to Medusa of how angels and humans shouldn't mix in this way. The less exposure to them, the better, and nothing would change her opinion on that.

Dionysus swayed towards her. The bottle of wine swung in one hand, the other broke off rose branches, tossing them between Medusa and him. The broken twigs spread out into grapevines, slithering towards her.

Dionysus swigged the wine. He let out an exaggerated *ahhhh*. "If one doesn't mind her sass, those vines will prove beauty is skin deep, like the humans say."

"You've become like them, unworthy of your wings, of your immortality. I can no longer stomach your presence."

Medusa's wings rose into a collage of ocean blue and night black. She sprung to the air. Not more than ten feet up, vines coiled her ankles and yanked her down, slamming her hard onto her knees. Vines wrapped around her torso, her neck, her forehead, pulling her down on all fours as if bowing to Dionysus.

"What are you doing? Release me," she demanded.

"But we're just getting started."

The vines dug into her, worming in and out of her body. Such agony flooded her as another pricked and entered her chest, shooting out through her shoulder blade, spearing the ground behind her, yanking her down onto her back.

Himeros and Pothos stood at either side of her, grinning down at her with such wickedness, firing up Medusa's desperate attempts to get loose. Dionysus stood at the end of her feet. The vines forced apart her legs.

"I have come for a taste of a different *wine*." Dionysus tossed the empty bottle aside. "One that will be loud and pleasurable to the ears."

"You're not thinking straight. None of you are." Medusa tugged with everything she had. "You're drunk, you've become primordial like the humans. Dammit, will you listen for once?"

"There," Dionysus said. He motioned with one hand, and the vines dragged Medusa up against the rose hedge, her arms wide, legs straddled. The thorns dug into her skin, which her flesh quickly healed over, keeping her in place. "Now where were we, my dear? Ah yes, you embarrassed me by dumping me in front of my father, his entire Council. You made a laughingstock of me." He squinted at her. "Time to return the favour."

"Hephaestus, help. Hephaestus! Dionysus and —"

A vine slithered over her mouth, gagging her.

She gnawed at the vine to no avail, tried head-butting each of them when they got close, but the vines kept her head rooted against the rosebush, slithering across her eyes. They did unspeakable violence to her and because her skin healed quickly, this encouraged them to do more sinister acts. The vines closest to her took turns blinding her sight, while their horrid whispers, the forced entries sped her down the road of madness, to a place no angel had gone. Something festered inside, darkening her, and the only pleasing images that stayed with her were of Lucifer. The thought of him was the only thing keeping her remotely together.

Dazed and confused, she hollered Lucifer's name. Pleaded with him to —

"He's not coming," Dionysus whispered, licking the side of her face. "Wait — What's happening to you? Those eyes. Your skin."

Dionysus pulled back from her sight. Sudden sunlight blinded her as the vines were abruptly cut from her. She collapsed from weakness. The pieces of plant inside her crumbled to dust.

"Lucifer," she said, to the silhouette against the sun.

Helped to her feet, the refreshing scent of citrus and lily flared her nostrils. The silhouette took a clearer shape and colour.

"Medusa, what have they done?" It was Athena. "You'll pay for this." She spun around. "Cowards. I'll cut away all your virility and feed it to the harpies."

Athena unsheathed her sword and stabbed the ground in front of Medusa, hands clutching the hilt.

"Who first?" she shouted.

Dionysus pushed himself out of the thorn bushes where he had been thrown by the looks of it, areas of his skin trickling blood, his royal purple rag torn apart.

"Sister, I was exacting revenge for her transgressions against me."

"You're not my brother. All I see is Poseidon in you."

Something was creeping inside Medusa, just beneath her skin, especially in the scalp area.

Athena grabbed the end of Dionysus's wing and pulled him forwards, clotheslining him to the ground, then she bashed his nose with the hilt of her sword, keeping him flat on his back.

She turned to Himeros and Pothos.

"He made us do it," Himeros shouted, tucking the loose end of his toga behind him, looking at his twin brother for answers.

Dionysus screamed in anguish, pulling himself from the thorns.

The sight of all this excited Medusa when mere minutes ago such brutality would have sickened her. Dionysus's suffering fed whatever lurked beneath her skin, wanting out, wanting to introduce itself to everyone, wanting to play too. This wasn't her. These were not her thoughts. A sudden migraine blasted her skull, disorientating her.

"This is for Medusa." Athena tramped Dionysus's bloodied face over and over, as if she were trying to erase his visage for good.

Medusa loved her for it. She wanted Athena to bash him to seconds from death. Lucifer couldn't be here but how poetic that his adopted daughter had come to her rescue. It seemed preordained, a signal from the universe. Athena kept tramping away in such anger there was a danger she might stomp him to death. Wouldn't bother Medusa a bit . . . what was wrong with her . . . such dark thoughts.

"How does it feel to be helpless?" Athena shouted. "Sniveling weakling." Dionysus's face was unrecognizable. "I'd do more things if the commandments permitted."

Medusa said between heavy breaths: "Kill him." The itchy feeling beneath her scalp moved up into her hair. She looked at her hands, plum blue in places.

"Hephaestus, help!" Pothos shouted. "Medusa and Athena have gone mad and are going to kill us."

"As you wish," Medusa hissed. "Help will not get here in time. Time for Medusa to have some fun."

She slowly rose, staring down at Pothos. Hate and anger filled her. They had defiled her. She would never live this down. People would be whispering about her as she passed by. Who would want her after this? Would Lucifer? What had she done to deserve this? The fury, the dread of being alone forever, of not having Lucifer once he found out about this almost broke her. The shame of it all, to be wronged like this. Within seconds she relived every vile act they had subjected her to.

She wallowed in pain, transforming, the plumb-blue bruises on her skin turned colour and spreading into lizard-green stains with specks of purple—what was happening? Her soul darkened, eyes glowed ruby red, hair thickened into black vipers, as if they had gnawed their way out from a disturbing place in her mind, their birth anything but painless. They hissed, lashed out with fangs wide, and lethal saliva dripped, sizzling the grass.

"What—" Dionysus shouted as Athena released him while looking back at Medusa in amazement. "A Gorgon!"

No! Gorgons were just a fairytale for younglings. She couldn't be one yet here she was, a hideous thing no one would want, especially Lucifer—they had taken Lucifer from her. They took any chance of happiness. They would pay for this.

Medusa's viper hair stretched out and coiled the necks of Himeros and Pothos, pulling them close to her stare, and slowly, their bodies turned to stone.

The vipers tightened around their rock-necks, squeezing their heads off. She swatted their stone bodies, tumbling them into pieces. She stomped the stone head of Pothos into bits and dust. Then she stamped the face of Himeros.

Before Dionysus could suffer the same fate as his cousins, a gentle force pulled her away from her murderous rage.

"You!" Medusa's eyes widened at the sight of the Almighty, armoured. "You made us like this." She charged at their king. "For Lucifer," she shouted. "I'll drag you to Hell as a gift to him!"

The Almighty grabbed her by the throat. Parts of his skin briefly turned to stone. That was fear in his eyes. He tossed her aside. She landed on all fours. The vipers hissed, poison saliva dropped from their fangs and stretched within her eyesight.

"What happened here, Athena?" the Almighty hollered.

"The three of them did unspeakable things to Medusa. Why has she turned into that?"

"A defense mechanism." He looked down with genuine pity at Medusa. "Every female angel has this Gorgon gene, but it is only brought forth by distress from the vilest of act that no male is permitted to do according to my commandments. She is virtually unbeatable now. No male will have his way with her again."

"That's a curse, not a cure," Athena shouted.

No chance at Lucifer?

"Change her back," Athena said.

"Everything must take its natural course. Near our species she will turn into that."

"How's that fair?" Athena said. "And what of Dionysus?"

"He goes in first."

"My Lord, I didn't kill anyone," Dionysus objected, "Please. Not there."

"The liquor is good in Hell, too," the Almighty said. "Enjoy. But if I were you, I would fly far away. She will be following soon after."

Dionysus screamed as the fiery portal pulled him in. He reached out, first screaming for mercy then spewing hate as his body ignited in flames.

Medusa would gladly follow along—but the Almighty was coming too.

"Face me!" she screamed.

As the Almighty turned, she gored him into the portal.

She would help Lucifer defeat him.

She would win Lucifer's heart.

Yes, she would.

The Golden Age of Hell

Lilith

Lilith sat cross-legged, hands limp over the armrests of her throne. Lucifer's seat was empty. The throne area was set within the crown of Crimson Peak. Within the cavernous interior of the mountain, thousands of demons hung upside down like bats. That was where the metropolis Blaze City came into play, carpeting the entire circumference of the mountain, spreading out into the Plains of Woe, offering refuge to the remaining horned beasts. Hell's indigenous inhabitants were Lucifer's special project. They were coming along nicely.

Every angel, including Cronus, had moved into Blood Tower, its name symbolic of angels being of one lifeblood regardless of tribe or house. Atop Blood

Tower the Council of Thirteen met. Lucifer kept it simple, a round table with thirteen chairs. No Great Tablet with commandments. He was up there now having a meeting with Hades, getting updates on the recent discovery of moly, a plant thought only to exist on Heaven's throne planet Elysium.

The variety here was blackish red in the leaves unlike its green counterpart, but its effects were similar. Its tuberous root was the ambrosia and its heavenly white flowers the nectar. Hell had whispers of home, they just had to look for them. What else was on those other planets? Or hidden on the throne planet Tartarus?

Presently, Lilith was entertaining grievances from angel and demon alike. Persephone had just left, pretending to be looking for her uncle, having an urgent message for him, her way of trying to get into that private meeting and under Lilith's skin no doubt. She was always wiggling her way into events to be closer to Lucifer, even back home, always watching from a distance in crowds during his speeches. Always tagging along with Hades on any missions involving Lucifer.

It was impossible to read Persephone, no emotion. She gave away no thoughts. A great disappointment to the House of Zeus, an impregnable mind was the only gift Persephone had. However, there was more to Persephone's game than just being a devoted follower of Hell's king and Lilith would expose her. Cronus's bloodline were a calculating bunch, dedicated to their mission in becoming the Order's new royal family. Athena was the only trustworthy one of the bunch as far as Lilith was concerned.

What else were Lucifer and the suddenly congenial Hades talking about up there? It was driving Lilith mad. Why couldn't they have had their talk here in front of her? Hades held a one-thousand-year-old grudge against Lucifer for crucifying him. Now he was suddenly chummy? Huge red flag there. The other thing they would be discussing was Hades' discovery of fire-breathing horses on a nearby planet and his claim to them. The arrogance.

It was hard to believe so much time had passed since they had been banished here. She had it figured out that one day of Heaven equalled thirty-three days in Hell, with one year in Heaven equalling thirty-three years in Hell. And they were no closer to finding a way out of here after all this time. They explored surrounding planets but without a portal maker, things were moving slowly on that front. Hell was more than just a galaxy.

They had tried pleading with Hephaestus to free them with all manner of bribes. They concluded that he couldn't hear them in here. Or he didn't dare disobey the Almighty. There were angels who religiously said the name of Hephaestus during their everyday duties, hoping that a short window of time would occur, allowing the portal maker to hear them.

And there, Dragons Den, a coal-black mountain loaded with caves where dragons slept after being today's food gatherers; others watched for potential prey from the large ledges expanding from their lairs. The summit was where the present leader slept, Lucifer had willed the mountain into existence from nothing and the firebreathers showed their gratitude by not burning angels anymore and leaving Blaze City alone, but once a demon left its safe haven it was fair game, unless it was accompanied by angels.

If only they could ride the firebreathers, they could explore four times faster with no energy spent. But how could you reason with them when they didn't have a constant leader? There they went again, fighting for the top of the mountain. The present dragon king and the challenger gnashed their teeth and hissed at each other, filling the air with their bloodcurdling roars. The challenger flipped the king into the side of the mountain, sending others scattering like crows. No dragon kept the seat of power for long. Lucifer took this as a good thing, it meant they were all equal in immense strength. Lilith saw it another way. With no dragon ruling long-term, being king was just a title, a social status among firebreathers, nothing more.

The former dragon king dropped to the floor of the basin. Ash puffed out from impact. It would lie there awhile to heal, dragon scat occasionally splattering it, then scramble its way back up the ranks. The new dragon king landed atop the mountain waiting for its challenger. Lucifer wanted to force them to accept dragon riders, beat it into them if necessary, but Lilith reminded him that this would be no better than Hades contempt for the demons. Assuming they could succeed with brute force — physical confrontation was a way of life for these flying lizards.

Was Lucifer really having a meeting up there or was he having a rendezvous with another female? Mad thoughts born from a vision haunted her of Lucifer sitting next to another female, much of her body shadowed, but enough of it seen for Lilith to know it wasn't her. She expected a time to come when she would lose his heart to another. Immortality was the eventual killer of every love. The more she had this vision, the crankier she got with him. He chalked it up as Hell getting to her and she just needed to find something to —

A fiery portal opened before her with a flaming Dionysus tumbling out of it, rolling along the lava-fissured courtyard, the flames dying down from his wings with each complete rotation. He slammed into Lucifer's throne a burnt mess. He stuttered for minutes about Medusa becoming a Gorgon and the Almighty casting him and Medusa here . . . The fact that the portal remained opened meant his story must be true. Seconds here were minutes there.

Where was Lucifer? Why hadn't he seen the portal? It appeared to be a one-way portal with its flames lashing out at the thrones. The demons were on their way, yet Lucifer's attention remained stubbornly on Hades.

"Well, hello there, Old Fella."

The Lord himself was tackled into view by a vile creature with a head full of hissing and acid-spitting vipers.

Was this real? After all this time, revenge was served to them like this. Lilith would distract the Old Bastard long enough for Lucifer to get here, then the fun would begin.

Conflicted

Athena

A thena pushed through the portal with the flames having no effect on her, warming her armour, nothing more. No skin burnt. All her hair remained. She was impenetrable to most things. Regardless, she hurried—not just to protect the Almighty, but to keep her adoptive parents from doing something stupid. Assuming that was where they were portalling to. Rumours had it, the Inferno was as big as the Heaven dimension, if not bigger. If she saw Lucifer, she would embrace him lovingly, as she would Lilith, regardless if the Almighty approved. Maybe Hell would look appetizing, prompting her to remain there. What had Lucifer once said during one of their sword-playing games?

"Better to rule in Hell than serve in Heaven under insufferable and mad rule."

Now or Never

Lilith

The snake-haired Medusa had just presented Hell with the greatest possible gift, making her an automatic ally. She pounced at the Almighty, and the vipers fanged the shoulders and neck of Heaven's king, two latching into his face. She clawed and head-butted him—a feral thing, far removed from the dazzling beauty she once was. It couldn't be her.

Dionysus was drunk, liquor heavy on his breath.

"Medusa!" Athena shouted, holding her sword out, her armour throwing off threads of smoke. "This isn't you. Stop."

"Athena?" Lilith couldn't believe her eyes. It was really her daughter, what a sight to see. Surely an automatic ally. "That thing can't be Medusa."

"She was beaten and raped by Dionysus and his cousins changing her into this." Athena stopped next to Lilith. "She has killed Himeros and Pothos in a blind rage."

"So it begins," Lilith said with a heavy sigh. "Our fall."

Unless she slew the king of angels, supplanting Lucifer as the new liege. Then maybe the Order had a chance.

The Almighty grappled with Medusa, parts of him turning to stone, then fading back to skin again.

"I don't understand how she turned into this."

"The Gorgon gene exists in every female angel." Athena looked ready to go in and aid the Almighty. "The bedtime stories are true."

"Is that your justice?" Lilith shouted.

The Almighty hurled Medusa aside. She landed on all fours.

"Punish us with that." Lilith motioned at Medusa, who hissed up at her. "Seems you have a hate for us females, couldn't think of something better than making us ugly to the sight of everyone. You have the mind and vindictiveness of a youngling."

"Here's another follower for Lucifer," the Almighty shouted, as the fiery portal softened into purplish blue. "Assuming my son can subdue her. I see he hasn't fixed that mouth of yours. It's been a thousand years here, and you are still a mirror image of the last time I saw you. No younglings? How many miscarriages now? Without a blood heir, how much longer will he remain with you?"

"You bastard."

He grinned, the gesture scarcely noticeable in that beard, just enough to agitate her, his words sufficient proof that he was reading her mind, learning how to get under her skin, breaking his covenant with the Order. She was sure of it.

Medusa howled in pain as her talons stretched out more, her blood dripping on the ash rock. She pounced at him with her legs clamping him. The vipers fanged his skin, injecting their acidic venom. Blood trickled into his beard, reddening it in places.

"Athena!" their Lord boomed in desperation.

He was weak if calling for help. What had happened to their mighty king? Parts of him were turning to stone. Medusa's talons ripped away at his back and wings.

Demons and angels converged upon the throne area. Surely Lucifer was among them, but Lilith didn't see any golden sparkle drop from the top of Blood Tower. Even in this bleak, fiery place, he shone brightly.

Athena looked back to the struggle before her. She raised her sword. To do exactly what? And there, Medusa, who spoke Lucifer's name so affectionately, it was no secret she crushed on him. Could it be her sitting on the throne next to Lucifer? Lilith's replacement to bear him a child? No, Lilith would be the mother of his younglings. Not this bitch. Not any bitch. She charged at the Almighty with sword drawn, his back to her. She ignored Athena's screams for her to stop. He was weak enough to strike. It was now or never. There was no waiting for Lucifer.

She pushed her sword through them both. Medusa would recover—so would the Almighty. She just wanted him on his knees so she could make him capitulate.

The Almighty hollered in such pain that it rattled Lilith's bones, sent shivers through her, as if he died, they all did. That was silly thinking. He was no better than them. Medusa wheezed, her head fell back, and the vipers whipped out in a frenzy.

"Hephaestus," the Almighty rasped. "Michael is needed."

There was their answer. Hephaestus had been ignoring their pleas over the centuries. It also meant reinforcements were coming. It was now or never.

"Mother, what have you done?" Athena lowered her sword, slowing her approach.

Lilith withdrew her blade from the Almighty's back.

Medusa tumbled to the magma-cracked ground. The Almighty hunched over, barely standing, then he fell on top of her. His head turned sideways, with one eye glaring up in Lilith's direction. His wounds started to heal, the stone patches fading into wrinkled skin.

Lilith placed her sword on his neck. "Surrender the throne to Lucifer."

"You will have to behead me."

"Don't try me, Old Fool."

"You started this. Finish it if you can."

"Damn you."

Athena's sword moved Lilith's blade from the Almighty's neck, keeping it at bay. Other portals opened, with Seraphim pouring through with Michael leading.

"Daughter?"

Athena teared up. "I'm sorry, Mother."

"You dare." The Almighty glared up at Lilith, his eyes blackening.

"Athena, we can finally finish this. You are of the House of Lucifer, not his."

The Almighty tackled Lilith, and she lost grip of her sword. He lifted her to the dark orange sky of daylight, crimson lightning branching out while she head-butted him, and punched him. He squeezed tighter, caving in her armour.

"The things I am going to do to you, Lilith." His eyes darkened into a squint.

Desperation came over her. He would take this out on not only her, but on Lucifer, and all of Hell. She had no choice. May Lucifer forgive her.

She unsheathed the dagger hidden in the armpit of her armour.

"For the House of Lucifer."

She rammed the dagger into his eye, then hammered it in with her fist. He screamed in rage, rattling the sky.

She punched it in deeper. "Die, you fossil."

THE ALMIGHTY WITH A BLOODIED EYE

JAMES PYNE

A Dagger in the Heart

Lucifer

Lucifer spirited towards the throne area, Hades at the right of him, both with their swords drawn. Confusing emotions came from everyone, including Lilith. With so many portals opening, it looked like an invasion was happening with five hundred new minds entering the scene. He did not infiltrate their minds, instead, all their thoughts briefly flooded him, which always happened when it came to new arrivals into Hell. One was his father. And Michael. And the hive mind of the Seraphim. And two others, Medusa and Dionysus, one of whom was angry with murder on their mind, the other fearing for their life. And Athena, his beloved daughter.

Hell's forces formed a shrinking circle, converging on the throne by foot and air. There weren't enough of them to make a dent in a fully weaponized legion of Seraphim. Too many of Lucifer's warriors were away on assignment. How could he have known this day would come? So Father got bored, did he? Decided to come and make trouble. He would regret that. Lucifer had grown in strength since their last encounter. A thousand years stronger.

"Lilith, no." Lucifer felt Lilith's sudden fear, her dread, her desperation, her call out for him Lucifer inside his mind. An image of his father's bearded face, vengeful eyes. "No!"

He could see them now, with them a little higher than Lucifer's approaching army. His father grasped Lilith by the throat. Lucifer could feel his father's uncontrollable hatred, his malicious intent — a spike of intense pain and loathing. His father howled in agony, yanking Lilith's dagger from his eye.

"Father, no!"

His father powered her down in front of their thrones. Bits of rock spat up. His father raised Lilith's dagger and impaled her heart with it.

"Lilith!"

His father looked up, one eye socket a gory splash of red and black. He backed off from Lilith, stumbling, like he was adjusting to seeing with only one eye. His father's emotions had never been so clear. Shock at what he had done. Regret. Was that fear coming from him? Not for his life — for the future of the Order.

Lilith coughed up blood; the knife remained embedded in her heart. His father looked at his hands and down at Lilith. He turned away from Lucifer's approach, head down, stopping at a newly opened portal to Heaven, looking up over his shoulder at Lucifer, his lone eye tearing.

All were in disbelief at what had just happened. Michael took his helmet off as did every Seraphim. Athena stood still, in front of the Almighty, her head down. Hell's angels looked at Lucifer, waiting for his move, their weapons ready. Demons circled above.

Lucifer landed into a run and fell to his knees beside Lilith.

Blood seeped down from both corners of her mouth. Her breathing was shallow, and tears down her face as her colour paled.

"Lilith, stay with me."

"I — tried — I love you Lucifer."

Images of their first kiss slammed into his mind, their first time looking into each other's eyes, that moment when he knew she was the one for him. He was now seeing it from her sight and could see the love in his eyes for her.

The images blacked out.

She died in his arms, her mind, and her emotions cut off from him, the detachment from Lilith became the worst emotional pain he had ever experienced. A horrible empty feeling that quickly filled with rage and confusion.

"Lilith." He tried willing her alive. Nothing. He looked up at his father. "Bring her back."

"I can't."

"You mean you won't."

"I'm sorry my son."

Before he turned away from Lucifer, tears streamed down one side of his bearded face, blood wormed down the other cheek.

Lucifer slowly rose to his feet.

"Face me, Father."

"I did not want this. She initiated."

Athena hurried toward Lucifer, looking down at the lifeless body of Lilith but was willed into a portal before she reached them, her arms out to Lucifer.

"Father," she shouted, disappearing.

"You coward. Fight me!" Lucifer's chest heaved, the rage in him was of nothing he had felt before.

His father backed into a closing portal.

Michael and the Seraphim backed into theirs.

"I will tear him apart." Lucifer unsheathed his sword and marched towards the one Michael was backing into.

"Move out of the way, Michael or I will cut you down."

Michael didn't unsheathe his sword.

Seraphim made a wall in front of Michael as they all backed into nearby portals.

"He killed my wife. It's my right."

"Lilith stuck her sword in his back, then daggered his eye with every intent to kill him," Michael shouted, backing into the purplish swirl of the shrinking portal, "I'm sorry for your loss—old friend."

Lucifer's forces charged at the portals, but not one of them made it back to Heaven as the last dimmed and closed.

Lucifer screamed to the sky and the planet Tartarus shook with his fury. The fire lizards scattered from Dragons Den. Volcanoes erupted. He turned back to Lilith's corpse. "Father, I forsake you from this day forward. I will kill you. I swear it."

A Killing Machine

Medusa

Lucifer staggered with grief towards Lilith, passing Medusa, whose viper hair started shrinking back into black and red hair. Her skin began fading to its freckled milky white in places. She was becoming herself again in the presence of an angel, but only briefly as Lucifer walked on. Her monstrous form returned in full force, an agonizing process every time it seemed. How could it be? The Almighty said it was permanent when in the presence of her kind. Was Medusa's love for Lucifer the cure? Or his genuine feelings for her the remedy?

Lucifer knelt before Lilith. In such a fragile condition, a vulnerable state in the eyes of many, the way they looked at each other, they sensed that Lucifer was prime to be overthrown. All were too scared to make the move.

Dragons circled above as if considering attacking until Lucifer glared up at them. They scattered. That was power, even in his frailest state, angel and dragon feared the mighty Lucifer. Every one of them—except one. Persephone, the only one to stand up for the banishing of Lucifer and Lilith, watched the king of Hell like her next prey. That was how it looked to Medusa who wouldn't let that happen.

It was Medusa's turn to be at Lucifer's side.

"I sense your wish to dethrone me," Lucifer said in a distant voice. "You fear me. Follow me not out of dread. I don't want such rodents groveling before me. Follow me only because you believe in my vision." He looked down at Lilith. "One my beloved Lilith died for. Follow me because you hate my father as much as I do. Follow me if you want your dignity back, want to see your families, your old friends, your loving partners." He paused, looking down at Lilith. He gently closed her eyes. "Something I won't see again."

"Lucifer." Medusa placed a hand on his shoulder. Her hand returned to its pale colour, the vipers faded into hair, her pitch-black eyes lightened to ocean blue.

Lucifer looked up at her. "Medusa?"

"It breaks my heart to see you in this state. Both of us are victims of your father's cruelty." She knelt before him; and the vipers sank from view. "He'll suffer slowly for this. He's a hypocrite now for not banishing himself to this place. Word will get out about this back home and they will rebel. How can they not take your side now? You will have two armies joining together against your father when we return."

She would be the supportive one. It was too soon to try to win his heart. Persephone gave Medusa a brief scowl.

"What did he do to you?" The dismayed expression on Lucifer's face when he asked that.

"It is he who did this to me." She pointed at the slowly recovering Dionysus, slouched over against Lucifer's throne, still burnt from portalling here. The liquor weakened his recovery.

"She killed Himeros and Pothos," Dionysus shouted, trying to pull himself up with the help of Lucifer's throne, falling back down. "She killed her own kind. She deserves the same fate."

"Take your hands off that," Medusa shouted. "That will be as close as the House of Zeus ever gets to sitting on that throne."

She marched towards Dionysus, grimacing as she changed back into her Gorgon form. She refused to howl in pain and look weak in front of Lucifer. The future queen of Hell would be tough, and fearless like its last empress.

Hades stepped into view, sword drawn, ready to strike her down.

"Hades." She slowed into a strut towards the thrones. "You're of the same blood that cursed me with this form. I'll get to Dionysus, through you, then. Your family has been nothing but a curse to the Order. I will hunt you all down, turn you into stone, smash you into nonexistence."

"What madness spills from your mouth," Hades said. "Are Dionysus's accusations true?"

"Just like a male, ignore the fact that he and his cousins defiled me at the whim of their cruel minds — me, a female. Not important enough in the eyes of the House of Zeus." She stopped her approach, almost close enough for her viper hair to strike. "Yes, the House of Zeus is two less. Before this day is out, three more less." She looked over at Persephone when saying that. "The first of today's three will be you, Hades, brother to the treacherous Zeus. I will scatter at his feet stone pieces of each of you so that he may know his bloodline is done."

Hades looked back at Dionysus, then down at Lucifer, and back to her.

"I'll put an end to this sudden death plague," Hades said, "by ending you."

He charged at her with sword ready to slay her down. She leaned away from his swipe, and the vipers lashed out, twirling around his sword arm, the rest around his neck, pulling him to her face. He glared into her eyes. His fists reddened to release fireballs, then horror came over him as his skin grayed and turned to stone. She slowly backed off as the vipers uncoiled from him.

The terror remained in Hades' stone eyes.

Dionysus had those eyes right now.

She spun-kicked his head with a clean sweep, to everyone's shock and awe. It bounced on the courtyard. Medusa stamped it into dust.

"One less brick in the House of Zeus."

Angels and demons backed away. Part of her liked that power. The other part worried about what Lucifer would think—no, he would see the benefit of ending the presence of the House of Zeus first here, then in Heaven.

"Uncle!" Dionysus shouted, standing on his own, suddenly showing courage to fight her.

She knew better from the way he looked around. He was hoping someone would intervene before she reached him.

"Another brick to smash." She looked at the real threat, Persephone, whose eyes widened, her wings spreading for flight. "Then her." She focused back on Dionysus. "Flee, Persephone. I'll catch up with you shortly. This will only take a minute."

Before she could solidify Dionysus into stone, the ground opened beneath her. Wings failed her as an invisible force slammed her hard onto her back. Rocks moved over her, pinning her down.

Lucifer stood at the edge of the crater with Lilith wilted in his arms.

"Lucifer!" Medusa reached up.

"It seems my father has made two monsters this day." He looked down at her in dismay, as if she were a monster even in her angelic form that she had transformed back into. "You've killed without a second thought. And you would again if left the chance. You've made that clear."

"I was trying to protect you. The blood from the House of Zeus will betray you. Please. I love you, Lucifer. I always have. Don't do this. Don't do this!"

The rocks slowly tumbled, gradually pinning her until only one small space remained, through which she could see Lucifer's disgusted face. A rock slowly closed over, leaving her in darkness, leaving her with that haunting look of disdain.

The Law of the Land

Athena

They were back on the blue planet.

"You murdered Lilith in cold blood." Tears streamed down Athena's face. The temptation to strike him down was there, but Lilith had gone for the kill. All had seen it.

"What's done is done." The Almighty stood before a portal to home, his back to her. Mount Olympus tower over them.

"You exiled Medusa for killing one of our own. Now banish yourself, too."

Hell appeared to be a place of never-ending struggle. How bad the Inferno must be for one of the banished to try killing the Almighty. But Lilith hadn't appeared insane. No, her actions were those of a sound, calculative mind.

"It's because of me Lilith is dead." Athena took her hand off her sheathed sword. "I shouldn't have let my heart get in the way, should've helped you quicker when you asked for it."

"No, Athena." The Almighty didn't look back. "Do not carry that in your heart. This is on me. You showed your allegiance today like no other has since Lucifer's better days. Three of the Order died today. I take the blame." He looked back at Athena with an expression of severity. "From this day forward, you are now the extension of my justice on this planet. Every district is under your watchful eye. You are judge and jury. Michael will alert all district leaders. Do what you see fit with my full support. I know you will do the right thing."

"But I didn't . . ."

He disappeared into the closing portal.

". . . damn you to Hell."

She screamed a mix of anger and sorrow at the spot where the bastard had stood. He had dropped her at the foot of Mount Olympus for a reason, he did nothing randomly. Angels flew in and out of their caves near the cloud-covered peak. She was the law then. Fine by her. Athena darted up to the summit, where the coolness of clouds refreshed her. She landed into a fast walk at the pantheon, wings lowering. Two guards stood between every space within the columned building. At her approach, two guards crossed their halberds, allowing her no passage.

She withdrew her sword and powered it down through the halberds. They withdrew their swords. Guards between the other columns looked ready to swarm her.

"Really?" she said. "Your swords would barely scratch me."

"Allow her passage," the voice of Zeus echoed.

Both guards reluctantly stepped aside.

She stepped down into the pantheon. Statues were carved out of the backside of the columns of Zeus, his brothers and sisters, his parents, his offspring, even Hephaestus, all except Athena. It didn't bother her in the least. She would only obliterate such a statue anyway.

"Athena, you have the look of war on your face."

"Lilith is dead because of your seed." She stopped at the throne steps.

"What are you talking about?" Zeus sat up in his throne, with its backrest of stalagmites almost touching the ceiling.

"Our Lord killed her. It all happened because of your damn seed."

"How do you know this?"

"I was there."

"In Hell? Which of my seed sparked all this?"

"An intoxicated Dionysus and his equally inebriated cousins horribly maimed and raped Medusa. Something triggered inside her, transforming her into a Gorgon and leading to her killing Himeros and Pothos."

"A Gorgon? And Dionysus?"

"Banished to Hell along with Medusa, where our Lord killed Lilith—who tried to slay him. All involved are dead or banished to Hell because of your bloodline. I'm ashamed to be part of it."

"His madness knows no limits. Now he kills us. And do you still stand by his side, Athena, after the murder of . . . your mother?" Zeus stood up. He casually walked down the twelve steps leading to his throne. "The House of Zeus disowns the memory of Himeros, Pothos, and Dionysus for their gross misconduct but it does not condone the murder of Himeros and Pothos. The hearts of all angels will have a glaring emptiness with Lilith's absence. We will hold a ceremony worthy of a queen. For six days there will be silence amongst us."

"Your fake tears wouldn't fool the blind."

"Athena, you must let go of your hatred for me." Zeus ambled towards Athena. "I know I've failed you as a father. But these dark times will compel us all to lay down our abhorrence for each other." He loomed over her and clasped her armoured shoulders with both hands. She shrugged them away. "Come now, surely you see we have a common enemy. Don't you want to avenge your mother's death? Your . . . father's sorrow?"

Athena glared up at him, tempted to raise the point of her sword to his throat. The authority was hers to do it. To mark his face with her sword. But he hadn't done anything wrong—yet. When he did, she would be there to stop him.

"Daughter, let it go."

She screamed: "I'm not your daughter!"

LUCIFER MOURNING THE DEATH OF LILITH

Cinnamon Eyes

Lucifer

When Lucifer's teardrops splashed on Lilith's bloodied chest, their blood and tears mixed, dripping onto a barren piece of land a few miles from Crimson Peak where Lucifer had decided to bury her. From those droplets spread a tiny slice of beauty in Hell's fury, a garden containing Lilith's favourite trees, bushes, and flowers. And every year the Forbidden Gardens expanded with the iron gate and fences dragging along the soil, stopping in their new position.

Today, Hell banged at the gate but didn't dare cross into the Forbidden Gardens. Fire stretched over but never licked the eternal blossoming trees. Dragons flew over but never landed, never exhaled random fireballs onto Lilith's resting place. An onyx tombstone at the head of her grave with her interred in a rose-tinted glass coffin. She had been laid to rest in the armour she died in, both hands clasped to her sword forever. An angel's corpse did not rot.

Lucifer knelt before her grave. He tried to will her alive, like he did at every visit, waiting for her eyes to open. What he would give to feel the pounding of her heart against his ear. For her to send him visions from the other side, to give him direction and purpose again. She had died before he could tell her one last time that he loved her, something he hadn't done nearly enough.

No one flew over the Forbidden Gardens on the anniversary of her passing. None could see him in this pitiful state again. Thirty-foot tall thorn rose hedges surrounded the garden, with rose vines blanketing the gate door. Due to the angle of her grave placement, not even those in the Blood Tower could see him. They left Lucifer to his one day with Lilith.

Lucifer had left Cronus in charge. The Elder could not take his eyes off Medusa's burial site, knowing she was still alive down there. Last year he dug up the area trying to get to her, but every time he was close, the rocks gently gave way beneath a sleeping Medusa, sinking her from his grasp. No angel would die again. Never would another suffer like he and Cronus had suffered.

The wrought iron gate squeaked open. Who dared come in? Before Lucifer could push himself up, a white-gowned Persephone appeared. The gate creaked closed at her passing. She had lost her beloved uncle, Hades, that day at the hands of Medusa's mad revenge. Persephone was the first to see Lucifer in this state.

Blossoms floated down on her like snow, mixing into her hair. They had never fallen before, not even during the worst hellstorm winds. Yet her mere passing added to the beauty of the place; it was a remarkable sight. Lucifer felt guilty for thinking that. She stopped and smelled the narcissus flowers. Then he remembered why he was here and looked away from Persephone's approach and back down at Lilith's grave, one hand on the glass lid above her chest.

Persephone knelt at Lucifer's side. It wasn't in him to tell her to leave. He saw her watching from a distance when he gave his speeches. She would find ways to go with him on expeditions. All the single females pursued him, wanting royal status. Except Persephone, the smart one. The one who studied him from the shadows, her pale, rosy-cheeked face pushing out of the darkness just long enough to get his attention, then sinking back from view.

She gently squeezed his shoulder.

"No one is to know of me in this state, understand?"

"It is between us."

"I'm lost even now, after all these years."

She whispered into his ear. "Then let me find you."

Lucifer looked up into her cinnamon-brown eyes, where he saw the promise of a new home.

Coming Defeat

Athena

Zeus had kept his promise with the other districts following his lead. During the first six days statues of Lilith popped up everywhere and paintings of her escapades were shared along with fond stories of her being told. They remembered her as a fierce warrior, a devout lover to Lucifer, and a favourable stepmother to Athena.

The seventh day involved the most athletic of all districts to come and display their raw strength, agility, and precision. The Olympic Games had first started back on the throne planet Elysium and were a personal favourite of Lilith's. Zeus decided to introduce the Olympic games to the humans. The biggest coliseum on the planet accommodated humans and angels alike, sitting amongst each other, at the insistence of Zeus. Athena was among them.

The shadow of Mount Olympus was slowly slipping away as the sun came back into view. Athena knew what Zeus was aiming for. He was dragging this on for seven days to make sure it burnt deep into their souls, so that when he came for their support against the Almighty, they would remember how he had murdered Lilith in cold blood like it was yesterday. This was step one in uniting them against a common foe under his flag of ambition.

"Where is our Lord?" Zeus asked from his temporary throne. Hera was noticeably missing, as she was unamused by Zeus's infidelity to her. Rumour had it that he had impregnated a fair number of humans, something Athena was looking into. "I ask you all, why isn't he here to show his respects?"

No one said anything. It was in their eyes. They were ripe for supporting a cause that would lead them all to ruin, but not if Athena had anything to do with it.

"Today, the greatest of each district compete for bragging rights," Zeus continued with Poseidon standing at his side in a loincloth, "in memory of Lilith who appreciated the games more than anyone else. If only she had lived to see her beloved husband partake in the games, but he was too busy being his father's son."

"You attack Lucifer's character!" Athena shouted from the stands. "Attack my father like that."

Everyone around Athena looked at her. She overheard them whispering about her arrogance due to her new title as the living law of the lands. She didn't care what anyone thought.

"Honourable Athena, I meant nothing by it. My heart is heavy for his loss and the suffering upon him. My apologies. No disrespect intended."

Poseidon egged her on with that smirk of his. Why the Almighty didn't keep that dog chained in the courtyard was beyond her.

"And now I present to all of you each district's champion. First, my brother, Poseidon, whose throne city, Atlantis, is a sight worthy of envy."

Poseidon leapt from Zeus's company and landed amongst the other contestants in the arena. "I haven't yet chosen the champion for my district. Perhaps all of you can help me with that?"

Angels chanted the name of the hulking Kratos, who was Zeus's bodyguard, never seen, but always watching. The loudest name chanted was Zeus's.

"I'm humbled by your faith in me," responded Zeus. "So be it, if the other competitors don't object, I shall participate." The other eleven, the likes of the slender Anubis, the big-eyed Tyr, the blue-skinned and six-armed Kali, the mammoth Quetzalcoatl, and the rest, all nodded with approval. And of course, Poseidon agreed. "So be it, I enter as the twelfth and final competitor."

"Not the last," Athena bellowed, standing up amongst the spectators. "That will be my honour."

Zeus stood up from his throne. "What district do you represent?" He chuckled. "Ah yes, the Forbidden Zone. I don't object and I'm sure the dragons would be proud to have you represent them."

"I represent my father's district."

"What?"

"He cannot be here to defend his name. You imply he was a coward. I, being his daughter, have the right to represent him."

"Fine, Athena. You may stand in for the . . . Inferno District. If the others allow it."

At first, silence, whisperings among mortal and immortals, then angels and humans alike chanted her name, and it grew, until the entire coliseum roared her name. The competitors nodded in agreement and welcomed her down, much to the chagrin of Zeus who crouched, then sprung to the air, landing amongst the other competitors, shaking hands, patting some on the back, always politicking.

"Come now, Athena," Zeus shouted. "Why must you drag out your entrance by walking down through the crowd?"

"So you might all linger on your coming defeat."

Dragon Fire

Lucifer

L ucifer had considered Persephone a spy for her grandfather, Cronus, perhaps even an assassin. The family was tight like that. It was no secret Cronus wanted the throne. Lucifer received enough images and feelings from him to conclude that. However, he never sensed any feelings of deceit coming from Persephone. Though her gift was the blocking out of any intrusions, she allowed Lucifer to read her emotions. A genuine warmness was all he got from her. The only image he ever got from Persephone was her denouncing the banishment of Lilith, Lucifer, and Calliope with Lucifer's father waving her biting truths away. Angered that no one took her seriously, she slapped her king with everything she had. Imagine that. Such courage.

"I must confess, Persephone." Lucifer slowly walked with her beneath the canopy of dragon wings, part of their wedding ceremony. The lovers were partially nude with their wings armouring parts of their bodies. "I was sure you'd try to pull my heart from my chest while I slumbered, out of your devotion to Cronus, or your father."

The firebreathers attended without any coaxing needed. Lucifer finally connected with their minds. Still, he couldn't civilize them like he had the demons, but their latest leader had agreed to partake in the ceremonies with its best hunters as a gesture of thanks for raising Dragons Den for them so many years ago. It was a start.

"I understand, Lucifer. But I have no zeal for the ambitions of my bloodline. Now a confession from me. I've watched from the shadows as you walk into the dragon flame of every new dragon monarch. A curious thing."

They were confessing secrets as was the tradition. The end of the dragon-made tunnel neared. The dark orange and black of the sky could be faintly through the veiny dragon wings. A shooting star blazed over.

"You seem to know all my secrets already, Persephone."

"Why do you willingly walk into their flames? To show dominance?"

"Faith."

"Huh?"

"That they will see I'm not a threat and worthy of their respect."

They stopped at the end of the tunnel. The matriarch of the dragons stood on all fours, its head leaning into them, big orange eyes, smoke puffed from its nostrils.

"Hold my hand tight, Persephone, and show me how much faith you have in our love. I will never let any harm come to you, not even from dragon fire. Walk willingly with me into this wall of flames."

Persephone let go of his hand as the dragon exhaled its fire.

"I'll walk into these flames alone, knowing your love reaches further than physical touch."

A Good Ole Fashioned Spanking

Athena

Poseidon flipped Athena aside in a showdown of pankration, an ancient game among the Order involving muscle strength and boxing. Tap one's opponent out or obliterate their face. It was one of the favourites of Zeus and the rest of his line.

Poseidon tossed her aside again.

She landed on all fours; dust flying up. Zeus had just defeated the hulking Quetzalcoatl in an epic match of strength and wit that would be talked about for ages to come. The winner of this match would face Zeus. This was a submission match, not something easy to achieve against someone like Poseidon. It was tempting to let him win and watch the brothers pummel each other—and they would for the sake of their egos.

The other part of her scoffed at such an idea. That side of her was win at all cost, with honour, if possible.

Poseidon put up his fists, mocking her. "Come, Athena. Not so tough without a sword and shield, are you? Before this day's done, I'll spank you over my knee."

To be put in such a vulnerable and ridiculous position for all to see? That would not happen to her, no matter what. She sideswiped his boxing stance with a sweep of her leg, then punched him in the face. It hardly affected him physically; still, his expression shifted into anger. He came at her fast. He tried wrestling with her, but she avoided his attempt, sweeping his leg with everything she had and by the looks of it, she shattered bone. He winced and labored to remain upright. She jumped on his back, wrapping her arms around his massive neck, her legs interlocking just beneath his ribcage. She held on tight as he staggered while his knee healed.

"Off me, worm."

He tried to pry her loose. Grabbed her hair, yanked at it. It wasn't enough to get her to let go. It fact, it only strengthened her determination. The crowd booed at Poseidon's dirty tactics and began cheering for Athena. She could withstand his punches and whatever physicality he dealt her, but if he got a hold of her, she would not get away and the game would be over.

"I'll stomp you into submission." Poseidon tried to flip her off. "I can break you with enough time."

She leaned in and whispered, "You dumb brute, you're wearing yourself out. You're making this too easy."

Poseidon growled in such anger that the coliseum fell into silence. He jumped in the air and fell on his back, knocking the wind out of Athena, who gasped for breath but still clung tight. He tried getting back up, but she wiggled her body to counter his attempt. By the time he got onto all fours, he hardly had any breath and collapsed, passing out. One last exhale and she released him. The temptation to ram his face into the ground was there, but she would lose the favour of the crowd if she did that. On his back, she turned on her buttocks and spanked his rump once.

The crowd roared with laughter.

She looked up at Zeus resting in his throne, raking his bottom lip with his teeth. She motioned with her hand for him to come for his spanking.

Defective

Lucifer

"It will come." Lucifer clasped his arms around Persephone's waist as they looked down from their bedroom balcony into the growing Blaze City spreading from the mountain slopes of Crimson Peak and into the Plains of Woe. He had civilized the demons and more came by the day, moving in, becoming part of a bigger thing. It was something they had never had before.

Persephone stared over at Dragons Den. Two firebreathers fought for leadership. There was still much work to be done with them. Each generation became more curious about the angels, but none had yet allowed an angel to ride it, scorching any who tried. A day would come when angels and dragons would be one fighting force.

"I'm beyond maturity, Lucifer. No one has gone this long without showing at least one exceptional gift."

She was right. The longest before Persephone had been Aphrodite whose pheromones alone could make an army fall to its knees — or fight to the death for her hand in marriage. Aphrodite had been a few years past her maturity, whereas Persephone was thousands of years overdue. All she had was her immortality and hidden mind, a good gift to have, but not enough in her eyes.

"They whisper that you're crazy to have chosen me as your new wife. I'm defective, they say. What kind of younglings would I birth, they ask."

Lucifer turned Persephone to him.

"I don't care what others think. You've done more than any other with all their powers." He kissed her. "You've mended my broken heart."

Bullseye

Athena

Zeus had handily beaten her in pankration. She won the horse-drawn chariot race, a new addition to the Olympic Games for the humans' amusement. After it was all said and done, the tiebreaker was the throwing of a spear into a shooting target and getting as close to the bullseye as possible.

"They are on your side for now," Zeus said of the crowd of mortals and immortals looking down at them.

"Everyone" — he threw his arms up and down, urging the crowd — "cheer for my daughter. Against all odds, she has made it to the finals."

Athena glared at him for calling her his daughter as the crowd cheered her name. Anger almost got the better of her. But of course, that was his intent, to throw her off her game. Nice try.

Zeus held the spear up in perfect form, waiting for the nod to throw it from his son, Hermes, the fastest angel alive. When given, he released it with pure poetry of motion. It hit the bullseye.

"Perfectly centered!" Hermes shouted.

The crowd went silent.

"What's wrong, daughter? You have a sour look. Does your *coming defeat* taste so bitter?"

Athena pulled out the spear stuck in the ground next to her. Glaring up at Zeus, she held the spear up and before Hermes could yank Zeus's out, she whipped hers forwards, splitting Zeus's in half.

"I'm not your daughter," she shouted over the applause and cheers of the crowd.

A Bloodline Further Severed

Lucifer

"Calliope," Lucifer said, as she landed before the thrones. Persephone sat at his side. "Where have you been? I've sent many search parties out for you."

"Calliope thinks Brother is a little too protective." She had rid herself of the rock armour and now donned something lighter. "Who is this? Where's Lilith?"

The mention of Lilith stung his heart.

"She has been murdered by our father."

Anger resurfaced in him until the warm touch of Persephone's hand clasped over his.

"Father was here? He killed Lilith? And what of him?"

"He cowardly left."

"He'll pay for this." Calliope glared at Persephone. "But you replace Lilith with *that*?"

The way Calliope spoke those words, in such an arrogant way, it sounded as if she thought Persephone was garbage. Persephone's warm grip softened, like she was ready to fly off in shame. He grasped her hand firmly.

"You speak personally, like you're inside her head."

"There's not much in there, hardly any depth, unless she's blocking Calliope from seeing her true intentions."

"Mind your mouth, Calliope."

"She's up to no good. She's a product of Zeus's loins. That alone should be enough for you to shun her, yet you marry this filth and insult the memory of Lilith. Their bloodline can't be trusted, now they have one foot in the door thanks to your naivety."

"Enough!"

"She's right, Lucifer," remarked Persephone.

"What do you mean she's right?"

"I am the daughter of your enemy."

"Zeus's hate for me has nothing to do with you."

"I'm useless, no special abilities to complement yours."

"Calliope has had enough of the pity party. She's pulling at your heartstrings like only a female can."

Lucifer only felt sadness coming from Persephone, and fear born from the prospect of losing him. That would not happen. He squeezed her hand tighter.

"If you continue attacking her character, then it's best you return to wherever you've been."

"Calliope comes with great news, to be shared only once this treacherous thing is carved from your life." Calliope withdrew her sword. "By force or willingly leaves. She's unworthy to be sitting in Lilith's place."

"Calliope!"

"This thing will not stain our bloodline."

"Tame your sword now."

"The one beneath my feet would be a more suitable mate than that beastly thing."

She could even sense Medusa buried far beneath, protected from the magma in a coffin of stone. What other abilities was she hiding?

"I said lower your sword," Lucifer repeated.

The anger coming from Calliope was overwhelming. Those feelings coming off her were genuine. Her madness, her distrust for anything or anybody had grown to insane proportions.

Lucifer stood up and withdrew his sword, slowly, hoping before its tip showed, Calliope would have retired hers. That didn't happen.

"You choose her over your sister?"

"Respect my decision and I'll forget this. You're in shock from the loss of Lilith and the news of me having a new wife. I understand. A lot of things have changed since you've been gone." He motioned at the

Forbidden Gardens way down there, standing out in all its breathtaking colours. Apple trees had grown taller than the stone wall. "Save your anger for our father."

"You blind fool, Calliope's protecting you. I'm all you have here."

"You will not harm her."

"You would strike Calliope down for that thing?"

"Stop pushing."

Tears ran down Calliope's face. "All you males are alike. Traitorous. Stupid. Blind. Calliope will never let another male betray her." She pointed her sword at Lucifer. "Guard her well. If Calliope comes across her, Calliope will show her pain unimaginable."

"You're not thinking straight, Calliope. I can help you."

Calliope's wings unfurled. The demons scattered from her wake holding their heads, whining. Whatever she was doing to them dropped them to their knees.

"Don't try to find me." She sheathed her sword. "Don't send anyone after me. They won't be coming back if you do."

Such threats by angels were once considered grandstanding. These days when an angel uttered them, Lucifer took it seriously.

Calliope flew towards the Forbidden Gardens and dropped from sight. After a time, she reappeared, swooping over, tears dropping from her face, landing next to Lucifer's throne where from the ash, sprouted a red lily. She bolted towards Dragons Den, veering from it, but not before all the dragons dove from their ledges and followed her like she willed them to do so. Then they dispersed, as if she released them, sending a message to Lucifer.

There was no coming back from this. The sister he loved was dead, replaced by this unpredictable, hateful thing that could turn on an ally at the mere paranoia of betrayal. Lilith had warned of this day from one of her visions. The scent of lily filled the area.

Lucifer bowed his head in sadness until the warmth of Persephone's hand squeezed his.

A History of the World in the Clouds

Athena

The powerful gust from Zeus's wings ruffled Athena's hair and chilled her neck. She had turned her back to him at his landing.

"You purposely embarrassed me in front of everyone. Face me."

She didn't turn to him. She had been waiting on the edge of Mount Olympus, marveling at the beautiful effect the sun had on the columns of the pantheon, like a king's sparkling gold crown. The higher clouds were odd shapes that resembled parts of the blue planet and were believed by the humans to be telling the history of the planet through sky pictograms. A unique new cloud was added with each deserving new event or living thing. It would be something the Almighty Ego would do. She smiled at the thought of seeing her likeness someday up there.

"For now you're their champion. Enjoy it while it lasts. Their memories are short."

"I don't care about their praises."

"Then what do you want? Power? A district of your own to rule? Are you coming to collect for the years I wasn't your father? Is that what this is about? A cherub's bitter revenge against her selfish father? Fine, I shall carve a section of my district for you to rule over in your image."

Athena looked down at the lower clouds that had no imagination to them.

"I don't seek a throne." Her wings spread out. "But I will enjoy the day you're knocked from yours."

She dropped into the coolness of clouds, what a heavenly feeling.

Chaos Bringer

Hera

Five centuries had passed since Hera and Zeus and the rest were assigned here. New younglings had been born on this planet. New marriages had been forged. Poseidon had slayed a giant dragon of unbelievable size that had escaped the Forbidden Zone, but not by his hand, by laser technology the angels and humans created to protect Atlantis from giant sea creatures and whatever else might come their way. It was only in Poseidon's district where humans were encouraged to advance in such ways. Around the rest of the globe, the humans were treated like children, enlightened on trivial things, nothing more, as the Almighty had wanted. The problem with that was Hera had predicted — though Zeus took credit — after centuries of this kind of treatment, the humans now worshipped the angels as gods.

Hera sat next to Zeus in the coliseum, the shadow of Mount Olympus hanging over them. It was here they would meet with the highest-ranking mortals of each village in this district and listen to their concerns. It was also here where the Olympic Games had taken place since the inaugural one in honour of Lilith. They were presently waiting for expected company in nothing more than colourful tunics. His was a swirl of a black and red. Hers was a swirl of green and blue. They had just recently remarried after centuries of separation. Hera did it for the status, rather than love this time around, but she still had strong feelings for Zeus. He wanted to make his house stronger with the reunification of their families and she liked the perks that came from such an amalgamation.

They loved each other in their own manner, but Zeus's brand of devotion had its good and bad side, and the bad stung deeply, compelling Hera to seek revenge. Not physically. She would get him where it hurt. He had been biding his time ever since the harsh banishment of his brother, Hades. The indignity he had felt for not trying to physically intervene was nothing compared to what Hera had in store for him. Zeus woke many times screaming his dead brother's name and she would shush him back to sleep, playing the part of a supportive partner. Just now he vented about how stupidly he just stood there, not reacting quickly enough. Starting today, he would begin amending that wrong, according to him.

"That look," the grey-haired and bushy-bearded Zeus said to Hera. "His burnt face haunts me, pushing me in the only direction I can go. Imagine the kind of heat needed to burn him. I shudder at the thought."

"What you've done is appalling." Hera's seldom rivaled beauty had both sexes sneaking looks her way. She was mid-thirties in looks when compared to the humans.

"You're free to interact with them too," Zeus said. "Your jealousy would not have been matched by mine. I would have encouraged such interaction."

"Is that what you call it? Nothing personal, just business, right?" She leaned forwards and let out an exaggerated laugh. Her curly hair fell into her eyes and swung away as she sat back up. "I wouldn't accept their inferior seed and you know that."

"There they are now." Zeus was a proud-looking father. It sickened her. He would rue the day. She would get the last laugh.

A legion of Nephilim marched into the arena in full battle gear. Their facial helmets were patterned with various creatures like the wings of an eagle along the top, and its beak bending over between their eyes, while others had ornate dragon scales. Some bore monster faces from the myths of their tribes.

"And why are these abominations here?"

Though their relationship wasn't the most intimate, the fact that these abominations standing below her existed mortified her. It couldn't get out who they were. As far as everyone was concerned, they were an army of the best warriors the mortals had to offer.

"They're here because I want you to meet them. They're ripe for knowledge. My intent all along was to train them in my art of battle."

"They're a constant reminder of your infidelity to me."

"The female humans were nothing more than vessels for my seeded army. I didn't do this behind your back."

"An inferior army." Hera sat back, crossing her legs. "And you did it without my blessing."

"Inferior? That would apply to most angels mating with the humans, my dear." He leaned over the arm of his throne closest to hers. "A secret not shared until now — our immortality is passed on to what you'd consider inferior beings. They're blessed with many of my strengths and abilities, and a few pleasant surprises. They only need my nurturing, my wisdom, my — "

"Your blind ambition, too, Husband?"

"What do you mean?"

"What if they turn on you?"

He said nothing.

She continued, "Your heart desires dominion over everything our Lord has created. And this is your plan? He knows everything. He knew you would do this before you even existed. He—"

"He knows only what is set before his eyes. He's no better than us." Zeus glared at her. It was easy pushing his buttons. "He can't see the future of everything and everybody. All he has on us is experience due to existing for much longer than us. What may seem new to us, is an old idea to him, that's why he appears all knowing. But some things are still new to him. He didn't see Cthulhu coming and he didn't see Lucifer turning on him at that moment. I saw the rage in his eyes after he banished Lucifer to Hell. Do you think someone knowing everything, including the future, would show such emotion?"

"You're right." Hera humored him, or else there would be thunderbolts exploding all over the place from his own brand of juvenile rage. "No doubt he has seen such deception many times before and is expecting you to be the one who comes knocking. You're wasting your time. Enjoy the position he has given you. You're the king of all districts here, the leader of the Council of Twelve on this planet. Even Poseidon was freed to appease you. Why isn't this enough?"

She liked her present status. She didn't want to lose it because of her husband's lust for unobtainable power. She appreciated his ambition, it was part of the attraction to him many eons ago, but this was too much. He was playing his own kind of god and it was going to explode in his face.

"The universe is a mess, Hera. Does it seem to have been created by a sane mind?"

"It exists as it does," Hera said, "to cut all of us with sharp lessons that the strongest heal from, becoming greater beings of enlightenment. Imagine a place where everything was perfect, where there was no chaos. What lessons are to be learnt from such an easy journey?"

"Well, my dear" — Zeus grinned — "I'm about to bring the chaos."

Best Behaviour

Aphrodite

Aphrodite exited the portal and landed into a strut. Every week angels came back to refresh themselves from assignments. Today however, she was not one of those vacationers. She had been called back from District 1 for a distinct reason and she knew exactly why. Big Cranky didn't miss much, but she suspected it was because of spies, not because of his omniscient mind.

The other arriving angels took to the skies and headed in the direction of Rainbow Ridge or to one of the many botanical gardens. That left the glorious Michael in plain view, her reflection growing clearer in his sparkling armour at his approach. She bedded a lot of angels and they all had a special place in her memories, but one of Michael's stature, of his purity, she had never dated. And never dared try, believing it would take more effort and time than she was willing to give. But she had been around awhile and settling down with someone worthy of her affection was in the wind. A youngling or two would be nice and to be the mother of Michael's firstborn had a nice ring to it. It might even be scandalous to some.

"Michael. Warrior Michael. It's an honour having you greet my arrival. Shall we?"

She held up her dainty-looking hand. one that packed a punch, as many aggressive males had found out. Aphrodite chose her mates, not the other way around. And her sexuality was her knockout punch, her heart-thumper, her hook-line-sinker. But this guy, he wasn't that easy, making him that much more desirable. To use her pheromones would be cheating. Aphrodite would reel him in with no tricks. Well, none of the magical kind, at least. She smirked at that.

Michael kept his helmet to his side and walked with her.

"Must you be like a rock at all times?"

"I'm here to escort you to the Hanging Gardens."

"No throne talk? I'm disappointed. I was hoping Big Cranky would spank me over his knee." She winked.

"You should take him more seriously. He's not so kind with clemency these days."

"That's an understatement. Hell is shouting back, no shit."

"Do try not to profane so much in his presence. You know how he hates that."

"Of course, Michael." Her virgin-white wings spread out, their black edges looking like they had been dipped in ink. "Anything for you. I'll be on my best behaviour." She gave him another exaggerated wink. "I promise."

Similar Arrogance

Hera

"The sight of them haunts me with your infidelity," Hera said. She sat in her throne, in her tunic coloured in swirls of summer hot days, as Zeus's fully armoured legion of Nephilim marched into the coliseum at her request.

"They're a necessary plot twist to his ending." Zeus was referring to his planned defeat of the Almighty, Hera guessed, although Zeus had made it clear he would first unchain Hades from the Inferno and get the Big Guy's attention.

Zeus stood up from his throne. "And where's my favourite son?"

The Nephilim stood silent.

Hera remained seated. "You offend them, Zeus." The Nephilim acknowledged Hera with a gentle bow of their heads. "Picking favourites always leads to jealousy and betrayal and great wars. A different approach is needed."

The shadow of Mount Olympus darkened the area, covering one third of the district this time of day.

"Where is your leader?" she continued. "The one chosen without proving himself, unless of course" — she looked up at Zeus — "drinking oneself to a stupor and bedding every harlot in this district is proof of greatness. Your chosen one seems like a chip off the old block."

"You speak too soon." Zeus sat back down.

A mountain of muscle swaggered in. He hardly wore armour, and what he did wear was treated like decoration — spiked elbow and knee pads, foul-smelling moccasins, a leather loincloth barely covering his bulge. A war axe hung from one hand while he chewed on a meat drumstick held in the other. He was barbaric. But there was also intelligence in him, more than he was letting on.

"Hercules," Zeus said, "why are you not properly dressed for this affair? My wife has requested this meeting, the least you could have done was dress accordingly. And after she's finished, I have some things to discuss with you."

"Father," Hercules said, looking up. His long hair traced the contours of his muscles. "We are of your bloodline. We're immortal and in no need of armour. Mortals cannot harm us."

"His arrogance reminds me of somebody." Hera rolled her eyes.

"Enough." Zeus glared at her. "His attitude complements his immense strength. It rivals almost everyone in our Order."

"Are you saying he's as mighty as one of us?" Hera asked. "This scandal before us? Not one of them has wings. They're immortal prisoners on this planet if we don't carry them from here to there. They're eternal babes, hardly a force to take down him." She was referring to the Almighty. "And this" — she motioned at Hercules — "the embodiment of your strength, that's it. He can smash mountains. Clap air to blow over trees and buildings. Pound cracks into the ground that swallow up cities. He could be formidable, but there's nothing up there in that head of his. He's —"

"I'm not an idiot" — Hercules tore into the drumstick — "I just don't care about all of this. I walked in last, following my sisters and brothers because I'm no better than them." He looked up at Hera: "Just like your *kind* is no better than us."

Hera sat up from her slouch. "Are you going to stand for this arrogance?" she demanded of Zeus.

"It amuses me," Zeus said, "to see you so annoyed by what you consider *an eternal babe.*"

He leaned towards his wife, smirking.

"You see, my dear . . ." Zeus tried to hold her hand. She pulled away from the armrest. "What you see as egotism, I see as confidence."

"Many in your precious new army can produce thunderbolts. Some can raise the dead. Others can open the fabric of time, seeing minutes ahead, or reaching back into the near past. One can open portals, though lacking the knowledge of specific coordinates, having them reach no more than a radius of a mile but it's still a useful tool under the right leadership. Yet you choose that big lug as their leader?"

"I have my reasons."

"Then let him prove himself."

"Don't push it, Hera."

"A challenge," Hera shouted down at Hercules. "Twelve tasks that you must finish. You may even choose one brother or sister to accompany you on each task."

"I need no one's help." Hercules smirked at her in such a way she wanted to punch it into nonexistence. "I will crush any obstacle. Even you." He pointed at Hera with his war axe.

"He holds that axe up with honour." Hera barely looked at Zeus. "Like it's something he earned, unbreakable steel bestowed upon a babe." She looked back down at Hercules. "Finish the twelve labors and then we'll dance."

"I did not sanction this." Zeus pounded his fists on the armrests of his throne.

"Father, I'm not afraid," said Hercules. "I accept her challenge. And I promise you, after the twelve labors I will put her in her place and spank her over my knee. The embarrassment of it will stain her reputation forever. Losing to an inferior immortal and spanked by one. Imagine the *scandal*."

He gnawed into the drumstick.

"When I'm done with you" — Hera smirked — "you won't even be able to spank your — "

"No need for vulgarity, my dear." Zeus patted her hand.

The Temptress

Aphrodite

Michael followed behind the Almighty and Aphrodite in the Hanging Gardens. She didn't come here much because she never wanted to leave. Why couldn't everything be this beautiful all the time?

She looked back at Michael. Those eyes of his. Were the most masculine, the most dangerous. Aphrodite wanted to conquer them at the sight of her smile. And she would. She flirted with suggestive eyes and a playful smirk, the kind a warrior would like. On the way here, he had mentioned how different she was since her days of being his protégé. Being forced into marriage with her half-brother, Hephaestus, put things in perspective, and those rumours of her infidelity were started by jealous competition.

"How could I not grant the man his wish?" Aphrodite said to the Almighty, sometimes looking back over her shoulder at Michael.

"Rules are rules," their Lord said. "You must kill your creation. Michael will accompany you."

"What kind of punishment is this?"

"You misused your gift. Instead of discouraging a mortal from making a temple to you, from adorning his land with statues of your likeness, from praising you as a goddess, you awarded him by bringing one of the statues in your image to life."

"It was the most realistic depiction of me ever made, so lifelike it felt like it was desperate to breathe, in hellish limbo between inanimate unreal and living. Such art deserved appreciation only an angel can give. Think of it, the only mortal to sleep with an image of me. I would've slept with him myself, but your rules forbid such interactions. Speaking of laws, I don't recall one forbidding bringing statues to life?"

"There are rules against being worshipped as a god. End your creation. Then return with Michael."

"Please, don't have me do this. I'm not a killer."

She wasn't. It was why she had quit on Michael many centuries ago, during her first mission to wipe out an army of mortals who were genociding the rest of the planet's population. At first, she had been all for avenging the deaths of the innocent. The sight of the carnage enraged her, to think such beings out there could be so wicked to their own kind. She felt her first bloodlust, the scent of mortal blood was intoxicating, she had never felt such a mind fuck. Pain for them, pleasure for her. But once she came down from that high, the gruesome sight of what she had taken part in, all those dead at her hands, reminded her who she wasn't.

"Please don't make me do it." She stood in front of the Almighty. She couldn't risk awakening that hunger, that addiction again.

"For someone who has killed the hearts of many"—he leaned back into his throne—"this shouldn't be a problem."

The Hydra

Hercules

Hercules wasn't dumb. He just saw no point in most of the things angels and humans did. He agreed with his father's philosophy that, regardless of ability or creed, all were cut from the same energy, that some were more blessed than others, nothing more, nothing less. But then his father had to go all hypocritical with his desire to become the Supreme Being of all life. The other thing Hercules had inherited from his father was his super ego, and if challenged, he would prove the doubters wrong no matter what it took.

"Thank you for the gift, Mother," Hercules said to Hera who hated it when he called her that. He stood within the coliseum with the rest of the Nephilim standing at attention behind him. He donned the golden hide of the Nemean Lion, its skin impregnable to most weapons wielded by mortal or immortal. He had knocked it out with one punch, and cut the lion's skin away with its own claws. The upper part of its head, still attached to the hide, functioned as Hercules's new helmet, the lion's two front fangs resting on his forehead.

"These tasks are tiresome." Hercules stood in the coliseum arena waiting for the next challenge. Hera and Zeus sat within their exaggerated thrones. He had already completed ten of the labors. Some were pointless, like cleaning out the filth of a cattle stable, which was supposed to humble him, but instead, he out-thought Hera and with a few pounds of a fist on solid ground, created a brief detour for a river that washed out the stable for him. Without a doubt, resisting the sexual whims of nymphs was his most challenging task so far.

"You're still as arrogant as ever," Hera said, in glistening black armour with spiked elbow and shoulder pads worn only during battle. It was a clear message to Hercules, a fight he welcomed.

"You're inflating my ego, Mother, with these lame tasks." Hercules crossed his arms over his meaty chest. "Not grounding it. Maybe we should do battle and forget the remaining two tasks."

"Insolent—"

Hera jumped from her throne and before Zeus could pull her back, she dove at Hercules with her wings spreading out. She snatched at Hercules and before he could swat her with his club or free fist, her touch weakened him. She carried him to the clouds, then dropped him, but not before yanking his lion armour from him. He cursed her all the way down. She followed him just out of reach of his club-swings. He landed hard on a field of tall grass, sending dirt flying up.

Hera landed next to him. Her wings wrapped around parts of her body like a second armour. She tossed his lion armour at him, grinning.

"How's that for grounding your ego?" she said. "Your next task is to cut the nine heads from the Lernaean Hydra."

"Never heard of it." Hercules tossed the lion armour aside and pushed himself to his knees, leaning over his firmly planted spiked club in nothing but his loincloth. The coliseum was far away in the horizon, dwarfed by Mount Olympus and the mountain range running along it like a sleeping dragon.

Zeus landed next to her.

"That's because I just created it."

Hera's greatest gift was the creating of magical beings from anything.

Hercules staggered to his feet; dirt fell from him in sheets. There, from a distance, he spied the sparkle of the Nephilim marching in fast.

The ground rumbled behind him. He turned to see a mountain of clay burst bruise out of the wheat field. Hercules stood his ground, the scent of earth and fish heavy in the air. Nine serpent heads sprouted from the lump of clay, muscular legs took shape, tormented faces pushed out of it, then sank from view, appearing in other areas of its massive frame. Colour spread throughout it, a greenish blue with streaks of blood red. It was an opposing height. The way its fanged mouths opened in anticipation of tearing his flesh away gave Hercules pause for thought.

"You defeat it when all heads are cut off and none grow back. Once severed, a head grows back in seconds. So be quick with it."

"What?" Zeus said, standing ahead of Hercules. "An impossible task."

"Losing faith in your number one son?" Hera sashayed toward her new creation.

The nine heads shuffled in their own directions, venom dripping in long thread from their fangs.

"And how will he do that?" Zeus asked.

The neck of one head gently slithered around Hera as she turned back to Zeus and Hercules.

"With their help," Hera pointed at the Nephilim stomping into the field fully armoured.

They ignored Hercules when he halted them with his hand, only stopping when Hera raised hers. He had to earn their allegiance. Fair enough.

"I feel generous," she continued. "Pick eight to assist you, there's no shame—"

"I will do it myself, Mother."

"If you call me *Mother* one more time . . ." Hera scowled, filling Hercules with much amusement. "I will—"

"There's no way you can do this task on your own." Zeus looked at him with fatherly eyes. "Accept her offer and choose your eight best."

"I got this, Father."

Besides, he needed to prove to the Nephilim that he was a worthy warrior to lead them.

"That's his weakness," Hera said, kissing one of the heads of the hydra.

"My weakness?" Hercules said.

Hera kissed each of the serpent heads in turn. "How can you lead an army"—Hera looked back at him—"when you refuse to acknowledge their strengths?"

She waved Hercules away and motioned at the white-haired Nephilim. "These ones can create thunderbolts that can be thrown simultaneously to cut the hydra's heads off. And these," she said of the red-haired ones, "can incinerate the hydra stumps, slowing down the heads from growing back. And this one can—"

"Fine," Hercules said, walking up to one of his Nephilim brethren. "Assist me by lending me your sword." The blond-haired Nephilim reluctantly did so. "All of you stay back. As your leader, I will lead by example."

He confronted the hydra.

It stood up on its hind legs and each of its heads let out a bloodcurdling screech, not in sync. It dropped to all fours and the ground shook. One head snapped at him. He leaned back, avoiding its fangs, and with one clean sweep its severed head bounced on the ground, blood spraying all over Hercules as the stumped neck snapped lifted away.

"The taste of inevitable victory!" he shouted at Hera, dodging another set of teeth, cutting that head away only to see the first stump open into yellow eyes, then a mouth open up into crooked fangs. It shot out into full view and came down at Hercules, who cut it away again.

"Stubborn," Hera shouted back.

The hydra tried to stomp at Hercules with one of its elephant-like feet. He caught it, pressing it away long enough to step back as it stamped the ground. Dust flew up.

"An entire army awaits your command," Hera said. "Yet—"

"Oh, shut up!" Hercules shouted.

He ran at the hydra, ramming himself into its huge frame, knocking it over on its side. The monster started to push itself back up. Hercules positioned himself to the side of it.

"Why will you not humble yourself?" Hera said. "There's no shame in—"

"How do you do it, Father?" Hercules hollered, waiting for the hydra to lean forwards to push itself back up. "It is a wonder you've not gone mad from her continual harping."

One foot punched the ground, sending dirt and grass upwards. It started pushing itself up with the side of its belly still to Hercules, its clumsy movements leading to all its heads slightly leaning forward. He twirled, then released the sword at the greatest momentum.

It cut through all nine heads in less than three seconds.

The hydra fell dead at his feet.

"And the last task, Mother?" Hercules kicked one of the decapitated heads Hera's way.

APHRODITE

JAMES PYNE

One Clean Swipe

Aphrodite

In black rose armour, clasping her sheathed sword, Aphrodite approached Pygmalion's humble home as if approaching death. Michael walked at her side.

"They are to be destroyed too," Michael said of the statues of her likeness within the yard of rose bushes and apple trees.

She said nothing.

Michael wasn't as cold-hearted as he acted. Those eyes of his sometimes watered, however lightly, when tragedy came upon someone he cared about. She saw his glistening eyes when Lucifer was dragged into Hell. It pained Michael inside, not that he would admit it. And the state he had been in when returning with the unthinkable news of Lilith's death . . . His walk was not in rhythm with his usual march. When someone shouted, "What about the death of Himeros and Pothos?" he shouted back, walking more steadily, "They deserve unmarked graves."

She knocked on the wooden door of the humble dwelling. The eaves of the thatched roof dripped water from recent rainfall. The door creaked open. The middle-aged Pygmalion beamed at the sight of Aphrodite.

"Aphrodite, I'm glad to see you." His expression soured when seeing Michael. "What brings you this way?"

"I've made a mistake and must fix things," Aphrodite replied.

"What have you come to do?"

"I shouldn't have done what I did, Pygmalion."

His eyes widened. "No, she's mine. She's pregnant. You can't."

This surprised Aphrodite. She didn't know her creations could reproduce. That meant she had stolen a spark from the Lake of Souls. In the end, it didn't matter. It ended today.

"I'm sorry, Pygmalion, I have no choice."

"Galatea, run!"

"What's wrong, Pygmalion?" his wife asked from within the house.

The likeness of Aphrodite hurried into sight wearing a virgin white gown.

"Run, do what I say."

Aphrodite brushed by Pygmalion, who tried to pull her back. She shrugged him aside. She looked into her own eyes, frightened, mortal. So this was the expression Aphrodite would wear if facing death. Humbling. It was wrong to do this. She also didn't feel like a one-way ride to Hell or whatever punishment the Almighty had in mind. Galatea's eyes were full of life, full of fear for her unborn child.

"It's like killing myself."

Aphrodite pulled her sword out, seeing her reflection in those terrified eyes.

"But you gave me life." Galatea held her stomach. "I'm with child."

"I'm a monster, Michael, no better than our king."

Aphrodite beheaded Galatea with the quickest swing possible. Blood splashed onto her armour and face, and she wiped it away before it wormed into her mouth. The strong metallic scent of human blood flared her nose, tempting her. She turned as Pygmalion fell to his knees in front of his dead wife.

"I hate you," Pygmalion shouted in a pitiful cry, pulling Galatea into his arms. "Damn your kind to Hell."

"Good," Aphrodite said. "Spread the word, we're not to be worshipped. It's for your own good. It can only end in tragedy."

She turned back to Michael.

"Why do you hold it in, Michael?" Aphrodite got in his face. "It's in your eyes. There's emotion in them. Let it out! Speak your mind. Ask yourself, why did that move you? How many have you erased from life, yet this small moment has stirred you?" She turned away from him. "What a monstrous ego. How can you follow such lunacy? How can you enforce every commandment without an iota of doubt?"

Pygmalion wailed in grief behind her as she sheathed her sword, and said, "I'll get your blood boiling, Michael. I'll get emotion out of you yet like only Aphrodite can."

Cerberus

The Nephilim

ercules had defied her at every turn. No matter what challenge she put in front of him, he did things his way, and never how she imagined each challenge playing out. Regardless, the end-result was as she had expected. It led them to this point. The thing annoying her the most was Zeus ribbing her every chance he got. That would change after the bombshell she was about to drop.

Zeus was presently unamused as he and Hera stood before the foot of Mount Olympus. The Nephilim behind them, in full military gear, stood at attention. Angels not interacting with the humans today watched from the big, orangish-red rocks of the area. Word had gotten out about the challenge. Just like Hera hoped.

Their son, Ares, watched with great anticipation. Neglected by Zeus over the years, he was quite jealous of his father's love for Hercules, a halfling of all things, garnering so much fatherly affection. And there, all by himself, his face the colour of dark tea, was a disinterested Hercules sitting on a molar-shaped boulder in full body armour.

"Not this," Zeus said. He also wore his armour, his hair avalanching into his curly beard. "He's not ready. And with so many watching. How did they all find out?"

Hera smirked over the fact that she had encouraged Ares to tell all his friends. "It was you who gave me creative control, Zeus. Well, I want an audience for this."

One thing about Zeus, he was true to his word. To a fault, which was why he seldom gave it.

"Anything but this." Zeus turned away from Mount Olympus. "With so many watching. They'll figure out that they're immortal."

"You're afraid he will be utterly defeated, that's the real worry here." Hera smirked at Zeus, who briefly glared at her, then looked up at the sky for answers. "Or is it because you're afraid he'll succeed where you have failed?" She folded her arms, grinning. "Where you've failed so many times."

"You provoke me." Zeus's fists turned blood red, with sparkles of lightning forming.

"And you cheated on me, no matter how you spin it."

His fists softened back into a bronze tan. "I'll treat this as a test run then. It will give Hercules and the rest a taste of what they will have to face in the battlefield against our kind, if such a day comes." He looked over at the Nephilim, lowering his voice. "It doesn't humour me that you chose this as his final challenge. You're trying to embarrass me, to steal the thunder from my —"

"It humours me that you brag up Hercules so much until now."

"They'll figure out that he and the others aren't mortals."

"So that's your fear."

Zeus had told everyone the Nephilim were the best mortal warriors in the district that he was taking under his wing. Ares had rolled his eyes at that.

"Get it over with," Zeus said, leaning against the boulder Hercules was sitting on.

"Not even a 'good luck,' *Father?*"

"Lower your voice."

"Despite this shame to declare me as your son, I won't fail where others have."

The look Zeus glared at Hercules was one Hera knew well—he wanted to send his son flying to the moon with one solid uppercut.

There were three known ways into Hell. The first was a one-way ticket by the Almighty's wrath, but burning alive in the Inferno's throat wasn't appealing to most. The second was via the portal master, Hephaestus, who wouldn't dare defy the Almighty and wasn't much of a fan of his father, Zeus, anyway. So that left one other known way: challenge Cerberus to a fight. It was a recent option for those who wanted an opportunity to free a loved one. However, only one angel could be liberated at a time.

"Cerberus!" Hera shouted at the base of the mountain. She unsheathed her dagger and sliced the palm of her hand. "I bring forth your challenger, Hercules." She smudged her bloody handprint on the rock and backed off. "Open up to us, mighty Cerberus."

The ground rumbled. A sudden wind blew orange dust everywhere. The shaking of Mount Olympus led to more angels flying down out of curiosity. Everybody loved watching a match against Cerberus. The bottom of the mountain cracked, then opened into a tunnel of pink and red walls, wet like the inside of a throat. At the back, giant cathedral doors resembled tonsils. The cathedral doors would only open at the request of the victor over Cerberus. So far, those doors have remained shut since their creation.

Hera sashayed towards Zeus, still leaning against the boulder next to Hercules. She leaned at the opposite side of her husband and smiled up at Hercules, who was still chilling on the boulder like none of this was a big deal.

"You must defeat Cerberus whatever way you can," Hera said. "My advice? Swallow your pride and enlist help from your—"

"I need no help against —"

A hulking, ominous Cerberus pushed out of the living wall of pinkish-red, stretches of the wall's flesh snapped from his body. He stood bare-chested in a golden skirt, his bronze-muscular skin glinted from sweat, lava-eyes within a face shaded by sweat-drenched hair hanging just past his shoulders. Cerberus was known as the dog of war for his tenacity in battle and his ability to morph into a canine-faced menace. A devout follower of the Almighty, he never left his post, though he could if he wanted to. There was, however, a catch to that: he would lose his virtual invincibility and he really liked being indestructible. An addiction he just couldn't kick.

Cerberus's shadow stretched out into the sunlit ground and stopped at the boulder Hercules sat on. No angel lasted long with Cerberus. His touch drained an opponent's energy into submission in no time, though he preferred stretching a fight out for amusement's sake. Especially when it involved Zeus, one of his favourite dance partners. Angels had even tried ganging up on Cerberus with the same pitiful results.

"My advice," Hera said. "Don't mock him. He's a Shapeshifter. You don't want to meet that side of him . . . Does he Zeus?"

"Scary looking, is he?" Hercules rolled his eyes.

"Laugh if you will." His audacity was endless. "If he starts morphing into the dog-faced demon—run."

"You're telling me to run from a dog. You must be joking."

"Two other canine-faces will form within his chest that will tear away the flesh of his enemy while he bear hugs them, eventually putting them out of their misery by ripping away their throat with the teeth of his main head."

"Sounds excessive."

"My advice, Hercules," Zeus whispered. "Lure him onto the soil of our dimension, he will gradually weaken and be prime for—"

"No offense, Father." Hercules slid off the boulder landing between Zeus and Hera. "But how can I take your advice when you've lost to him how many times?"

The First Move

Aphrodite

Aphrodite unsheathed her sword and started cutting down the statues made in her image. How degrading making her do this.

"This is emotion, Michael." She hacked off a marble head. "This is anger." She kicked the statue over and stomped its chest, cracking it into pieces.

Michael stood there, hand resting on his sheathed sword, keeping his usual stoic nature. Whatever emotion tried seeping out, he buried it deep inside him.

"Maybe I'll bring them all to life and let them run off into the wilderness in spite of him."

"I wouldn't advise it."

She turned and shouted, "Stop being so serious! Stop taking everything literally."

"So much emotion. You've been around the humans too long. I'll help you destroy them if you like?"

"What a gentleman you are. How about helping me understand you?"

"I have no time for your mind games."

"You could be so much more. Greater than Lucifer." That bugged him. It was in his eyes. A tactic she would use against him during future arguments to throw him off track. "You've got to stop holding things in. You're rotting inside.

"You're stalling."

"Stalling for what, for you to grow a heart, to stop doing everything by the book? I don't care about these statues." She swatted one aside, and watched the pieces splay out at her feet. Another statue shouldered over. "I don't care about art made in my honour. Or temples built to garner my favourable attention. Or the stories the humans already tell their youth of me."

She sauntered towards Michael, kicking another statue down on her way.

"I've watched you grow into a juggernaut. I was sure you'd become something special—and you have—but there's so much more to you. I want you to experience a feeling you've never explored." She clasped his armoured waist with both hands.

He looked away, head down.

"I see how you look at me, Michael. Not like the others. You see me more than an object of desire. I've always appreciated that, but I didn't know what to do with it. Didn't want to take the time to explore that part of me with you. But I'm ready now. When you greeted me at the portal today, that same look was in your eyes."

"You're married to Hephaestus."

"For show. To keep him happy. My father's making up for how he treated Hephaestus during his youth. It's strictly platonic. I needed a break from dating. Hephaestus isn't functioning down there anyways."

"That's more than I need to know." A hint of annoyance was detectable in his voice. "Zeus just wants to stay on the good side of the only other portal maker."

"You're right, Michael, and I'm sick of being part of his game."

"Are you sure you're not playing with me now?"

"Take that back."

"Still two more over there." He motioned at the remaining statues.

"You cold bastard."

He smirked.

"You think it's funny." She turned with her sword in hand, only to have Pygmalion impale himself on it.

She gasped in horror. "Pygmalion, what have you done?"

"If I can't be with her in this life," Pygmalion said, his eyes softening, as if at peace. "Then I will be with her in the next."

He slipped from the sword and fell dead at Aphrodite's feet.

"A rare kind of love?" Michael said, with a look of confusion, staring down at Pygmalion's corpse. He looked at Aphrodite. "True love?"

"Yes, Michael." She placed a hand on one side of his face. "Finally, you see."

She would get emotion out of him, introduce him to a new world only she could unveil to him. She was Aphrodite. And she would have the most powerful warrior as her own.

CERBERUS VERSUS HERCULES

That Grin

Nephilim

"This isn't your fight, boy," Cerberus shouted at Hercules, hunched over within the living pink and red of the Inferno's mouth. "Let Zeus fall before me for the twentieth time so you all may see how great he really is. I want to hear him beg to be thrown back to his dominion just one more time."

"I will humble you!" Hercules shouted, glancing back at Zeus, who looked estranged by his failures being revealed to all present. He focused on Cerberus. "And you will kiss the feet of Zeus and beg him for your life when I'm done with you."

Cerberus waved Hercules away. "You're nothing but a few seasons old." He turned to the wall he had pushed out of, and his flesh started rejoining with it.

"You'll regret those words." Hercules jumped up into the stuffy heat of the tunnel, surprised to find the surface was spongy. "Turn and face me."

"You got fight, I'll give you that. Have it your way."

As Cerberus turned, Hercules tackled him with everything he had. Cerberus shrugged him aside. Hercules bounced off the fleshy wall that started pulling at his skin. He tore away from it.

Cerberus drove his sword between him and Hercules into the gummy surface. Cerberus's strength had Hercules rethinking his next move. Brute power wasn't going to work here, it was like slamming into a deeply rooted mountain, which was what others had remarked about Hercules. He pushed himself back up, wondering if Cerberus could take a punch straight on the nose?

"You can use my sword," Cerberus said. "All you have to do is get past me." He stepped in front of his blade. "It's the only thing that can maim or kill me inside my playroom."

Hercules took a swing at Cerberus's smug face, but Cerberus caught his fist, squeezing tight. Hercules squinted; never had he felt such pain before. He tried to punch Cerberus with the other hand, but he snared that attempt too.

"You're about to kneel before me, youngling," Cerberus said, the lava-glow of his eyes wide. "On your knees."

Hercules stood his ground even with the mighty force pushing down on him. The muscles in his arms and legs bulged and burned, his back felt like it was going to snap in half, but he refused to give in.

"I see Zeus defied the Almighty's decree and mated with a human." Cerberus looked past Hercules, who could well imagine the look on his father's face. "And all of them too." He nodded at the legion of Nephilim. "All of you are products of Zeus's lack of regard to the commandments."

Cerberus head-butted Hercules, almost knocking him out. Hercules held on, until Cerberus drained his energy from him and tossed him aside.

"No matter," Cerberus shouted at Zeus. "Anything inherited from you is gone from him. He's of mortal strength now, just like all of you who have challenged me." He grinned down at Hercules. "Should I end the heartbeat of this abomination?"

Hercules tried to crawl out of the tunnel, only to collapse. Outside, Zeus pushed off the boulder where Hera remained. Thunderbolts stretched from his fists.

Cerberus laughed. "He's not just a pawn. You do care for him." He picked up a disorientated Hercules and lifted him over his head. "I am bound by the Almighty's decree. I kill no angel, but this blasphemy is fair game. However, his grit has impressed me. You can have him back. Are we done?"

He tossed out Hercules who landed hard and rolled to the leather boots of the Nephilim. Hercules looked up at his fellow Nephilim, male and female warriors. They looked down at him, indifferent.

"Cerberus mocks our father." Hercules pushed himself up, his strength returning. "He mocks our bloodline. Mocks us. I have never asked to be your leader. But I ask you now, follow me in there and prove to our father, to Hera, to every other angel here today that we deserve their respect."

None answered. They just stared straight ahead.

"I know you don't like me. I know you're relishing this moment. Me, asking for help. One thing I do know, you all want to be part of a greater glory. There, it stands waiting. There, is where *legends* are born. Not one of us is better than the other. One army. One soul. What say you?"

They collectively stomped their war boots. Swords were drawn, shields raised into position.

"Let us free Hades for our patriarch and become worthy of joining the House of Zeus."

Hercules turned. He felt his immortal powers returning. Weaponless, he shouted a drawn-out war cry while leading the Nephilim into the Inferno's gaping mouth.

"It's their war, Zeus!" Hera shouted. "Stand down."

"Zeus is welcome to join in," Cerberus shouted over at Hera, before focusing back on Hercules. "You all have my word I will not morph into my beast form. Already it's an unfair advantage for me.

Cerberus retrieved Hercules's sword and rested it on his shoulder, motioning with his other hand for them to hurry up in such a mocking way that Hercules couldn't wait to punch that grin from his face.

The Good Soldier

Michael

Michael resented the fact that Aphrodite had seen him in this state. They were returning to the throne planet. He did his best to keep the walls up, something Lucifer had to destroy. The day Michael knew he and his teacher were going in separate directions had happened eons ago on a now barren planet by the hellish fury of Apollo. But in the olden days, this yellow and black planet was vibrant with life and it was where Michael saw for the first time how spiteful the Almighty could be towards his only son.

Lucifer and Michael stood on a ledge high up on a mountain. Below them, plumes of smoke streaked the sky like claw marks. The invaders were dragging out the slaughter of villagers, having their fun first.

"Ethnicity is all that separates them," Lucifer said of the invaders dragging the screaming females into huts while the males were gutted or beheaded. "Divine intervention is warranted. We are sworn to protect the innocent. Yet we watch without a qualm?"

"Your father's orders are to observe and report back. Nothing more."

"Doing nothing makes us murderers, too, Michael."

"We're bound by his commandments."

One of the killers held a bawling infant upside down by the leg and swung the baby against a tree.

Lucifer unsheathed his sword. "This is what I think of his commandments."

When the Almighty found out that Lucifer had massacred the entire mass of genocide bringers, there was a silent rage in those eyes. Michael knew something significant was about to happen. He expected punishment, too, for not stopping Lucifer. How could he go against his mentor? The angel who had taken him under his wings and made him the warrior he had become?

"Your interference with the planet's natural evolution has left me with no choice," the Lord said from his throne. "I must erase the stain you left. They worship you as their saviour. Their god. Their protector. Their civilization will revolve around the idea of you now. This cannot happen."

"You can't destroy an entire planet out of pettiness." Lucifer put one foot up on the bottom step as if he were going to charge up at his father. "It kills you that they love me. You can't have that, so you'll erase them. But I'll always know. And I'll never let you forget how you killed billions of mortals because of your wounded ego."

"And you'll watch it happen."

Michael had agreed with Lucifer that day. He never told him. Not because he feared retribution. Not because he didn't want to admit that Lucifer was right. To Michael, the commandments were sacred and must always be followed, regardless of opinion. The whims of the Lord were always carried out, regardless whether he understood them or not. But today, walking alongside Aphrodite, as they entered the portal to the throne area, he wasn't so sure about any of that anymore.

The Dog of War

Nephilim

Hera watched as one of the Nephilim, a female, remained outside the tunnel as per Hercules's request. It was Olympia. She wasn't a fighter, but she was still part of the plan. Hera had a fairly good idea what Hercules was up to. Zeus kept those thunderbolts alive, burning his skin, with every intention of throwing them at someone. Hera remained leaning against the boulder, with no intention in getting involved. She had planted the seeds of teamwork in Hercules's brain and by the looks of it, they had finally sprouted. Would it be enough for victory? A part of her was pulling for Hercules and his army to win. The other part wanted to see Zeus fall to his knees from defeat yet again. The cheating bastard.

"Finally, he gets it," Hera said.

"What do you mean?" Zeus said.

"Stubborn like his father," Hera said. "I suspected it would take all twelve challenges for him to humble himself, to become the true leader of this army."

"I was to train them for this day, not you."

"And you would have trained him, and the rest of them, for failure." She smirked. "I lost count after five attempts. It was time for a feminine touch. Now watch and be humbled, my unfaithful husband." She pushed off the boulder to get a better look at Zeus's face. "Lose or win, you will be humbled in some way, that must eat you alive."

Cerberus stood solid, feet slightly unmoving with every Nephilim that came at him, including Hercules, his touch drained them of their angelic ability, leaving them mortalized. He bounced them off the fleshy walls, launching some of them back into Zeus's dominion.

"Relentless and tiresome." Cerberus grabbed one of the Nephilim by the face and squished, tearing flesh and bone away. The soldier dropped dead. "Still don't get that message."

He batted Nephilim against the walls of the tunnel, which they became adhered to, struggling to get loose, screaming as their flesh pulled away from them. Their bones collapsed in piles of ruins.

"Your army's defeated," Cerberus shouted to Zeus. "Call them off or I'll kill every one of them. Or should I be addressing someone else as the leader of this relentless swarm of mosquitoes?" He looked at

Hera when saying that. "They're mere mortals here in my domain, yet they keep buzzing around me."

Hercules punched Cerberus's face with the strongest of mortal might, nothing more than a leaf to a powerful wind.

"Aren't you ashamed, Zeus?" Cerberus swatted Hercules as if he were nothing but air. "Have all those defeats at my hands weakened your passion for personal glory? Come here and face me like you did the first time, assured victory in your hungry eyes. I miss that version of Zeus, not the pitiful one in my sights today."

"Your ego is your weakness," Hercules said, semi-kneeling with one hand over his knee.

"Delusional. Look at all of the beaten around you."

"Here it comes." Hera gave Zeus a matter-of-fact look.

"What?" Zeus glared. "They're defeated. Admit you did no better."

"Olympia!" Hercules shouted at the only Nephilim outside the tunnel. She was not a fighter, but she was unique in the manner that she could open portals. He shouted, "Now!"

A blue portal opened behind Cerberus.

Hercules and those of the Nephilim who could, tackled Cerberus into the portal. It closed after his entrance and then reopened near Olympia. Cerberus landed on his back. He staggered up with two Nephilim on him. He rolled them off, appearing briefly blinded by the sun. He lumbered towards his dominion. Hera sashayed towards him. His enhanced strength was fading, leaving him with the angelic strength he had been born with, which was above average but nothing like he had possessed in there.

Hercules stepped out of Hell's gateway and started in a slow run, picking up speed as he speared Cerberus, knocking him back over, dust clouding them. Hercules rolled off to one side and by the looks of it, had spent his remaining energy, and was now slowly regaining his immortality and strength while on all fours. A thunderbolt slammed into Cerberus, sending him back down. Another thunderbolt splashed out sparks after hitting Cerberus. Another. And another as if Zeus had a thunderbolt for every defeat Cerberus had handed to him.

Hera wondered when Zeus would stop pelting Cerberus with stunner bolts, changing it up with harsher ones. Though Cerberus wasn't very strong physically outside Hell's gate, he did heal quickly, allowing this confrontation to drag on longer than it should.

"Stealing the thunder from your son," Hera said. "From them." She motioned at the Nephilim, beaten down all over the place. "What will they think?" She looked back at the other angels, where Ares stood, disgust clouding his face. "What will your real son think? You know, the one you've neglected. Poor Ares, what does he see? A father—or someone pitifully selfish?"

Zeus glared back at his wife, then down at Cerberus. "With a sword or axe you are the Dog of War, but without one, and out here, as great a warrior you are, you're nothing but something for my shadow to cross over."

Zeus jabbed two thunderbolts into Cerberus's shoulders, pinning him down.

"Now to free my brother." He looked down at Hercules, who was regaining his footing. "Make sure he doesn't get back in there."

Zeus shouted to all, "I won't just free Hades. All will return from Hell even if I have to hold those doors open myself until the last angel comes home."

Finally, there was Zeus, the Zeus whom Hera dreamt of. Liberator of all.

Zeus entered the jaws of Hell with Hera at his side. She accepted his hand and squeezed it tight. They stood before the two great doors while the Nephilim helped each other out of Hell's gate.

"Open to Hades," he shouted at the doors. The doors roared open to a scene of volcanoes erupting in the distance. Dragons glided between the forks of lightning in a dark orange sky. A hump of dirt stood before them, long ago piled but by the looks of footprints in the loose, red soil, it was regularly visited.

"Hades!" Zeus shouted. "Come forward."

"Your brother died at the hands of Medusa," Cerberus said from outside. "He died thousands of years ago as time in Hell runs faster than it does here. Hades is only remembered by Cronus."

Hera turned to see Hercules stomp Cerberus back down.

"How long have you known?" Zeus asked, in a calm yet menacing voice.

"Since it happened, I'm connected to everything that happens in Hell. The things I know that you never will, would fill volumes."

"All those times we fought, and you didn't tell me?"

"It was not my business to tell you."

"I will kill you."

"Zeus, stop." Hera grabbed him by the arm, but he shrugged her away.

The doors of Hell closed before a dragon could fly through. Its flames spat through the chink in the door before it roared shut with Hera waving away the fireball into smoke.

"I can't free the rest?"

"Only the one you ask for." Cerberus laughed.

"I'll kill you with my bare hands."

Zeus pushed Hercules aside as he jumped at Cerberus, pounding his face into a mess of flesh. The parts he wasn't hitting anymore began healing while Zeus kept wailing away in uncontrollable fury.

"Zeus, enough!" Hera shouted.

Everyone watched in shock at Zeus's unhinged state, the nonsensical things coming from his mouth. She could understand his grief for the loss of a brother, assuming Cerberus was telling the truth, but the direction he was heading was going to get him banished to Hell.

"Zeus!" Hera shouted. "His face."

"Yes," Hercules shouted. "Pound it into mangled flesh."

But Zeus didn't hear her, or Hercules as Cerberus's face morphed into a snarling, dog-faced demon with the blackest of eyes, exaggerated fangs that could tear away the sturdiest of armour. He chomped into one of Zeus's fists and tore away at it.

Zeus raised his semi-severed hand, dangling strips of flesh. Already showing signs of healing fast, he couldn't stand up quickly enough before Cerberus's jaws clamped into Zeus's armoured thigh, his incisors and canines penetrating what should have been impregnable metal.

"I will slay you like the beast you are." Zeus raised his fist high, a thunderbolt protruded from it.

A great shadow passed over as Zeus tried to stab Cerberus's pointed dog snout with a thunderbolt but before impact, the Almighty grabbed that fist and tossed him aside.

Someone must have said Hephaestus's name, informing him of what was going on. There was a snitch amongst that crowd of angels, and Hera would find out who it was. In the end, it was good that they ratted out Zeus before he ended up banished to Hell for murdering one of their own.

"Your House continues to stretch my patience," the Almighty said. "First Cronus. Then Hades. Dionysus. And now you."

"Hades is dead by the hands of Medusa. Did you know this too? So be it, banish me to Hell so I may avenge my brother's murder."

"The knowledge of the tragic loss of your brother is punishment enough," the Almighty said. "But there will be consequences, it's not only you who is breaking my commandments."

The Almighty helped Cerberus to his feet. He had by now transformed back to his angelic form, except for those hungry looking eyes.

A portal opened in front of them.

"Hold your head high. You were true to me, always. Now go. See old friends and family."

Before Cerberus entered the portal, he looked back at Zeus. "I should like to taste your blood again."

Hera winced at the sight of Cerberus's present face. It was still angelic, but more disturbing than his hybrid look ever could be.

"And as for you." The Almighty looked to Zeus as Cerberus entered the portal. "You have two choices. Hell. Or . . ."

"Or what?" Electricity spread throughout Zeus's fists.

He wouldn't dare.

"Or your beloved Nephilim will be portalled to an undisclosed location."

"How can you make me choose such a thing?" Zeus stood his ground.

"Choose. Or I will."

"Father?" Hercules said.

"Do it." Zeus said, unable to look at Hercules or the rest of the Nephilim.

"How can you be so cold?" Hera couldn't believe how quickly he had decided. "Your own blood?"

"Father! We're your daughters and sons." Hercules's voice was cut off as he was the last of the Nephilim to be sucked into the portal, then it shrunk from sight.

The opening within Mount Olympus rumbled closed.

"Your last chance." The Almighty's wings spread out. "And the portal connecting Heaven and Earth shall be from this day onward closed until you make things right."

"You're punishing everyone?" Hera said.

"None are innocent with the state of this planet. Fix it. Or I will. And none of you want that."

The Almighty faded into the portal and it closed behind him.

"You find this funny?" Zeus said to Hera, his eyes watering for her brother. He didn't need to tell her.

"No, not the death of Hades. A great tragedy." She knelt her head in respect as others did. She looked up slowly. "The House of Zeus, like the House of El, is crumbling away. Who will outlast who?"

Hera wrapped her arms around Zeus and kissed him briefly. Her arms slid from his bulky shoulders. "I was grinning because of your humiliation at my hands. Selfish of me, I admit." Way up in the daytime sky, the giant portal between this planet and its moon dimmed into nothingness. "And at what price?"

The Opening

Aphrodite

The Almighty had just returned. Aphrodite and Michael had been waiting for him. He skipped walking up the steps, and glided up to the dais, turned, and plunked himself into his seat of power. The heartbeat of the black crystal throne pulsed brightly. Fingers curled at the ends of the armrests, knuckles white, their king inhaled deeply at the sight of Aphrodite. He gazed down at them for what felt like a long minute of uncertainty for all.

"Is what I asked, done?"

Before Aphrodite could speak, Michael stepped forwards.

"Yes. She did not pause."

"Refreshing to have one of my decrees carried out without incident. It's rare these days."

"I didn't enjoy it."

"I'm sure you didn't, Aphrodite. It would be difficult to kill one's image."

"True love was murdered today. Something rare in the universe, killed by my hands."

"If you had heeded my words, none of it would have happened. No sorrow. No tragic ends. If the others had listened, that portal would remain open."

The portal to the blue planet shrank from sight.

"The planet closed off, why? What's happening?" Aphrodite thought of her father, Zeus, of her uncle, Poseidon, her half-brother, Ares, and most of her siblings and relatives. All stationed on the blue planet. She was cut off from them. "You're punishing the innocent. Only a select few have disobeyed your commandments. You close them all off? For how long?"

"As long as it takes for them to make things right."

"Then send me back there, to be with my family."

"You will remain here."

A surge of anger filled her. "You bastard."

The Almighty's eyes widened.

"You control freak. You psycho."

"I shall reunite you with some of your family if you like?" A flaming portal opened midway up the steps. "You have some catching up to do with your grandfather, I believe?"

"I'll give you a better reason to send me to Hell."

"Aphrodite." Michael held her back and addressed the figure on the throne. "She's emotional, an unfortunate trait of hers. Forgive her, my Lord."

"Her bloodline is a curse upon me. They have been given more chances than any other House."

"My Lord, I've never asked you for anything. I've always done anything you asked without question. I ask this one time, please, show leniency to Aphrodite."

The Almighty sank back in the throne, looking away from Michael and briefly down at her.

"From this day forwards you are responsible for her."

"Thank you, my Lord."

"They have a way of getting inside your head. Be mindful of that, Michael. Such feelings could be the ruin of you."

Aphrodite scowled at Big Cranky but not for too long. She wasn't going to push her luck, especially now that her fate was tied to Michael. There was an opening, but that door was not open wide enough yet. It would take more pushes, however gentle, to creak open the door to his heart. But she was Aphrodite and she always got what she wanted.

THE RISE OF ZEUS

JAMES PYNE

Unlimited Power

Zeus

The bright, full moon floated closer to the pantheon. Zeus stood alone, having given his personal guard, Kratos, a night off, although Zeus wouldn't be surprised if he were still watching his back from somewhere.

Maybe that wasn't such a bad idea. With the portal closed, some districts might send an assassin to take him and Hera out. Nonsense, of course, but many did blame them for recent events. They would see things his way soon enough. Being cut off from friends and relatives would in time make their ears friendly to his words.

But this evening he was mourning the death of a brother. Zeus had requested Poseidon's audience; he

503

would give him the unbearable news himself. Where was their father, Cronus, during this? Where was Lucifer? The Almighty?

"My brother is dead because you wanted it to happen!" Zeus shouted up at the night sky, as clouds frothed into view. "You never loved any of us. Not even your own House. We are all nothing more than amusement for your bored, sick mind." Tears streamed down his bearded face. He had never cried before, not even during his youngling years.

"Hades!"

His brother's name echoed throughout the mountain range below him.

The upper clouds darkened the moon.

Zeus whipped thunderbolts down at the mountains, chipping away at the peaks. He lost control and kept whizzing thunderbolts with no target in mind, no reasoning behind it. The more he did it, the angrier he became.

He threw his arms out and raged at the sky, falling to his knees, weeping.

"Hades!"

Waves of sorrow and hatred hit him. His fists squeezed tight, fingernails drawing blood. He felt a buzz through his body and before he could react, lightning branched from the sky and entered his fists, his entire body, then the sky released him, and he hunched over on all fours.

"I did that?" He stood up, looking at his blistered hands.

It wasn't the Almighty's doing, he was sure of it.

So much energy buzzed inside him. It wanted out, like he had to dispel it soon or he would split into pieces. He quickly got to his feet and stood at the edge overlooking one of the taller mountains. He pointed his fists downwards, streams of electrical bolts flooded from him, from his eyes, his fists, triangulating into one spear of lightning that obliterated a mountaintop.

"What power is this?"

Hidden in him all along? The death of his brother had brought it out, his one last, loving gift to Zeus.

"Old Fool." He smirked at the sky. "You've given me an army and you don't even realize it."

It would take time but most of their hearts would favour Zeus. Those who stood in his way —

He raised his arms, and clouds rumbled above with lightning illuminating them into an angry orange and red.

—would be struck down by Zeus's might.

His hands reached to the sky. He willed the clouds to feed him. Electricity rooted down into his hands, and his body buzzed with unlimited power. He balled up his fists, raised them to his eyes. No one would laugh at Zeus ever again. This was what the Almighty had feared Zeus discovering. He pointed both fists at a lower mountain and released branches of lightning into it, shattering it into a billion pieces of rock.

There would be a day when he would do the same to the Almighty. But first, he needed time to build his army.

Dragon Tamer

King Lucifer

The most recent king of the firebreathers tumbled from Dragon's Den. It slammed into ledges, scattering other dragons into flight. They glared up at Lucifer with flaming yellow eyes, like they considered challenging him for top spot. He'd had enough of their fighting and settled it once and for all. He would teach them to function as one and not as individuals. Then he would handpick a leader for them to follow. Until then, he was their king whether they liked it or not.

The view from here was magnificent. It was tempting to make this his throne area. Now, that would be an exclamation mark to the rest of Hell. Demons streamed in and out of Blaze City. The place was teeming with life, with culture. Hell's original

507

inhabitants would do anything for Lucifer. Blood Tower loomed on one side of Crimson Peak and the Forbidden Gardens on the other, in vibrant colour and unmatched beauty. His focus went back to the throne area where Persephone sat, cross-legged, watching and waiting for his return. She was frisky tonight.

Lucifer flew from the peak towards his throne to claim his wife for bed.

He heard the sound of rocks falling behind him. The sound of flesh colliding.

Hell's king looked back to see the dragons spiralling upwards towards the peak, gnashing at each other, ramming into each other, blowing fire and venom.

"The universe wasn't built in a day," Lucifer said under his breath, landing into a walk in the direction of his beloved Persephone, who stood up to embrace him. He glanced down at Lilith's grave garden. "Just like my revenge."

THE INFERNAL STRUGGLE

Now that you're through...

...please leave a review.

Reviews are extremely important to authors, especially us independent ones. They help with Amazon rankings, allowing us more exposure, and tons of other things. We really appreciate those who take the time to leave a review. After all, you already bought my book and now you're taking the time to review it. That's awesome of you. I can't thank you enough!

SIGN UP FOR MY NEWSLETTER

FOR SPECIAL OFFERS, GIVEAWAYS, BONUS CONTENT LIKE EXCLUSIVE SHORT STORIES AND EXCERPTS, UPDATES BY THE AUTHOR, INFO ON NEW RELEASES AND OTHER GREAT READS:

www.mothmanpublishing.com

James Pyne is a Nova Scotia based author of mostly epic dark fantasy, though he sometimes strays into other literary realms. The last few years he has seen his work in over a hundred magazines and anthologies. A blue-collar worker his entire adult life, he tends to keep to himself but on occasion he will visit other countries and get himself into some misadventures— Japan, Argentina, Spain will never be the same. Add him on any of the social media platforms listed below and shoot him a message. He loves hearing from the fans so don't be shy!

Website: www.mothmanpublishing.com
Facebook: www.facebook.com/jjamespyne
Instagram: www.instagram.com/pyne_james

Made in the USA
Monee, IL
22 December 2022

23427091R00284